The Samurai Detectives

The Samurai Detectives

Volume One

SHŌTARŌ IKENAMI

Translated by Yui Kajita

PENGUIN BOOKS

PENGUIN BOOKS

UK | USA | Canada | Ireland | Australia
India | New Zealand | South Africa

Penguin Books is part of the Penguin Random House group of companies whose addresses can be found at global.penguinrandomhouse.com.

Penguin Random House UK,
One Embassy Gardens, 8 Viaduct Gardens, London SW11 7BW

penguin.co.uk

Kenkaku Shōbai by Shōtarō Ikenami
Original Japanese edition published in 1973 by SHINCHOSHA Publishing Co., Ltd.
First published in Great Britain by Penguin Books 2025

001

Copyright © Ayako Ishizuka, 1973
Translation copyright © Yui Kajita, 2025

English translation rights arranged with
SHINCHOSHA Publishing Co., Ltd., Tokyo in care of Tuttle Mori Agency, Inc. Tokyo

The Translator's Note is not included in the original Japanese edition.

The moral right of the copyright holders has been asserted

Penguin Random House values and supports copyright.
Copyright fuels creativity, encourages diverse voices, promotes freedom of expression and supports a vibrant culture. Thank you for purchasing an authorized edition of this book and for respecting intellectual property laws by not reproducing, scanning or distributing any part of it by any means without permission. You are supporting authors and enabling Penguin Random House to continue to publish books for everyone.
No part of this book may be used or reproduced in any manner for the purpose of training artificial intelligence technologies or systems. In accordance with Article 4(3) of the DSM Directive 2019/790, Penguin Random House expressly reserves this work from the text and data mining exception

Set in 11.5/14.5pt Dante MT Pro
Typeset by Six Red Marbles UK, Thetford, Norfolk
Printed and bound in Great Britain by Clays Ltd, Elcograf S.p.A.

The authorized representative in the EEA is Penguin Random House Ireland, Morrison Chambers, 32 Nassau Street, Dublin D02 YH68

A CIP catalogue record for this book is available from the British Library

ISBN: 978-1-405-97576-6

Penguin Random House is committed to a sustainable future for our business, our readers and our planet. This book is made from Forest Stewardship Council® certified paper.

Contents

Translator's Note   vii

Chapter 1	The Swordswoman	1
Chapter 2	The Oath of the Sword	44
Chapter 3	The New Geisha	76
Chapter 4	The Four Rulers of Izeki Dojo	108
Chapter 5	River Suzuka in the Rain	145
Chapter 6	Kinchan of the Painted Brows	179
Chapter 7	Assassination by Poison	214

Shōtarō Ikenami (1923–1990) was a bestselling Japanese author famed for his multi-million copy selling series of historical fiction novels. Over his lifetime, he won the Yoshikawa Eiji Literary Award and Naoki Award for popular literature. Over a dozen of his works were adapted for film and television, and his work remains exceptionally popular in Japan.

Yui Kajita is a translator, illustrator and literary scholar, originally from Kyoto, Japan, and currently based in Germany.

Translator's Note

Yui Kajita

Shōtarō Ikenami is one of the titans of Japanese historical fiction, and *Kenkaku Shobai* – widely considered to be his greatest work – balances light-footed entertainment with literary weight, humour with wisdom, and sword-clanging action with the quiet current of the seasons.

While I hope readers can jump right in and get carried away by Ikenami's storytelling, there are some basic historical details worth going over in brief. The **Tokugawa shogunate**, or Edo bakufu, was the military government of Japan established by Tokugawa Ieyasu, which lasted for 264 years (1603–1867): a long era of peace and economic growth after many years of civil war. The **Shogun** was the de facto ruler of Japan, residing in Edo Castle (in present-day Tokyo), though nominally appointed by the Emperor (a figurehead seated in the Imperial Palace in Kyoto).

In the four-tier hereditary class system of the Edo period, warriors were the ruling class, followed by farmers, artisans and merchants – with an outcast group below the fourth tier which included people with professions that were deemed 'unclean'. Some of the most powerful members of the warrior class were the **daimyo**: the 270 or so feudal lords who controlled most of Japan's land. Ultimately subordinate to the Shogun, the daimyo were divided into three categories depending on how close their ties were to the Tokugawa family. **Hatamoto** were high-ranking samurai who served the shogunate directly. Unlike the lower vassals of Tokugawa, daimyo and hatamoto had the right to an audience with the Shogun. Samurai were bound by a strict hierarchy and code of conduct under their lord. A **ronin** was a masterless samurai.

The status and income of those in the service of the shogunate were measured in rice: **koku**, a crucial unit, was the amount of rice that could feed one person for a year, equivalent to about 150 kilograms (330 pounds) or five bushels. For instance, a daimyo's domain was worth at least 10,000 koku, while a 'greater hatamoto' had an income between 1,200 and 10,000 koku. Lower down on the social ladder, another level of income mentioned in this novel is forty **tawara**, or straw bags of rice, which was enough to cover the annual living costs of eight people. Such salaries could be collected in either rice or money.

The **ryo** was the unit of currency in the form of an oblong gold coin. According to the narrator, 'Fifty ryo was a considerable sum: in those days, commoners could easily live for five years on that kind of money.' One ryo was equal to four **bu**, sixteen **shu**, or 4,000 **mon**.

The samurai class were privileged to wear two swords, inserted between the sash-like belt around their waist called **obi**: a long **katana** (the blade measuring 27–30 inches long on average, and about 40 inches including the hilt) and a short **wakizashi** (the blade 12–24 inches long). Shorter blades, such as **tanto** and **kozuka** – straight blades in between a dagger and a knife – were also carried for self-defence. A samurai's formal dress usually included a pair of swords and a **hakama** (wide trousers worn over the **kimono**), but Kohei, our protagonist, likes to keep it casual with only his wakizashi, kimono and loose **haori** jacket. Forging katanas is a fine art, and the swordsmiths mentioned in this novel are notable figures from history.

Chapter 1
The Swordswoman

I

The bamboo grove swayed in the cold wind.

In the western sky, heavy clouds hung low, extending over the rice fields to the distant horizon, the rift between its grey banks tinged with the hazy glow of sunset.

For some time, a flock of northern wrens had been flying around the stone well without a moment's pause, their liquid trills ringing in the air. The young master of the house watched their flight in total stillness.

His physique was as sturdy as a boulder, but his face, still visible in the gathering dusk, looked younger than his twenty-four years, and his dark skin gleamed like tanned leather stretched taut.

The young man's eyes glinted with a certain intensity underneath his thick brows. He gazed at the small, nimble wrens flitting about without betraying a hint of boredom.

The smell of broth wafted from the kitchen.

These days, he had been living solely on this simple scallion miso soup, accompanied by a small side dish of pickled daikon, for both breakfast and supper.

The young man's name was Akiyama Daijiro.

It was nearly half a year since Daijiro had established his own dojo of the Mugai-ryu school of swordsmanship, nestled in the grove of trees near the Masaki Inari-myo shrine on the outskirts of Asakusa, where the river of Arakawa turned into Ohkawa and snaked around the land.

'Look. From now on, you've got to do everything by yourself. I won't look after you any more.'

That was what his father, Akiyama Kohei, had told him before helping him build a modest dojo of his own. The dojo was about 530 square feet, and Daijiro lived in the two rooms across the hall from it: a six-tatami-mat room of about a hundred square feet and a three-tatami-mat room of about 50 square feet. They were sparsely furnished. The wife of a nearby farmer took care of his meals.

She soon appeared from the kitchen and padded up to the well where Daijiro stood motionless. She gestured to let him know that supper was ready, and then without waiting for a response promptly turned on her heel to go back inside.

The woman was mute.

Daijiro finally went inside.

When he began to eat, his eyes lit up like an artless child's; his big nose twitched, sniffing the broth in pure delight, and his thick lips seemed to focus their full attention on embracing the freshly cooked barley.

By the time he finished his meal, darkness had already fallen.

So far, not a single pupil had entered his dojo, and the only person who regularly came and went from Daijiro's house was the farmer's wife – but this evening, a rare and mysterious visitor crossed his threshold.

The visitor was a middle-aged samurai in impressive attire, and he introduced himself as Ohgaki Shirobei.

Daijiro had neither seen nor heard of this man before.

Daijiro invited Ohgaki to the larger room and poured a cup of plain hot water for his guest. There was no supply of tea in the house.

At first Ohgaki's eyes roved over the bare room and Daijiro's clean yet rather simple clothes, but soon his face split into a broad grin. 'I witnessed your skill with my own eyes this summer, at Lord Tanuma's mansion,' he said.

Daijiro nodded. He recalled the occasion.

This Lord Tanuma was Tanuma Tonomo-no-kami Okitsugu, who belonged to the Council of Elders, or roju: the group of highest-ranking officials under the shogunate. Tanuma had won particular favour with the current tenth shogun, Tokugawa Ieharu, and it was generally acknowledged that his rapidly growing influence outstripped any other's. This spring, Tanuma received an additional income of 7,000 koku from the Shogun and was appointed as a daimyo ruling over the Sagara domain of Totomi province worth 37,000 koku. Rumour had it that he'd begun as a vassal with a mere 300 koku to his name. It was fair to say that his was an extraordinary rise to power.

In the summer, a sword-fighting tournament had been held in Tanuma's secondary mansion. About thirty swordsmen tested their skills against each other – some were masters who had their own respectable dojos around the city of Edo, and others were proud representatives from various domains.

It was unprecedented that a young, nameless swordsman like Daijiro was allowed to compete, and yet, on the day of the event, Daijiro defeated seven opponents in a row. Although he lost his eighth match against Mori Kurando – a retainer of Sanada Kou, who ruled Matsushiro of Shinano province worth 100,000 koku – Daijiro was still a dark horse whose remarkable skill became the talk of the day. He had made his debut in the world of swords with flying colours and in the Shogun's own castle town of Edo, no less.

Daijiro suspected it was thanks to his father that he'd had the chance to appear in this ceremonial tournament.

Now, let us return to the night in question. Ohgaki Shirobei, the unexpected visitor, claimed to have seen Daijiro's bouts at Tanuma's tournament.

'Indeed, your performance was truly admirable,' the guest went on. There wasn't a trace of falsehood in his tone.

'And may I ask what brings you here?' Daijiro asked quietly.

'On account of your accomplishment . . .' Ohgaki leaned in, his knees edging forward on the tatami floor. 'I would like to request your assistance in a matter.'

'Yes?'

'It will be for the good of the people, for the common good.'

'Hmm . . .?'

'I ask you to put your excellent skill to good use.'

'Do you mean a match?'

'Well, something along those lines . . .'

'What exactly do you have in mind?'

'I would like you to strike a certain individual and break both of their arms. *Not* sever them. Only break their bones.'

'I don't follow . . .'

'If I may be so bold, please . . .' Ohgaki paused and pulled out a small bundle wrapped in a silk cloth from the fold of his kimono. 'Here is fifty gold ryo.'

Fifty ryo was a considerable sum: in those days, commoners could easily live for five years on that kind of money.

'Please consider it.' Ohgaki bowed, putting his hands on the floor in front of him. 'I wouldn't be here if I didn't have every faith in your abilities. I assure you, it is for the greater good.'

'Whose arms are you asking me to break, and for what reason?'

'I . . . I cannot say the name. If you are willing to assist us, we will guide you to the person.' There was a mole the size of an azuki bean on the tip of Ohgaki's nose, and he kept rubbing this lump with his little finger as he added, 'I understand this is not an easy request, but please bear in mind that if you carry out the task with success, you shall soon reap the rewards.'

Despite his rhetoric, Ohgaki flatly refused to divulge any information about the circumstances, the name of the opponent, and the person's whereabouts. No matter how Daijiro asked him, he remained tight-lipped.

Faced with Ohgaki's persistence, Daijiro finally drove him away with the words: 'I must refuse.'

II

The next day before noon, Daijiro went to his father Kohei's residence.

From Hashiba, which was just around the corner from Daijiro's dojo, there were two boats that ferried people across Ohkawa to Terajima. Two farmers were in charge of steering the boats. When one crossed the river and reached the village of Terajima, one could see a footpath that went between the rice fields and, beyond that, a dirt bank that stretched across the landscape. A scene unfolded just as it had once been described in a book: 'Upon the order of the authorities, three kinds of trees – the peach blossom, the cherry blossom and the willow – were planted on either side of the bank. Ever since, from the month of February to the month of March, the marriage of crimson, amethyst, jade and white amidst their boughs bears a striking resemblance to a curtain of gilded nishiki brocade adorned with delicate embroidery, and the view is aptly praised as profoundly exquisite.'

Places of scenic beauty and historical interest dotted the surroundings – there were the Mokubo-ji temple, the grave of Umewakamaru and Shirahige Myojin shrine, to name a few – and each season offered different shades of picturesque charm. Six years had already passed since Kohei had settled down in this neighbourhood.

To reach Kohei's residence, one followed the bank's path to the north. The house stood in front of a pine grove in the middle of rice fields overlooking Kanegafuchi, where the three rivers of Ohkawa, Arakawa and Ayasegawa met. It was a small house of three rooms with a straw-thatched roof, which used to be a farmer's cottage until Kohei bought and refurnished it.

Daijiro turned left off the path, cut across the pine grove and emerged in front of the open engawa, a wooden veranda which adjoined the private living room at the back of the house and looked out on the garden.

He found his father lying on the tatami floor.

If father and son were to stand side by side, Kohei's white-haired head would go just up to Daijiro's chest. But that wasn't because Daijiro was especially tall.

At present, Kohei was stretched out on his side, his head resting on a young woman's lap as she gently cleaned his ear. She was called Oharu, the second daughter of Iwagoro, a farmer in the nearby Sekiya village. Oharu wasn't especially tall either, but with Kohei's head on her lap, she looked like a mother coddling her little boy.

The name Kohei – with 'Ko' meaning 'small' in Japanese – suited him perfectly.

'The young master is here,' Oharu said to Kohei, in a rather casual manner.

'Mm-hmm,' Kohei murmured in a mellow voice that belied his years, though he would soon be sixty. His eyes were still closed in dreamy pleasure as Oharu groomed him.

'Good morning, Father.' Daijiro, who was neatly dressed in his hakama, greeted his father respectfully.

'Sit down,' Kohei said.

'Yes, sir.'

'I smell scallion soup.'

'Really? I don't smell anything . . .' Oharu cut in.

'No, it's coming from my son,' Kohei said, reaching out a hand to stroke Oharu, who let out a coquettish squeal. Daijiro looked away.

'Dai. What do you want?' Kohei asked.

'Well . . .' Daijiro told his father about the strange visitor from the night before.

Daijiro was aware that the only reason a young man like himself – having only returned to Edo at the end of February after a long absence from his father's home – had been given the opportunity to participate in the tournament and to show what he was capable of before Lord Tanuma and the other high-ranking officials of the shogunate was through the intercessions of his father, who was well connected in many spheres.

And so Daijiro felt obliged to speak to his father about the middle-aged samurai who had appeared at his door with a suspicious request after seeing his performance at the Tanuma mansion, just in case it was anything of significance.

'Hmm . . . Called himself Ohgaki Shirobei, did he . . .?' Kohei muttered when he had listened to the whole story.

'Do you know him?'

'No.'

'He was holding a paper lantern from Fujiro in Hashiba . . .'

'Oho. Sharp eye.'

'I only saw the mark by chance . . .'

'I suppose he took a boat from somewhere along Ohkawa, moored at Fujiro and borrowed a lantern there, then made his way to your house.'

'I think so.'

'Break someone's arms, eh . . .?'

'Yes.'

'Oh, how awful,' Oharu burst out, getting to her feet and pattering away to the kitchen.

Kohei's head had fallen to the floor from Oharu's lap, but he stayed where he was, never once opening his eyes.

'You weren't moved to accept his bidding for fifty ryo?' Kohei murmured. 'He wanted you to break a pair of arms, not chop them off, after all. It makes little difference. If you don't find a pupil soon, you'll be hard-pressed to make ends meet. We've been living in peace for more than a century now, thanks to the power of the Tokugawa shogun or whatever you want to call it. No war for more than a hundred years. It's a fine thing. So, Daijiro. In times like these, what the samurai carries on his side – along with his skill in wielding it – becomes another tool for getting along in the world. If you're not mindful of that, you'll starve to death.'

Kohei spoke calmly, as if he were mumbling to himself; the son watched his father's ruddy old face with clear, unblemished eyes.

The warm sunlight of early winter was glimmering on the water that flowed into the garden. The stream was drawn from the river around where it curved at Kanegafuchi, and there was a small boat floating on it. This was Kohei's boat.

Oharu brought a tray with some tea and sweets and offered it to Daijiro. It was first-rate tea, and the sweets were the 'Saga Rakugan' from Kyomasu-ya, a renowned confectionery shop in Ryogoku Yonezawa.

Daijiro sipped his tea and began to eat the sweets in a leisurely fashion. He appeared carefree, his movements utterly natural; not a whiff of his present life of poverty could be felt in his bearing.

Kohei's kindly eyelids flicked open, his needle-sharp eyes glinting for just an instant before they were closed again.

'Thank you for this. I will return now,' Daijiro said.

'Uh-huh.' Kohei nodded. With his little finger, he prodded tenderly at Oharu's thigh close by his side and said, 'Take Dai home on the boat, will you?'

'Sure,' Oharu said. She went down the garden, hopped on the little boat, picked up the pole and called out, 'Come, young master.'

'Thank you for the ride.' Daijiro gave a courteous response to his father and joined Oharu on the boat.

Since he was young, Kohei had devoted his whole life to the way of the sword, but now he seemed to be savouring his retirement.

Oharu steered with deft manoeuvres even when the boat reached the swirling currents around Kanegafuchi, and the boat entered Ohkawa without any trouble.

'How old are you again, Oharu?' Daijiro asked.

'Nineteen.'

'So, you've been living with my father for two years now . . .'

'That's right.'

'Hmm . . .'

Daijiro thought back to an incident about a month ago,

when his father had made a rare visit to his dojo. 'You know my maidservant, Oharu . . .' His father had begun.

'Yes?'

'I'm afraid I've found myself drawn to her. I don't have to tell you this, but I shouldn't keep secrets from you, either. Just letting you know.'

'Yes, sir . . .' Daijiro had managed to reply, but his mouth had hung open in bewilderment.

For the last four years, Daijiro had been away from his father, journeying across distant provinces to train himself in body and spirit. So when his father had told him, 'To tell you the truth, son – these days I've come to enjoy women more than swords . . .' Daijiro was quite astonished.

'It came to me like a revelation once you'd left, you see,' his father had continued. 'I knew then that it was time to close my dojo in Yotsuya and quit the blade.'

Daijiro, who had never really known a woman even now at the age of twenty-four, struggled to understand his father's words. Until six years ago, his father's day-to-day life had been more regular; he did frequent the mansions of various daimyos and greater hatamotos, for he had a knack for keeping up friendly relations in society, and he had no need to live frugally, but most of the time, he'd spent his days reading or eagerly training his pupils at his own dojo in Yotsuya Nakamachi.

He's like a different person now . . .

Daijiro turned his eyes away from Oharu as she guided the boat, swaying from side to side right in front of him.

She laughed happily.

III

That evening, Kohei asked Oharu to take him out on the boat and crossed Ohkawa to Hashiba. It wasn't to visit his son's dojo. He was headed for Fujiro, an elegant restaurant in Hashiba.

Though he was dressed informally without a hakama over his kimono, Kohei had donned a fine haori jacket and casually thrust a short sword into the obi around his waist – this wakizashi had been forged by Horikawa Kunihiro and measured nearly eighteen inches – and his white hair, which Oharu had smoothed down, looked neat and smart.

He stepped on to Fujiro's small wooden pier and said, 'Wait for me at home, Oharu.'

She nodded with a smile and glided back over the river and into darkness.

Kohei went through to a small private room at the back of Fujiro, ordered some sake and called Omoto, whose job was to entertain the guests. Kohei was a regular at Fujiro, so he knew her well.

'I hear you've been working hard these days, sensei,' Omoto greeted him with an arch smile.

'Doing what?' Kohei asked.

'Why, they say you've been strolling around Mokubo-ji holding hands with a girl who looks so young she could be your granddaughter.'

'Uh-huh.'

'How are you faring?'

'I'll have a hard time keeping up with her soon. The girl learns fast.'

'Oh, *sensei* . . .'

'Jokes aside . . .' Kohei paused, pinched out a small gold piece worth half a ryo and tucked it into the collar of Omoto's kimono. 'I want to ask you something.'

'What is it . . .?'

'Last night. A samurai came here – a portly fellow of about forty with a mole the size of an azuki bean on the tip of his nose – yes?'

'Gosh, how did you know?'

'Where is he from?'

'I have no idea. It was his first visit here. He came by boat from Oumi-ya, the boathouse outside the gate by Asakusa bridge – he just had a spot of sake, then he went out for about half an hour and came back again . . .'

'To return the lantern he borrowed?'

'Why, yes!'

'And after that?'

'He went back the way he came on Oumi-ya's boat.'

'Hmm . . .'

'Is anything the matter?'

'Oh, nothing . . . Come, pour me some sake, will you? By the way, Omoto – who's the lucky man who gets to share your company these days?'

'Naughty, *sensei*.'

The next day, Kohei had Oharu ferry him to Ume-ya, a boathouse in Hashiba. He switched to a new boat there and went down Ohkawa towards Asakusa bridge. He ordered the boatman to moor at Oumi-ya, passed through to their guest room and ordered sake. After a short while, he asked for another boat.

On Oumi-ya's boat, Kohei went back the way he came over Ohkawa. The boatman was a middle-aged man with a stern frown etched on his face that made him seem as though he knew the world inside and out.

Judging that the man actually did know *something*, Kohei held out a small gold piece to him and said, 'Do take it.'

'Much obliged . . .'

'The night before last, a man of about forty with a mole on the tip of his nose—'

'Ah, you mean Master Ohyama,' the man cut in before Kohei could finish.

'Ohyama . . . was that what he's called?'

'Indeed it is.'

'I was introduced to him some time ago, at someone's feast, but his name slipped my mind.'

'He is the steward of Lord Nagai Izumi-no-kami.'

'Ah . . . of course,' Kohei said knowingly, his face lighting up.

Nagai Izumi-no-kami Naotsune was a samurai of high rank – a 'greater hatamoto' with 5,000 koku in annual income – and he served as the Shogun's castle guard, among other duties. Although Kohei had acquaintances in numerous circles, he had yet to meet Nagai in person.

Kohei returned home before sunset.

Oharu came out to greet him and said, 'I popped by at the young master's place on my way home.'

'Did you now? What was my boy up to?'

'I spied him in that room with the wooden floor . . .'

'The dojo?'

'Aye. He was standing there all by himself, and he drew his katana . . .'

'Mm-hmm?'

'And he just stared at nothing, didn't move a muscle . . . Oh, it gave me the creeps.'

'So, he held his katana at the ready and simply stood there . . .'

'That's right. He could've stayed like that for hours, for all I know.'

'Hmm . . .'

'I wonder, is that how he spends his time every day?'

'Looks like it.'

'Where's the fun in that?'

'That's the thing with men. While we're young, we become enthralled even by the smallest things.'

'Huh.'

'As for me, nothing's more thrilling than being here with you.'

'Ah, that tickles!'

IV

The next morning, Oharu went to see her father, Iwagoro, who lived in Sekiya village and handed him a letter and an errand fee from Kohei.

Iwagoro set out at once.

Iwagoro and his wife, who had no less than eight

children, had been appalled and furious when they had discovered that Kohei was involved with their second daughter, Oharu. But since Kohei had proffered a suitable amount of money in offer for her hand and now took good care of them at every turn, they were delighted.

'I can't figure it out, though – how can a tiny old chap like him who knows only how to wave around a sword live it up like he does? Boggles the mind.' That was what Iwagoro, who wasn't yet fifty, often said to his wife, Osaki.

Iwagoro delivered the letter from Kohei to Yashichi, the goyokiki in Yotsuya Tenma.

A goyokiki was a private eye of sorts, who worked as a pawn of the Machi-bugyo – the magistrates who maintained order by overseeing the administrative and judicial matters of the area – but the goyokiki's detective services never went beyond that of an unofficial subordinate.

Now, Yashichi of Yotsuya was still in his thirties, but he had an easy-going, well-seasoned character; his wife ran a restaurant called Musashi-ya, so people in the neighbourhood affectionately called him 'the Musashi-ya boss'. There were plenty of goyokiki who flaunted the authority of the Shogun and pulled devious tricks behind the scenes, but not Yashichi. Yashichi was a rare specimen, one might say.

As soon as night fell, Yashichi showed up at Kohei's house, bringing little gifts of fish and vegetables with him. 'I came to stay the night,' he said.

'Thanks for coming all this way,' Kohei said.

'Your letter made me anxious. What happened? Please tell me everything.'

Back when Kohei had run his own dojo in Yotsuya,

Yashichi had come often as a keen pupil. They had kept in touch ever since.

'The year's end is just around the corner now,' Kohei said. 'Winters are getting harder every year – old age, perhaps. Well, have a drink with some natto soup and listen to my story, if you will.'

Oharu was staying at her parents' for the night.

Kohei proceeded to confide in Yashichi everything that had occurred. 'I could say it's none of my business and leave the whole thing alone, but it bothers me – it's odd he should've taken the trouble of coming to my son, too.'

'Very true.'

'As for my son, he did become a swordsman of his own free will, just as I did . . . but as you know, times have changed. Nowadays we can never let our guard down, so this incident makes me a little uneasy. I came up to Edo early on, and I've been knocked around in all sorts of ways in my time, so nothing can ruffle me, whatever happens. But my son – he's got the bulk all right, but he's too green to know both sides of the world. Well, seeing as he wanted to take up the sword and get out there, I pulled one or two strings in secret to help him get his foot in – but I wouldn't want him to get caught up in some shady business on that account.'

'Of course.'

'I know I'm too soft on the boy, but don't laugh.'

'I'm not laughing.'

'Do me a favour, Yashichi.'

'So, this fellow who called himself Ohgaki – the one who came to see the young master – you're quite certain he is the steward of Lord Nagai?'

'Most likely.'

'Lord Nagai's mansion is in Asakusa Mototorigoe, if I remember correctly . . .'

'Yes.'

'Very well. I'll look into it.'

'I owe you one.'

'Excuse me for a moment, sensei . . .' Yashichi, who had been sitting on the wooden floor by the sunken hearth, rose to his feet in one swift motion. Nature called.

Yashichi passed Kohei on his left, slid open the wooden door and was about to step out on to the engawa that led to the privy.

In that instant, Kohei seized the long metal chopsticks jutting out from the mound of ashes, spun around and threw them at Yashichi's back without a word.

The space between them was less than two feet.

Yashichi ducked without even a backward glance; the sticks whizzed over his head and pierced the shutter which screened the veranda from the garden.

Kohei grinned.

After a short while, when Yashichi came back from the privy, he was holding the metal chopsticks in his hand. He blithely put them back in the hearth.

Kohei filled Yashichi's sake cup to the brim and asked, 'Are you going to some other dojo these days to keep up your training?'

'No.'

'Hmm.'

'But . . .'

'But?'

'I *am* following your word – every day, from the moment I wake up to the moment I fall asleep, I'm always sharpening my intuition, no matter what I do.'

Kohei chuckled.

Five days later, Yashichi of Yotsuya appeared again at Kohei's home in the afternoon.

'Lord Nagai Izumi-no-kami's third mansion is in Fukagawa,' Yashichi began. 'The servants there are rather wild about gambling in their quarters . . .'

'It's the same everywhere these days.'

'I poked around there. I didn't find anything particularly alarming, but – sensei, I'd prefer it if you could keep what I'm about to say just between you and me.'

'Gladly.'

'The word is . . . Lord Nagai's heir is the young master named Ukyo.'

'Mm-hmm.'

'According to the servants, there's been talk of an arranged marriage for this Ukyo. And the intended is . . .'

'Go on.'

'Well, she is the secret child of Lord Tanuma, the roju.'

'What did you say . . .?'

V

That Tanuma had taken the adopted daughter of a doctor, Chiga Doyu, as his concubine had reached Kohei's ears as well.

This woman was particularly close with Shogun Ieharu's

concubine, Ochiho no Kata, and so it followed that Tanuma sought to cultivate friendships through his concubine with key figures such as Ochiho no Kata and Matsushima, the head of the ladies-in-waiting who held the real power in the Ooku, the women's quarters of Edo Castle. Tanuma took every opportunity to send gifts and other fineries to the attendants of the Ooku. It was said that his popularity among the women of Edo Castle was 'something extraordinary'.

The Ooku was the palatial living quarters of the women of Edo Castle, with the Shogun's official wife and concubines at its centre, and no men were allowed to set foot in the premises except for the Shogun himself. It was a special territory that housed hundreds of attendants and maidservants. The women of the Ooku wielded a covert but considerable authority and influence not only within the castle itself but also on the wider politics of the shogunate.

Tanuma had served the previous shogun, Ieshige, first as a page, then as a steward; not only was he later promoted to a daimyo, he had also climbed up to the highest rung of the shogunate when he attained the position of a roju. It was telling that a man like him with an esteemed career devoted such assiduous attention to maintaining his popularity in the Ooku. Rumour had it that all his efforts sprang from his fear that one day he might fall out of favour with the Shogun.

When viewed from outside, the politics of the shogunate seemed to revolve around Tanuma. Many daimyos and hatamotos who hungered after various kinds of profit and promotion tried to ingratiate themselves with the great Lord Tanuma. It was said that 'prodigious quantities' of bribes and offerings were delivered in a steady flow to Tanuma from such quarters.

Some gritted their teeth and grumbled over the state of affairs: 'Sooner or later, Tanuma's mansion will burst open with gold coins,' they'd say.

Since the most influential man in the Shogun's reign was carrying on in this manner, bribes were rife among the general public, too. The more principled – what one might call the honourable samurais – lamented this latest fashion. 'Truly regrettable,' they'd say. 'The world is going to the dogs.'

Now, it would seem peculiar that such a man, seemingly engrossed in furthering his political career, should take pleasure in the martial arts, but this was a fact. Tanuma held an unofficial tournament at least once a year at his secondary residence in Hamacho; he took pains to stay abreast of movements among the swordsmen of Edo, and there were quite a few who'd become retainers in the houses of daimyos through Tanuma's recommendation.

Tanuma would later write in his will: 'Spare no effort on studying the military arts; youths in particular shall apply themselves with eager commitment. Should they have zest to spare after their training, only then are they free to amuse themselves as they wish.'

In any case, it is safe to say that Tanuma was one of the largest patrons of the countless swordsmen in Edo.

At the tournament he'd hosted earlier in the year, he had taken note of Daijiro's sudden emergence.

'Who is he?' Tanuma had asked an attendant. When he was informed that the young samurai was Akiyama Kohei's only son, Tanuma murmured, 'Worthy of his father,' and nodded repeatedly in admiration.

Kohei had never had an audience with Tanuma, and neither had he done anything to attract too much attention in public. The fact that Tanuma knew of Kohei and his hidden prowess was proof of Tanuma's considerable interest in the world of swords in Edo.

Kohei heard all about this exchange straight from Lord Kinoshita himself.

Kinoshita Higo-no-kami was the daimyo of Ashimori domain in Bitchu province, worth 25,000 koku. He was a fan of Kohei's tales, so he invited him to his mansion several times a year and delighted in listening to Kohei's accounts of the latest gossip of the people and the goings-on in various provinces.

Since Kohei was used to walking all over Japan, he never ran out of stories to tell. Kinoshita was far from the only daimyo or hatamoto who took pleasure in hearing Kohei's anecdotes. In fact, every one of those lords was the elderly Kohei's patron.

Back to the matter at hand:

Kohei found nothing suspicious in the news that Tanuma's illegitimate daughter was due to marry Nagai Naotsune's heir. What troubled Kohei still, however, was that the steward of the Nagai family had paid a secret visit to Daijiro under a fictitious name and asked him to break a certain individual's arms for fifty gold ryo.

When Daijiro was still a child, Kohei had made a point of sending him away and having him go into training elsewhere, not beneath his wing. Nevertheless, Kohei hoped to help his son establish himself in the world as a fully mature swordsman, since that was the life Daijiro had now chosen for himself.

Of course, things were different now from the warring times of the Sengoku era.

No matter how strong a warrior one was, one needed a bit of worldly wisdom to get ahead, especially in a city as ruthless as Edo.

The large sum of money hadn't swayed Daijiro at all; he had refused to listen to the visitor who'd asked him to use violence on an unknown opponent for unspecified reasons. Daijiro, needless to say, had done the right thing.

Kohei had only been jesting when he'd suggested the contrary. Although inclined to always help his dear son, he never wanted to see Daijiro debase himself as a swordsman.

Several days later, Yashichi of Yotsuya returned with a fresh report.

With money for bait, Yashichi had fished out a servant named Takezo, who had been hired temporarily at Nagai's third mansion. Yashichi treated Takezo to some sake and managed to coax more particulars out of him.

According to this Takezo, the illegitimate daughter of Lord Tanuma had lain down one condition for her marriage into the Nagai family.

The daughter was called Mifuyu, and she was nineteen – the same age as Kohei's sweetheart, Oharu. Mifuyu had declared: 'I don't want any man who is weaker than me.' She had given her word that if Nagai's son, Ukyo, could defeat her in a sword match, she would marry him with good grace. But if not, she wouldn't. *That* was her condition.

'Hmm . . .' Even Kohei was tongue-tied at that. 'To find a girl like that in this day and age – who would've thought?'

'But it's a true story, sensei, from what I've gathered,' Yashichi said. 'That's why there's been so much fuss in Lord Nagai's household.'

'Is Nagai's son much of a fighter?'

'Not at all – the servants say when Master Ukyo carries a pair of swords on his waist, he teeters.'

'That's how it goes nowadays.'

'So, Lord Nagai is in a pretty pickle.'

'No wonder – if Nagai can pull Tanuma's daughter into his family, he'll enjoy the sweet juice without doing any work.'

'Well, Lord Tanuma is also very keen on this engagement, apparently.'

'Hmm . . . Is that so . . .?' After a brief lull, Kohei said, 'Thanks for your hard work, Yashichi. I really owe you one. Leave the rest to me. Feels a bit unfriendly just to hand you money . . . I'll return the favour when it's a good time. Say hello to your missus for me, and your little boy, too.'

VI

The current concubine of Lord Tanuma wasn't Mifuyu's mother.

Back when Tanuma had still been a close aide to the previous shogun, Ieshige – and soon after his much-awaited promotion to become the daimyo of the Sagara domain with 10,000 koku – Mifuyu was born from a waiting maid called Ohiro, who served his mansion in Kanda Ogawamachi.

That was how Ohiro had come to be Tanuma's concubine, but she died from an illness in the summer of 1760, the year after Mifuyu's birth, and so there were few people in the general public who knew of her existence.

Lady Tanuma, his official wife, was fiercely jealous of Ohiro at the time. Adamant that Mifuyu should not be kept as Tanuma's child, she sent Mifuyu away as soon as Ohiro died, to be adopted by Sasaki Mataemon Katsumasa.

Sasaki was restationed to Tanuma's new territory of Sagara, and he was to take Mifuyu with him. Though it wasn't a promotion, he received a bonus of one hundred koku.

'Do take care of Mifuyu for me.' That was all Tanuma had said to Sasaki, but since she was his first daughter, he deeply regretted having to part with her. He choked up as he spoke, and his eyes grew wet as they bore into Sasaki's.

Lady Tanuma was Tanuma's second wife. She married him after his first wife died, and she gave birth to his eldest son, Ryusuke, later known as Okitomo. She was the daughter of Kurosawa Mokunosuke Sadanori, a hatamoto with 600 koku; though the figure is small compared to Tanuma's present wealth, he'd had only 300 koku to his name as the commander of the Shogun's personal guard when he married her.

The couple were very close. Lady Tanuma wouldn't have been so jealous of Ohiro otherwise. Lord Tanuma couldn't ignore her demands either, since she had supported him as he climbed the social ladder.

Kohei heard about all this from a swordsman named Ushibori Kumanosuke, who was the master of a dojo in Asakusa Mototorigoe, where he taught the traditional school of martial arts called Okuyama Nen-ryu.

Ushibori hailed from Kuragano in Kozuke province, and he had moved to Edo about ten years ago. He had never married and devoted his life to the way of the sword, breaking new ground in his own way. Although his dojo was small, many of his pupils were from distinguished families.

Kohei had already been aware that Tanuma's vassals came to Ushibori's dojo for their training. Kohei and Ushibori weren't especially close, but each knew enough about the other.

About seven years ago, Kohei and Ushibori had had a match in front of Doi Noto-no-kami, the lord of the castle in Echizen Ono worth 40,000 koku, that had ended as a draw. The match had essentially been a test for determining whether the Doi family should appoint Ushibori as their official instructor of martial arts and, since Ushibori hadn't won, his appointment was called off.

It is a matter of conjecture why Kohei came to be Ushibori's opponent for this match; it might have been because the captain of the foot soldiers who served the Doi family was a pupil at Kohei's dojo, and this pupil called Yamamoto had petitioned Lord Doi to hire Kohei as their official instructor. The bout was, in other words, just as much of an opportunity for Kohei.

The contest lasted for two whole hours as they locked eyes and held their wooden swords in the lower position, with the blade pointing downwards at the opponent's feet. Neither of them moved an inch. It was impossible to determine the winner.

Later, though, Ushibori would tell his pupils: 'It was Master Akiyama who ended the match in a draw for me. Towards the end I was getting out of breath, and I simply couldn't stand it any more. But he stood his ground without batting an eyelid. That small frame of his seemed to grow bigger in my eyes until he was twice the size – no, three times – and at the same time, somehow it felt as if his body had slipped right into his sword. Well, there was nothing I could do. I suppose he made it a draw so that he could help me along in my career.'

After that, the two had met a couple of times at some feast or other.

Now, Ushibori greeted Kohei with delight, as they hadn't met in quite a while. He invited him into his home and offered him sake.

Still young at forty, Ushibori was good-natured and the type to lead his pupils by setting an example. Also, he wasn't much of a talker. Since Kohei could trust him, he told Ushibori the whole story without leaving anything out and inquired about Sasaki Mifuyu.

'Then is this young lady Mifuyu a pupil of yours?' Kohei asked.

'No, she trained under Izeki Tadahachiro over at Ichigaya. Master Izeki used to visit Lord Tanuma's mansion to give lessons.'

'He passed away last year, didn't he?'

'Yes.'

Izeki had been famous across Edo as a true master of the Itto-ryu school. According to Ushibori, Mifuyu had been his pupil and was known as one of the so-called 'Shitenno', the Four Rulers of the dojo.

'Impressive,' Kohei said.

'Well, you should have a look sometime.'

'At Miss Mifuyu, you mean?'

'You'll see why her future husband would have to be stronger than she is – anyone less wouldn't be able to handle her.'

'Huh . . . interesting.'

'But a steward of the Nagai family came to see your son, you say . . .?'

'I'm wondering if he was trying to get my boy to break her arms . . .'

'Hmm. If her arms were broken, even she would have to give up on fighting a match, and she just might agree to marry into the family without kicking up a fuss . . . Is that what they were after?'

'Nagai must be keen to make ties with Tanuma, after all.'

'Indeed . . .! So, what will you do?'

'Now that I can guess what's behind it, that's enough for me. My son turned down the money and sent him packing. Nothing more to it.'

'But what if . . . some other swordsman accepted the offer instead of your son?'

'Well . . . that's something.'

The two looked at each other. Silence fell over them as they became lost in thought.

VII

It was the 26th of December in 1777, and Mifuyu was on her way home after a training session at Izeki dojo in Ichigaya Choenjitani.

She was a swordswoman, and her appearance gave it away. Her hair was arranged in a slick wakashu-wage – a topknot style for adolescent boys – and over her slender yet toned figure she wore a short-sleeve kimono the colour of pale violet along with a hakama. Her yotsume family crest of four sharp squares marked her black silk-crêpe jacket, and she was barefoot under her silk-strapped sandals. Two narrow-bladed swords – one long, one short – hung from her waist.

Her breezy gait was clearly masculine, but she gave off a certain air of elegance as a maiden of nineteen would. Her thick eyebrows set at a determined angle, her sylphlike eyes fixed straight in front of her, she strode down the street with a bold step. The people she passed by couldn't help but glance back at her dashing figure.

Now that her revered teacher, Izeki Tadahachiro, had passed away, Mifuyu was considered one of the 'Four Rulers' of the dojo, taking up the role of instructor and ensuring that the place was well looked after.

Mifuyu had returned to Edo five years ago, when Izeki moved to the big city from the Sagara domain.

Izeki had lived in Sagara since the days when the territory had belonged to Itakura Sado-no-kami, and he had remained after the ruler changed from Itakura to Tanuma.

Mifuyu had begun learning the way of the sword at the tender age of seven. She was, truly, a natural warrior.

For a long time, she had believed that Sasaki and his wife were her true parents. But in time she discovered the truth about her upbringing when Lord Tanuma told her to come back to Edo. Lady Tanuma had softened enough by then to let her husband acknowledge Mifuyu as his child.

Mifuyu's adoptive father had no choice but to obey his lord's strict orders. He told her everything and sent her back to Edo. She was escorted there by Izeki; which soon led to him becoming a regular visitor at the Tanuma mansion, with Tanuma eventually building a dojo for him in Ichigaya.

Tanuma welcomed Mifuyu with wide-open arms. 'Forgive me for everything in the past. From now on, I am your father,' he said gently, hoping to win her over.

But Mifuyu gave him a curt answer: 'I am *Sasaki* Mifuyu.' After that, she clammed up and refused to speak to him.

Lady Tanuma stepped in, however, and after much coaxing, Mifuyu finally consented to becoming Tanuma's daughter. But ever since, Mifuyu had thrown herself into sword fighting with fresh fervour.

It was also around this time that she had begun to dress like a man.

Even Lord Tanuma, with his fondness for sword fighting, was worried sick for her uncertain future as she became increasingly androgynous.

Fed up with her father fretting over her, Mifuyu had left his Kandabashi mansion the previous summer.

Now, she lived in her birth mother Ohiro's family home in Negishi, looked after by an elderly manservant, Kasuke.

The house was the second residence of her uncle Kichiemon, her mother's elder brother. Kichiemon was a purveyor of specialist texts and owned a prominent shop called Izumi-ya Kichiemon near the Gojoten shrine in Shitaya, which supplied documents to the renowned Kan'ei-ji temple in Ueno and even Edo Castle.

On this particular day, Mifuyu dropped by Izumi-ya on her way back to her lodgings in Negishi.

Heavy clouds had hung over the sky since that morning, only to thicken into a grey mass in the afternoon. There was no wind, but the air was bitterly cold.

'You're out and about quite often these days,' Kichiemon said when Mifuyu came in. 'I beg you to mind your position – you have to be more careful.' Though she was his niece, he always found himself adopting a particularly polite manner when he spoke to her. After all, she was, first and foremost, the great Lord Tanuma's own daughter.

'I'd like to have dinner here before heading home, Uncle,' Mifuyu said.

'Isn't it time you returned to the mansion in Kandabashi instead?'

'When my marriage is arranged, I'll have to go back to Tanuma whether I like it or not.'

'Y-Yes, to be sure . . .'

'Of course, that's only if the man who is to be my wife can beat me in a sword match.' She chuckled.

The creases deepened in Kichiemon's old face. They'd had this conversation countless times already, but there was nothing anyone could do to change her mind. Even Lord Tanuma was powerless against her.

Kichiemon's family business had had friendly relations with the Tanuma house ever since his father's generation, and after his sister had given birth to Mifuyu, Izumi-ya had grown under Tanuma's auspices. Without Tanuma, he couldn't have dreamed of gaining the patronage of Edo Castle or Kan'ei-ji. He was so indebted to Tanuma that he felt it would be 'blasphemy' even to sleep with his feet turned to the direction of Tanuma's mansion – and in fact, he really did make sure he never did so.

As Mifuyu tucked into the assortment of dishes brought out for her on a footed tray – a clear soup with tofu, red tilefish marinated in miso paste, and so on – Kichiemon and his wife, O'ei, exchanged a glance with a helpless sigh.

It was around seven in the evening that Mifuyu left Izumi-ya.

She walked out into Ueno Yamashita, which was what one might call a temple town of Toeizan Kan'ei-ji. Kan'ei-ji was the head temple of the Tendai School of Buddhism in the Kanto region as well as the family temple of the Tokugawa clan. With Shinobazu Pond to the west and the wide road of Shitaya to the south, the streets were packed with all kinds of stores and restaurants as well as stalls for street performers, curiosities and tea shops. The town was alive with as much bustle as the busiest streets of Asakusa or Ryogoku.

Though it was a cold night, the end of the year was drawing near, and people buzzed to and fro, their lanterns swinging with their hurried steps.

From Yamashita, Mifuyu entered Kuruma-zaka Street and turned again, continuing down the path towards Sakamoto, with the forest of Ueno rising steep on her left and a row of residences for the shogunate's lower-rank samurai on her right. This street was part of the Oshu Kaido – one of the major Five Routes of the Edo period – which ran through Kanasugi and Minowa to the Senju-ohashi bridge; soon it was bright from the merchants' houses that stood on both sides, and there were many people passing by.

Once she passed the gate of Zensho-ji temple, Mifuyu strode left into the alley bordering the second and third districts of Sakamoto. In her right hand, she held a lantern she had borrowed from Izumi-ya; her left hand rested inside the fold of her kimono in a debonair, cheeky kind of way.

She turned right along the wall of Yoden-ji temple. This neighbourhood was darker, and the streets were empty. Clumps of trees and vegetable patches stretched out in front of her: a stark contrast from the bustle of the city she had just left.

She would soon be in the village of Negishi. It was just as a certain book had described: 'The village of Negishi, where bamboo thrives, lies in the shadow of the Ueno mountain, and it is a site of mysterious beauty, favoured by people of leisure. The song of the bush warblers born in this village has won the admiration of many far and wide.' A fair number of the houses dotting this area were holiday homes and hideaways of those with refined tastes.

Mifuyu reached the corner of Yoden-ji, instead of its wall, the dense grove around Kan'ei-ji now appeared on her right. She came to a stop.

'It's snowing...' she murmured, noticing the specks of white whirling down in the dark.

Just then, something fell over her head – not snow, but a fishing net. She tossed aside her lantern and took a step back to draw her long katana, but she couldn't pull it out all the way. The net closed around her as she staggered and struggled to break free. Four shadows darted out of the grove without a sound and attacked her with cudgels.

'Who—?! How dare you?' she yelled, but there was nothing she could do. They struck all over her body and she fell to the ground, before soon passing out.

'Pull off the net,' a tall samurai ordered.

The other three quickly untangled the net from Mifuyu's limp body and dragged her out. All of them were samurai. Their faces were concealed, and their sturdy footwear suggested they were prepared for a long journey.

'Show me her arms,' the same man said.

'Yessir.' Two men laid Mifuyu face down, extended her arms above her head and pinned them to the ground. She let out a faint groan.

Her lantern was burning nearby; one of them stamped out the fire.

'Good. And now to break her arms with the back of my sword,' the tall man said, unsheathing his katana. But then he lurched forward with a yelp and fell on one knee. A stone had shot through the air and hit him right in the face.

'Sensei! What is it?' the men stammered.

A small shadow approached them from behind, as swift and silent as a breeze. It casually picked up a cudgel from the ground and beat the trio right and left. Their screams were cut short in an instant as they all fell to the ground unconscious.

Teeth chattering with fear, the tall man crawled away and finally managed to stagger to his feet with his sword at the ready. The stone must have struck him hard; the tip of his blade was trembling.

'Put that away. It's pointless,' said the small shadow. 'Come back another day. The name is Akiyama Kohei.'

The man was clearly in shock; he turned on his heel and scampered off without a scrap of dignity. Kohei didn't pursue him.

'Are you all right?' he asked Mifuyu, who had come to and half risen from the ground. He flashed a mischievous grin. 'You had your guard down. If I hadn't been following you, you would've been in serious trouble.'

Mifuyu said nothing, her face turned away.

'Hmph. Not even a word of thanks?'

'Much obliged.'

'Your heart's not in it, I can tell.'

'What more can I say, Master Akiyama?'

'You know my name . . .?'

'I heard you say it to that scoundrel.'

'Hmm.'

The three men roused and started to flee. Kohei darted forward like a flying squirrel and struck down one of them with his bare hand. The other two ran away without even a backward glance.

'Master Akiyama,' Mifuyu said, 'why were you following me?'

'For three whole days.'

'I want to know why.'

'I was bored, that's why.'

'What did you say?'

'I see how it is. You're bound to stay unmarried for a good while yet. A wilder horse than I'd imagined.'

'H-horse?'

'Take care on your way home.'

With that, Kohei hoisted the unconscious assailant on his shoulder like he weighed nothing – though he was probably twice his size – and disappeared into the dark.

Even Mifuyu was at a loss as she stared wide-eyed after the small man.

The snow didn't settle that night.

VIII

Two days later in the afternoon, Kohei was chopping firewood at the back of his house. It was a clear, mild day without any wind. Sitting on a stone, he chopped the wood as effortlessly as if he were cutting paper with scissors. He barely moved the hand holding the hatchet. The tip of the blade only had to tap lightly at the log for it to split in two, then four.

A flock of plovers flew away, skimming over the dry reeds that grew on the bank of Ohkawa.

Oharu was out; her father had brought a batch of New Year's mochi for them, so she was taking some to Daijiro's dojo on the other side of the river.

A figure stepped out in front of Kohei. It was Mifuyu, dressed as a young man.

'I came to thank you for saving me the other night. I am grateful,' she said stiffly.

'How did you find me?'

'I asked Ushibori Sensei. I had heard much about you before, but I was so surprised that it didn't occur to me then – apologies for my bad manners . . .'

'There's always some danger lurking for anyone who wields a sword, even in a peaceful, carefree time like this. Are you prepared for that?'

'Yes, sir.'

'Here's a good case in point. Those men who attacked you weren't just any old gang prowling the streets . . . For whatever reason, a supposedly respectable lord with 5,000 koku has hired some rats to break the arms of a woman in the hope that she will marry his son. It's a downright circus.'

'None of them have the right to call themselves samurai . . .'

'Never mind. So, how about it? Won't you go back to Lord Tanuma?'

'If only . . . *he* weren't my father . . .'

'You disapprove of the roju's influence, is that it?'

'I think it's dirty.'

'That's politics for you – finding a sliver of truth in the muck.'

'I don't understand.' Without even a blink, Mifuyu stared hard at Kohei's face as he went on chopping wood. Soon, her eyes began to gleam with a certain intensity.

Kohei had his eyes on the logs. 'You like swords that much, eh?' he asked.

'Yes. It is my life.'

'Why is that?'

'When I stand with a sword in my hands, I never hesitate.'
'So you have doubts at other times?'
Mifuyu was silent.

'Do you dislike men?' Kohei asked before she could answer.

'I do. But you're different, Akiyama Sensei.' Her tone suddenly softened, and Kohei looked up in surprise.

She looked like a young boy in her wheat-coloured outfit, and her face was bright red. He stared at her, bewildered.

'I've never felt like this before,' she said. She turned her back on him and covered her face with her sleeves. Even Kohei was startled by this and half rose from his seat, his mouth hanging open. 'The other night . . .' she purred falteringly, her back still turned, 'you were amazing, sensei . . . When I saw . . . when I saw you do what you did, I . . .'

She whirled around and fixed her eyes on the bamboo thicket behind Kohei. Her hand was already on the hilt of her katana.

Kohei remained sitting on the stone and slowly turned around.

Five men rushed out of the thicket into the clearing and closed in on them with their swords drawn.

'The same sprats,' Kohei said, and without even rising to his feet he picked up one log after another and flung it at the men. He looked so nonchalant that he might as well have been tossing a handful of beans to feed some pigeons, but the logs flew straight at their faces and knees.

Four of the men staggered back with a groan. One even toppled over to the ground. A plain log could be surprisingly effective in Kohei's hands. Only one of them managed to dodge it: the tall man who seemed to be the leader of the pack.

With a fierce cry, the man charged at Kohei, swinging down his sword in one breath. Kohei swerved to the side and threw another log at his face.

'Damn it!' The man knocked it away with his sword and leaped over the pile of logs where Mifuyu awaited him with her sword at the ready. He dived to the ground to dodge her blade and quickly got back on his feet, raising his sword again. 'You bastard . . .!'

Mifuyu stepped forward to strike again, but Kohei told her to cover his back. She spun around and rushed to his side, just in time to face the four men who had recovered from the blows and were about to thrust their blades at Kohei.

'Come,' she said firmly, standing in their way. 'I am ready.'

Kohei looked up at the tall man and sat back down on the stone. 'I know who you are. You're Asada Torajiro from the Nen-ryu dojo at Honjo Yotsume. Your pupil – the one I caught the other night – spilled the beans.'

Asada's eyes widened, glinting with murderous intent. He quickly raised his sword above his head, ready to swing down.

Kohei's lips curled into a sneer.

Asada had taken a step forward, but now he retreated by three and lowered his sword to the middle position, his blade tilted at a slight angle.

Behind Kohei, Mifuyu was taking on all four men at once. She had kept them at bay, not giving them a chance to take a single step closer to her. That wasn't all: she had already incapacitated two of them by severing some of their limbs.

'Tell me, Asada,' Kohei sighed, sitting on the stone with a log in one hand, the hatchet in the other. 'You figured your pupil leaked your name, so you came here to kill me, didn't you . . .?'

'Shut it.'

'Who was it that offered you fifty gold ryo to break the arms of this young woman behind me, eh . . .? It's all right, you don't have to tell me – I know who it was well enough. But here's the thing, Asada. Did you stop to think who she could be?'

Asada gnashed his teeth, but he couldn't close the distance between them. He was paralysed with terror at the piercing, needle-sharp gleam in Kohei's eyes.

'It's a headache to see more and more ruffians like you here in Edo these days,' Kohei said. 'Hey, listen. This young lady is the daughter of the roju Lord Tanuma Tonomo-no-kami.'

The moment Asada's face contorted in astonishment, Kohei flung the log at him. He ducked, but the hatchet rammed into his head with a tremendous crack. As a shriek tore out of Asada, Mifuyu knocked the remaining two men unconscious with the back of her blade.

'Well done,' Kohei told her.

Asada's towering body swayed for a second, then fell to the ground with a resounding thud.

Stunned, Mifuyu stared at the fallen body.

Some time afterwards, when Oharu came back on the

boat, there was no one to be seen: Kohei, Mifuyu, Asada's corpse, and the four assailants had all disappeared.

It was only when dusk was starting to veil the land that Kohei returned home.

When Oharu asked where he'd been, he said, 'I found a big man lying dead by the roadside, so I went and buried him.'

'I'm sure that's a lie,' she said.

'Sure it is,' he said airily. 'A big fat lie at that.'

*

The new year dawned, and it was now 1778. For Kohei, it would be his sixtieth year; for Daijiro, his twenty-fifth.

On the 20th of January, a sword match was held between Mifuyu and Lord Nagai's son, Ukyo, at the secondary mansion of Lord Tanuma in Hamacho.

Ukyo faced Mifuyu, holding the wooden sword with a timid grasp. She quickly advanced towards him; when he flung his sword at her chaotically, she easily parried the blow and struck his right arm with such great force that it broke.

Moaning in pain, Ukyo was carried away to another room. On the way, he whispered to a vassal of the Nagai family called Mitsui: 'It's for the best. I can't imagine marrying a female Fan Kuai.' Fan Kuai was a warlord of ancient China, known for his extraordinary courage. In the end, Ukyo seemed rather happy about the outcome of the match.

Lord Tanuma heard about Mifuyu's victory upon returning to the Kandabashi mansion from Edo Castle.

'Well, I never expected Ukyo to win, but . . . oh, my

Mifuyu . . .' he muttered. 'Will there ever come a day . . .?' He heaved an exasperated sigh full of fatherly love.

As for Lord Nagai, he gave Ukyo a lengthy dressing-down. 'I won't consider you my son any longer,' he declared.

Nagai had been hoping to forge an intimate connection with Lord Tanuma and thereby secure a promotion from his current post – which he found rather uneventful – to the roju's second-in-command, which would have brought him much closer to the Shogun himself. Naturally, he was filled with regret.

On top of that, he and his steward, Ohyama Sahei, were tormented by the fact that Asada Torajiro and his pupils, who had agreed to ambush Mifuyu after Daijiro turned them down, had been missing ever since the year's end. When they considered what would befall them if this scheme of theirs were to reach Tanuma's ears, they were gripped by panic.

It was Ohyama who had proposed the scheme to break Mifuyu's arms so that she would give in and marry into the Nagai family. By the end of February, he had killed himself.

Mifuyu had grasped enough about their plot from what Kohei had said to Asada, but apparently, she never brought it to Tanuma's attention.

As spring drew closer, Mifuyu picked up a habit of crossing the river and visiting Kohei at home on the flimsiest of pretexts. He was at a loss. Whenever she looked at him, her eyes shone as if a secret passion were blooming.

Oharu noticed it and cried with jealousy. 'I don't like her. Please don't let her come here, sensei.'

As for Daijiro's dojo behind Masaki Inari-myo shrine, he still hadn't found a pupil.

He contented himself as ever with meals of broth and barley, one bowl of each. Every day, he stood in his dojo and trained all by himself. Sometimes he would fast for a few days and sit upright for hours on end in deep meditation.

The farmers in the neighbourhood gossiped among themselves: 'Have you seen that sensei at the dojo? I do wonder if he's been possessed by the sacred fox of Masaki shrine . . .'

Chapter 2
The Oath of the Sword

I

'Delicious,' Daijiro murmured.

There was no one around; he spoke only to himself.

This was a rare occurrence.

Daijiro continued to live alone in his small dojo by Masaki Inari-myo shrine on the outskirts of Asakusa. The farmer's wife went home as soon as she was done preparing his suppers. He would eat in silent contemplation, and after that, either read into the night or put out the light and meditate for long stretches of time. He never grew tired of meditating.

But he had never talked to himself before. If talking to oneself is an expression of one's loneliness, his habitual silence indicated that he was not at all lonely in his day-to-day life, even with such a spartan routine.

The miso soup on this particular day must have been exceptionally good to make him utter that word aloud. Ever since autumn last year, he had been living solely on barley rice and scallion soup. Tonight, the soup had some tanishi in it instead of just scallions.

Tanishi was a small freshwater snail with a dark, spiral shell, found in rice paddies, ponds and swamps. There was plenty to be foraged from around the time of year when frost began to thaw and the bare paddies were ploughed for the coming spring. One could pick the fattest snails, soak them in water to get the dirt out, and stew them in miso or dress them in a paste made with leaf buds of sansho pepper. 'Well, I'd say it's even better than miso soup with shijimi clams,' Kohei once said.

The tanishi soup came as a surprise for Daijiro; the farmer's wife had gone with her husband to gather them, and she probably brought some for him as a treat. Since he had been subsisting on scallion soup for so long, even he was moved to murmur in appreciation.

'Delicious,' he said again, carrying the soup and barley to his mouth in turn. His youthful face and deep-set eyes glowed with the sheer animal pleasure of consuming food.

His dojo had still yet to see a single pupil enter its threshold. His father had helped him build the dojo, but after that, he simply told him to manage on his own. Truth be told, Daijiro had barely any rice and miso left in the kitchen now.

Actually, he did take one pupil.

A hatamoto named Takao Sahei – who was worth 700 koku and owned a mansion in Yushima Uekimachi – had seen Daijiro's extraordinary skill at the tournament held at Lord Tanuma's secondary mansion last summer and sent his second son, Yujiro, to train under him. On the 18th of January, Yujiro had come, accompanied by a steward, to ask for admission to the dojo.

Daijiro had readily assented, and on the very next day,

he handed Yujiro a thick pole weighing over thirty pounds. Nearly six feet long, it was made of Japanese evergreen oak with a solid wire of iron metal embedded in it.

'First practise with this until you can swing it at least two thousand times,' Daijiro told him.

The twenty-three-year-old stopped at fifty strokes on the first day; on the second day, he managed a wobbly eighty strokes. On the third, he gave up at a hundred and slumped down on the floor.

'And you won't let me do *real* practice until I can get to two thousand?' Yujiro asked sulkily.

'Of course not,' Daijiro said bluntly.

From the following day, Yujiro didn't show up at the dojo. Since he had been training at another dojo and was already used to handling practice swords made of wood or bamboo, he seemed to have had no patience for Daijiro's way of teaching, regardless of where his father wanted him to go.

Nowadays, making a living from running a private dojo meant you had to know how to treat your pupils – and even humour them by letting them strike you once in a while.

And that was how Daijiro lost his very first pupil in just three days.

Still, with the money that Yujiro had paid when he started at the dojo, Daijiro managed to buy more rice and miso paste as well as pay the farmer's wife's wages, which he was supposed to settle once every six months.

When he ate, Daijiro chewed every mouthful until it turned into a soft pulp, so his meals always took a rather long time. Though it might appear tedious to some, it was one of his principles as a samurai, which he had learned from his father when he was young. In a way, it was the very first step in his training.

Kohei's wife and Daijiro's mother, Otei, had died from an illness when Daijiro was seven, so he took after his father in many of his habits.

When he finished his meal, Daijiro drank a cup of plain hot water in slow gulps, then quietly lay down on his back. This was something his father had taught him, too: to lie still with his eyes closed for about an hour after supper. This was his custom on an ordinary day, but he was also perfectly able to have a quick meal when there was a need.

The scent of spring suffused the night air. Heavy with warmth, the gloom shrouded everything beyond the small room in which he lay.

Suddenly, he opened his eyes. He sensed someone approaching outside; their footfall sounded different from Kohei's. It stopped in front of the dojo's door, and a hoarse voice called out, 'Hello?'

The door wasn't even barred. Daijiro stepped out on to the dirt-floor pit just inside the door.

'Is that you, Daijiro . . .?' the visitor asked from the other side.

Daijiro slid open the door to find an elderly samurai standing firm, dressed for a long journey. The old man was like a mulberry tree with an armour of frost at dawn.

'It's a pleasure to see you after so long,' Daijiro said courteously, welcoming him in.

'Indeed,' the old man answered. 'Daijiro. I came to ask you to be a witness to my death.'

II

The old samurai's name was Shimaoka Reizo.

If Daijiro remembered correctly, Shimaoka was three years younger than Kohei, so he should have turned fifty-seven.

Reizo and Kohei used to train together under the tutelage of Tsuji Hei'emon Naomasa, who had led a dojo of the Mugai-ryu school in the ninth district of Kojimachi.

The Mugai-ryu style of sword fighting was established by a man named Tsuji Heinai, who was from Masugi village in the Koka district of Oumi province. Heinai later took the name Gettan, though the particulars of this part of his life are lost to history.

Heinai was an eccentric man; generous and indifferent to worldly possessions; he refused to take any kind of payment from his pupils and hence lived in extreme poverty. It has been recorded that 'when he made his way to a pupil's home for a lesson, bits of cotton stuck out of the hem of his kimono, his haori jacket was worn thin around his shoulders and sleeves, and the scabbard of his katana was faded, the coat of lacquer peeling off . . .' By the time his dojo grew to more than two hundred pupils, his manner of living had improved somewhat, but whenever he had a little bit to spare, he freely gave it away to others in need.

Once, Heinai assisted the brothers Sugita Shozaemon and Yaheiji, who served the Ohno domain in Echizen province, in their attempt to avenge their father, Bansuke, by killing Yamana Gengoro. Thanks to his help, they succeeded. After that, Shozaemon let his younger brother take over the family and returned to Edo to become Heinai's disciple.

Heinai had never married, and in 1727, when he succumbed to an illness at the age of seventy-nine, Shozaemon inherited his dojo at Kojimachi and changed his name to Tsuji Kimata at the same time.

Kimata also remained a bachelor throughout his life and never had a child, so when it was time to pass on the dojo, he chose his favourite disciple, Misawa Chiyotaro, to be his successor.

Chiyotaro changed his name to Tsuji Hei'emon and took over the dojo. It was this Hei'emon that had taught Kohei and Reizo. People called them the 'two finest' pupils of the dojo, a pair as formidable as a dragon and a tiger.

When Kohei was thirty and Reizo twenty-seven, their master Hei'emon announced to them out of the blue: 'Live as you wish from now on.' He left Edo without any apparent purpose and became a recluse in the small village of Ohara in the Otagi district of Yamashiro province. He had neither wife nor child.

Kohei stayed in Edo.

Reizo accompanied Hei'emon to Ohara.

With that, the dojo at Kojimachi, which had been passed down over generations ever since it was founded by Heinai, the father of Mugai-ryu, finally closed its doors.

Reminiscing about those bygone days, Kohei had once told Daijiro, 'The Tsuji dojo had more than two hundred pupils at one point, but by the time Hei'emon Sensei left Edo behind, there were only seven of us, including me and Reizo. But we made up for our small number – you should've seen how we threw ourselves into training day and night . . . Even you wouldn't believe how far we went.' Kohei chuckled.

He never did tell Daijiro what their practice had actually entailed. As time had gone by, the number of pupils at the dojo had dwindled, most likely because they were fed up with the extreme rigour of their training.

In Hei'emon's view, he hadn't been particularly harsh in his teaching methods; he had merely endeavoured to impart the art of swords that had been passed down over generations. The only problem was that the pupils of his generation couldn't bear it any more.

Kohei, who remained in Edo, later opened his own small dojo in Yotsuya Nakamachi. 'That's when I became a different man,' Kohei once remarked with a faint, mysterious smile playing on his lips – but he said no more. Daijiro knew only the vague outlines of this period in his father's life.

Daijiro was born and raised in the midst of the thunder of crashing swords and roaring men in his father's dojo. At thirteen, when Daijiro told Kohei that he was determined to live as a swordsman, Kohei had said, 'Do as you wish. So far, I've been teaching you the basics: the essentials that you should know as a man. You're free to become whatever you like – I won't stop you. Though if you really want to learn the blade, you have to first leave me and enter another dojo.'

In Daijiro's fifteenth summer, Kohei sent his only son to his old master in Yamashiro. 'If Hei'emon Sensei has a look at you and tells you to go back to Edo, you listen to him and come right back,' he told Daijiro.

But Daijiro didn't come back. Apparently, the old sensei – in his seventies then – took a liking to Daijiro.

Daijiro trained under Hei'emon for about five years, deep in the mountains of Ohara. Ever the faithful disciple, Reizo was still by Hei'emon's side, and Daijiro served him as a second master. Daijiro didn't exactly complete his training; it came to an end when Hei'emon died from an illness.

'You should go back to Edo and follow Master Kohei's advice,' Reizo had told him then. Reizo himself departed for his hometown in the village of Shibamura in the Shiki district of Yamato province.

Now, it had been a full six years since Daijiro had last seen Reizo.

Reizo had travelled all the way from Yamato to Edo without stopping on the way, so Daijiro made a fire from some wood and drew a bath for the first time in a long while. When the bath was ready in the wood barrel tub, he urged Reizo to bathe and helped him wash his back. The old man was thin, but his body was firm and sinewy, as if it were fortified with strands of steel wire. Compared to his grey-streaked hair tied at the back of his head, his hardened body seemed to belong to another man entirely.

'How is Master Kohei?' Reizo asked, his voice easing in the steam of the bath.

'He lives on the other side of the river. I am sure he'll be delighted when he hears you have come, Shimaoka Sensei. I will go and let him know.'

'No need,' Reizo said sternly.

'You won't allow me?'

'I don't need to see him. It will be enough if you could be with me to witness my death.'

'I will gladly obey you, sir.'

'I will fight a duel with a real sword.'

'What . . .?'

'I have given my word, you see.'

'To whom? Where?'

'I need you to be my messenger. It's a bother, but I'd be obliged if you could go to my opponent.'

'Yes, sir . . .'

'This duel will be the third time that he and I cross swords. I doubt I will come out alive this time. It's the swordsman's fate. Right now, I live in comfort in the mansion that belongs to my elder brother, Shimaoka Hachiro'emon. He's the headman of Shibamura in Yamato, overseeing several village chiefs. I would want for nothing for all my remaining years. Though I'd been absent for a long time, the whole family gave me a warm welcome back – both my brother and his wife, their children, and their little grandchildren . . . My brother has enough wealth that it makes no difference to him to house an unmarried, unknown, ageing swordsman like myself. Seven years ago, when the venerable Hei'emon Sensei passed away in Ohara—'

'You said you will quit the blade and live out your life in peace, as an ordinary old man.'

'I did say that. However, that cannot be. My opponent hadn't forgotten our oath from ten years ago . . . A letter from him arrived in Ohara last spring, and it was forwarded to my brother's mansion.'

'Ten years ago . . .' Daijiro murmured. 'That was soon after I left my father and entered the dojo in Ohara.'

'Do you remember how I was away for about three months around that time?'

'Ah . . .'

'I see it has come back to you.' The deep wrinkles on Reizo's face softened as his mouth curled up for a moment before tightening into a thin line again. Daijiro finished washing Reizo's back and prompted him to soak in the tub again.

'Is this duel for settling a grudge?' Daijiro asked.

'You could say so.' Reizo's voice was calm, and his thin eyes betrayed no emotion.

'And your opponent – is it one man?'

'Yes. But he will have an attendant. I'm afraid I must ask you to be mine.'

'Yes, sir.'

'Listen carefully, Daijiro. It's the fate of the swordsman to see a duel through to the end whether he likes it or not. Your father knew this very well, so as soon as he reached the cusp of old age, he made an about-face, swift as a swallow, or so I heard . . .' Reizo chuckled. 'There's many a man who suffered bitter defeat against Master Kohei. And those who are defeated will keep challenging you until they win. Do you understand?'

'Yes . . .'

'Without conquering the one who crushed you, you can't recover your confidence as a swordsman. Without confidence, you can't face the world with your blade. All the more reason to triumph over that rival. There's no other way to go on . . .' Reizo sighed. 'Once a samurai, always a samurai – even those of us like Master Kohei and myself, who have left behind the world of duels, can't escape from them for ever. You are young, but you would do well to remember it.'

'I will.'

'What a world we live in, even in this age of peace . . .'

Daijiro was silent.

'However, I daresay there are certain joys that can only be found by those who take the way of the sword. So it was for the likes of me and Master Kohei when we were young.'

There was still some tanishi soup left. Daijiro warmed it up and cooked a fresh batch of barley rice for his guest. They made plans for the duel as Reizo ate. When the meal was done, Reizo lay down to sleep in the larger of the two rooms. Before long, Daijiro could hear his quiet, steady breathing. Daijiro couldn't get a wink of sleep that night.

In the morning, they breakfasted together. Daijiro got dressed for his errand as soon as they had finished, and soon after seeing him off, Reizo disappeared from the dojo, too.

For the first time this year, Kohei happened to drop by the dojo to check on his son. He saw that the house was unbarred and empty, went back home, and said to Oharu, 'Dai wasn't in this morning. I wonder where he could be – something rather unusual must have come up. What do you think, Oharu?'

III

Daijiro walked at a brisk pace. He was dressed formally in a crisp hakama, his hair neatly combed and tied back in a topknot. He wore an old-fashioned kasa, a flat wickerwork hat made of cypress. Within a couple of hours, he had crossed the Shin'ohashi bridge in Azabu, gone further south until he reached Sanko Hill and the gate of Saiko-ji temple that stood to the west of the hill. He passed a woman working on a farm and asked about the house he was looking for.

Under the gloomy sky, he slipped into a narrow lane that ran along the north side of the temple.

Back in those days, this was essentially the suburbs of Edo. Saiko-ji was hemmed in by a thick pine grove, and a small hill rose behind it. At the end of the small lane stood a simple construction that served as a gate. The gate was ajar, so Daijiro stepped in and took off his hat – but he stopped in his tracks.

He had heard the sound of a bowstring and the sharp crack of an arrow hitting a target. Like the temple, this house was surrounded by a dense grove, but when Daijiro turned left inside the gate, he came to a clearing that seemed to have once been a vegetable garden. In this open ground stood a young man practising archery.

He noticed Daijiro and lowered the arrow that he was about to nock. 'Who are you?' he asked in a high-pitched voice.

With a bow, Daijiro gave his name and said, 'I come as a

messenger from Shimaoka Reizo of Yamato. I would like to deliver a letter to Kakimoto Genshichiro Sensei.'

The young man said nothing and stared intently at Daijiro. There was a hint of something boyish about his face. His delicate, pale skin – one shoulder bare from archery practice – was flushed with the exertion, making him all the more striking. Though his lithe figure was of average height, his eyes were piercing.

The silence stretched on.

'Is Kakimoto Sensei at home?' Daijiro tried again, shifting his gaze to the straw-thatched house on the other side of the clearing.

'You can wait here,' the young man said, glaring up at Daijiro. His shoulder was still bare. He was being plain rude, but Daijiro didn't bat an eyelid.

The youth went into the house and came back in a few moments. This time, he had pulled up his kimono to cover his skin.

'I have asked Kakimoto Sensei. You said you're a messenger from Master Shimaoka Reizo, so he has told me to receive your message and pass it on to him.'

An odd little smirk flickered on his lips. The sight of this smile baffled Daijiro. It wasn't a disparaging sort of smile; if anything, there was a hint of flattery in it. Needless to say, the flattery wasn't directed at Daijiro.

'Here is the letter from Shimaoka Reizo. Could you please present it to Kakimoto Sensei and bring me his answer?'

The youth took the letter and withdrew again.

The air was still and silent. A great gingko tree stood on

the far end of the clearing, and an archery target was tied to it. Five arrows were clustered right in the middle on the black dot.

Is he a pupil here? Daijiro wondered.

There was no sign of anyone else. According to Reizo, Kakimoto was just over forty, at the height of his prowess as a swordsman. Daijiro had expected such a man to be at a dojo, but he could see nothing of the kind here – only the trees, the clearing and the small house in hushed solitude.

Though small, the thatched house had a picturesque look. It seemed too old to have been built by Kakimoto. Perhaps it used to be a retreat for an elderly person, which would have been more fitting.

The youth came out again. A trace of that peculiar smirk was still there.

'This is Kakimoto Sensei's answer,' he said curtly, handing Daijiro a letter.

The boy had no manners. He called his own teacher 'sensei' in front of a stranger. For a disciple, the teacher was supposed to be like a father; it was ridiculous to use such an honorific for a fatherly figure in the presence of others. It was clear from the inflections of his speech that he was fawning over his teacher and didn't care a whit what Daijiro thought. Daijiro inwardly shook his head at this behaviour.

He checked that Kakimoto's letter was indeed addressed to Shimaoka Reizo and took his leave with a quick bow.

The archer watched until Daijiro passed the gate, then went back inside the house. The house had four rooms, but there wasn't a speck of dust anywhere. It was old but well looked after, in stark contrast to the neglected yard.

There was one person in the back room – an obese, middle-aged samurai. His face was fleshy as though it were swollen, the colour of his skin like a sooty sheet of paper. His nose and mouth were thick, too, and his purplish bottom lip drooped down. He seemed to struggle to breathe.

This man was none other than Kakimoto Genshichiro.

If Daijiro could have seen him, what would he have thought?

This was Reizo's account of his second duel with Kakimoto, which took place ten years ago on Mount Tsukuba in Hitachi province:

'This giant man nearly six feet tall had an armour of muscles as hard as a boulder, and I thought I'd be blown away like a leaf just from the swish of his sword. The first time we fought each other was ten years before that, back when your father and I were still with Tsuji Sensei in Edo . . . But Kakimoto had changed completely in the span of a decade. At our first match, I knocked him down with a single strike of my wooden sword. At Mount Tsukuba, though . . . we held our blades at the ready and locked eyes for about four hours. In the end, we were both spent. So, we swore to meet again in ten years' time.'

There was no trace of the man he used to be in Kakimoto now.

He had been absorbed in re-reading Shimaoka's letter at his desk, but as soon as he saw the youth come in, he rolled up the letter and tucked it under the collar of his kimono.

A futon was laid out behind him, and the room was stuffy with the odour of medicine dissolved in warm water. Apparently, Kakimoto was sick.

'What is it, sensei . . .?' the archer asked tenderly. He sounded completely different from how he'd spoken to Daijiro; the contrast was like night and day. He snuggled up to Kakimoto and said, 'Please show me the letter, sensei.'

Without answering, Kakimoto hooked his arm behind the young man's slender neck and kissed him. The youth closed his eyes with a moan and wrapped his pale arms tight around the man's bulk. But he pushed Kakimoto away in a moment.

'We shouldn't. It's bad for your health,' he whispered, his eyes glowing in admiration.

'Silly boy,' Kakimoto groaned. Getting to his feet with a faintly bitter smile, he said, 'It's nothing to worry about. This letter is from an old friend.' His voice was deep and gentle.

'Where are you going, sensei?'

'The privy.'

As soon as he stepped into the narrow hallway, he let out a sharp cry and pressed his hands against his chest. 'Ah . . .!' It was almost a scream. He crouched on the spot, his face twisted in agony.

The youth flew to him and held him up. 'It's all right. Please stay calm – deep breaths . . .'

Kakimoto gasped between strangled groans.

'Be strong . . .' the boy murmured, laying his master down on the futon. He poured some medicine into his own mouth from the earthenware teapot kept by the pillow, and he gave this to Kakimoto, mouth-to-mouth.

The fit subsided, and when the boy made him take a different powdered medicine, Kakimoto soon fell asleep.

Reizo's letter had fallen in the hallway. The boy picked it up and opened it. Once he had read through it, he put it back under Kakimoto's collar and crept to the back door, where he ran into the old maidservant, who had just returned.

'Sensei has taken a turn for the worse. I will go to the doctor, Yamaguchi Gen'an, to get more medicine. Look after him while I'm gone,' he said, and rushed off.

It was past noon when Daijiro returned to his home in Asakusa. Reizo got back after sunset.

'I've been walking around the streets of Edo. It's changed since the last time I was here.' When he read Kakimoto's response, Reizo said, 'Good. The duel is set for the day after tomorrow.'

'And the place?'

Instead of an answer, Reizo showed him the letter. When Daijiro had read through it, Reizo's eyelashes fluttered slightly.

'The handwriting is Kakimoto's, but . . . it's a little different from the letter he sent me a year ago,' Reizo muttered.

'What's different about it?'

No answer came from Reizo.

IV

Supper was a feast that night, owing to the mute woman's kindness for Daijiro and his guest. It was a feast by Daijiro's standards, at least: asari clams lightly stewed with scallions and tofu.

'This is great,' Reizo said cheerfully, misty-eyed with nostalgia. 'The flavour of Edo. It takes me back.'

'Shall I fetch my father, sensei?'

'What for?'

'He would be so pleased to see you . . .'

'We haven't met for a very long time. It's been thirty years, perhaps . . .'

'Then there's even more reason to meet. I'm sure my father would—'

'Well . . . we are never the same after thirty years.'

'Do you think so?'

'You'll see it soon enough, Daijiro.'

'What will I see . . .?'

'Thirty years ago, when Tsuji Sensei left Edo to live like a hermit in the village of Ohara, Master Kohei and I went our separate ways as swordsmen. While he rode the current of the times, I deviated from that current and clung to the way of the sword that I'd always followed ever since I was young . . . I am still the same man as when I took my first step as a samurai, but . . . Well, Daijiro. I wonder what kind of path you will come to follow from now on . . .'

Reizo quietly drank up the sake in his bowl.

'And look at me now. Even though I'm almost sixty, I still trek all the way to Edo just to settle a match with an adversary from twenty years ago. If Master Kohei saw an old man like me, what would he think?' he said with a low chuckle, his face creasing into a smile.

It was an honest smile. He was neither ashamed of himself nor mocking Kohei.

'I'll tell you about Kakimoto Genshichiro,' Reizo went

on calmly. 'He is the younger brother of a man named Kakimoto Isaku – a samurai of the Shibata domain in Echigo province. Twenty years ago, Genshichiro was a swordsman at the well-reputed dojo of Ohta Magobei.

'He was young and full of vitality back then . . . He marched into our dojo with his head held high and demanded a match against Hei'emon Sensei.'

Daijiro held his breath. It was a story that no one had ever told him before.

'Master Kohei happened to be out. It was just me and Sensei at the dojo that day – there were so few of us left. So . . . I stepped forward to meet the challenger. And I took him down with one strike.'

Kakimoto had been twenty-four years old that day, leading four of his fellow pupils from Ohta dojo to 'crush' the Tsuji dojo, which was still a distinguished training hall even though it was starting to fall apart.

According to Reizo, Hei'emon hadn't even watched their match; he'd stayed in the back room, absorbed in a book.

Meanwhile, in the dojo, Reizo and Kakimoto had sat down in the formal position and bowed to each other, following the code of behaviour before a match. The moment they rose, Kakimoto's wooden sword was knocked out of his hands; as it flew to the ceiling, Reizo's wooden sword tapped Kakimoto's right arm.

Kakimoto blanched. He stood there, paralysed, for some time. His shame stung all the more because he had barged in with a confident stride and four fellow pupils in tow, but he never even saw the master of the dojo; instead, Tsuji's pupil had treated him like a child.

Eventually, he looked up and asked Reizo to fight again once ten years had passed – but with real swords.

Reizo accepted this without hesitation. 'I will remember,' he said.

After that, Kakimoto had left Ohta dojo and disappeared from Edo altogether.

Ten years later, at their second encounter on Mount Tsukuba, the duel had begun with a fierce volley of strikes from both sides, but neither allowed the other to breach his defence; they glared at each other for four hours until they had no more willpower or strength to fight. They withdrew their blades at the same time and swore to meet again in another ten years.

'If Genshichiro had defeated me the first time, he might have gone on to inherit Ohta Sensei's dojo and become one of the greatest swordsmen in Edo by now,' Reizo said, sipping cold sake. 'I imagine he must've sweated blood in his training over these twenty years. He lived in obscurity all this time with the single purpose of defeating me. I, too, have trained hard to be a worthy opponent for him. However . . .' Reizo reached for his sake, but his hand paused in mid-air. 'This time, I won't come out alive. I've grown old . . . Still, I will be perfectly satisfied to be felled by Genshichiro's blade.'

Daijiro was silent as he served more barley into Reizo's bowl.

Late into the night, before they went to sleep, Reizo unwrapped a small bundle and presented a short katana to Daijiro. It was an inscribed wakizashi forged by Echizen-no-kami Kunitsugu with a blade of about eighteen inches.

'Take it. As a keepsake – of me,' he said. 'Even if I

manage to win the duel, I doubt I can ever see you again once I go back to Yamato.'

'But this is such a famed sword . . .'

'Will you accept it for me?'

'I . . . I would be honoured to . . .'

'Thank you. This Kunitsugu was a gift from Hei'emon Sensei. I wanted you to have it.'

The sound of rain had seeped in without their realising, and Daijiro listened to its quiet echoes filling the room.

V

The rain had stopped by the morning.

After breakfast, which the farmer's wife had prepared for them, Reizo said, 'I'll be back before sunset,' and left the house.

Back in the old days, when the late Hei'emon had been travelling around from Kyoto to Yamato, he had stayed at Reizo's family house in Shibamura. Reizo had been seventeen at the time. Drawn to Hei'emon's admirable character, Reizo had followed him back to his dojo in Edo. For ten long years since then, Reizo had made Edo his home, so the city held many memories for him.

I suppose he's going to Kojimachi today – to see where the Tsuji dojo used to be, Daijiro thought, as he watched Reizo follow the path through the vegetable patches in the direction of Ohkawa. Reizo, wearing a flat wickerwork hat, looked tall as he strode on, his back perfectly straight.

He hasn't changed at all since ten years ago. To Daijiro, Reizo looked nothing like an old man. His old teacher was only three years younger than his father, but Daijiro couldn't help but notice how much older his father had grown.

After he had returned from Ohara, Daijiro had stayed with his father for about half a year, then left Edo again to journey across the land and further his training. His father had covered his expenses for him during this time. And in early spring last year, when he had come back to Edo for the first time in years, he found Kohei comfortably settled into his easy life of retirement. Daijiro had been taken aback by this change in his father; he even seemed to toddle a bit when he walked, and, besotted with a young peasant woman, he somehow had enough money coming in to idle his days away, hardly ever picking up his katana.

Daijiro had heard nothing about Kohei's hand in saving Mifuyu from the underhand scheme back in December. In fact, he had almost forgotten about the strange visitor to his dojo. When Daijiro had paid Kohei a visit at the beginning of the year, Kohei had kept the whole story to himself. Not even Oharu knew about this incident.

Now that he'd seen Reizo off, Daijiro began to feel rather restless. Reizo hadn't told him to do anything other than to 'witness' his death. Judging from their previous clashes, there was little doubt that Reizo's opponent would have grown even stronger by now. But Reizo, on the other hand, had been living in peace in his hometown, and of course he had aged by ten years.

It seemed to Daijiro that Reizo was fully prepared to accept defeat – that he even *wished* to be felled by this

Kakimoto, who had devoted twenty years of his life to overcoming him.

A man like that was bound to play fair in the duel, and Daijiro judged that there was little need for him to worry about anyone else coming to Kakimoto's aid during the match.

They had agreed to meet at six the following morning in front of the Korin-ji temple gate in Azabu. Then the rivals, with one attendant each, were to go to the field in Hiroo to commence their duel.

As usual, Daijiro started cleaning his small dojo, first sweeping the floor then wiping it with a cloth. Even this was a way of practising the Mugai-ryu technique of steadying respiration: the movements of his limbs and back had to be at one with the rhythm of his breathing.

Kohei had taught Daijiro this technique from a young age – not because he wanted to turn Daijiro into a swordsman, but because he wanted his only son to grow up to be strong and healthy. So, for most of his life, Daijiro had trained himself through cleaning in and around the house, and oftentimes, his body moved in harmony with his breathing without his being aware of it.

This morning, however, he couldn't get his movements to properly align.

He finished the cleaning and stood in the dojo. He unsheathed his katana – an Inoue Shinkai piece measuring slightly more than twenty-nine inches, which had been a gift from his father – and, with a fierce roar, started practising his strokes. But again, he couldn't concentrate.

Just after noon, he stepped out. He crossed Ohkawa to

the east and headed towards Kanegafuchi to visit his father. Though he went as far down the dirt bank as to make out Kohei's thatched roof beyond the pine grove, he stopped in his tracks.

Well . . . should I tell him about Shimaoka Sensei . . . ? Daijiro hesitated. Reizo had told him that there was no need to let Kohei know. He couldn't just ignore what his old teacher had said. *But . . . I can't help worrying about it. What if Kakimoto kills him?*

He couldn't quite make up his mind whether he himself should challenge Kakimoto to a duel with real blades, should Reizo be defeated.

As long as I accompany Sensei, I'll surely challenge Kakimoto to avenge him. It would be impossible not to.

But he wasn't sure whether that was the right thing to do – and this was what he wanted to ask Kohei.

Somehow I keep thinking about what I'd do if Sensei lost. A bad omen . . . Daijiro clicked his tongue and turned on his heel.

Yet he didn't go home. He instead wandered around aimlessly, not knowing where to go.

Pale sunlight filtered through the clouds. He could sense the stirrings of life in the earth around him as spring drew closer.

How unsettled I am at a time like this . . . I still have a long way to go as a swordsman. Even to his own mind, his immaturity was all too clear.

Eventually, he found himself in the precincts of Kameido Tenjin shrine, though he didn't remember how he'd got there.

I've got to pull myself together. He had to get back and draw a bath so that it was ready for Reizo when he returned. He wanted to offer his old teacher something special for supper on the night before his crucial match – a fish, at least. He turned around and hurried out of the shrine.

But once again, his legs carried him towards his father's house as if of their own accord.

Just as he was about to go down the dirt bank, he caught sight of someone who had apparently just left Kohei's house. Daijiro wasn't one to be easily startled, but even he had to stare wide-eyed at this figure in a short-sleeve pale violet kimono, a pair of katanas at his waist, and his hair tied back in a slick style befitting an adolescent man – for he was a stunningly beautiful young swordsman.

Daijiro had no idea that this was in fact a swordswoman dressed as a man.

Mifuyu walked up the bank and noticed Daijiro standing there. She glowered at him, her bold eyebrows furrowing and colour rising to her handsome face.

Who could this be . . . ? Daijiro looked back at her dubiously.

'What do you want?' Mifuyu asked sharply.

'Oh, nothing . . .'

'Then why do you stare?'

'Apologies – I didn't mean to be rude.'

She threw him a look of obvious disdain, then strode off along the bank.

What an odd fellow, Daijiro thought, watching her go for a little while. But soon he made up his mind and climbed down the bank. Passing through the pine grove, he went round to the back of Kohei's house.

That was when he heard Oharu crying.

Hmm . . .? He paused.

Oharu was shouting and weeping in a frenzy, while Kohei tried to soothe her in a honeyed tone. Her cries subsided in a little while; she murmured something in a teary voice, then a hush fell over them.

Daijiro shook his head. *I don't understand. Everything's a mess . . .*

He gave up on seeing his father and retraced his steps on to the bank, this time with the purposeful tread of a man who knew where he had to go.

VI

Having taken a boat across Ohkawa homewards, Daijiro also crossed on foot a smaller river called Omoigawa, which flowed on the outskirts of Hashiba. He kept walking along the stream, with a view of the grove surrounding Masaki Inari shrine to his right.

Rice fields stretched out before him, far and wide; it felt wide open especially at this time of year when the rice had yet to be planted and the land was bare. The damp smell of mud swelled around him, and the early-evening murk crept low over the earth.

A narrow path continued north through the fields, leading to Daijiro's house. The land belonged to Sosen-ji temple; the peasants who worked on the temple's rice and vegetable fields used to live in the house that Kohei had bought and refurbished for his son.

As Daijiro walked up the gentle slope of this narrow lane, his house came into view. The dojo stood at the front of the house; he could see the back door to his living quarters on its right, and the stone well a little way off. The grove of pine trees and kunugi oak darkened the back and the left side of the house.

Daijiro saw a silhouette of someone standing by the well. *Hmm? Shimaoka Sensei is back already.* He hastened, and Reizo, who had been washing his face at the well, seemed to notice him, too; he raised his hand and called out something, taking a few steps forward to greet Daijiro.

Suddenly a single arrow tore through the dusk and pierced Reizo's chest.

Reizo and Daijiro cried out at once. Daijiro sprinted to Reizo's side, drawing his sword and slashing away the second arrow that flew towards them. Glancing at Reizo, he immediately charged towards the grove on the left side of the dojo.

The third arrow whizzed through the air; Daijiro lunged into the trees at the same time. He could make out a slender figure in the shadows, his face hidden under a cloth. The man flung aside his bow.

'Who are you?' Daijiro came to a halt and challenged the assailant, who was now crouching in the gloom with his long sword at the ready. Even as he asked, however, Daijiro could easily surmise who he must be: the young man he had seen at Kakimoto's house. *He certainly was a skilled archer . . .*

Enraged, Daijiro advanced towards him. The archer was petrified. He emitted a low cry and was about to make a run for it when Daijiro's blade flashed in the dark.

The archer screamed as his right arm flew from his body.

Daijiro raised his sword to deliver the second strike, but he heard a terrible cry from the direction of the well. *Sensei . . .?* He couldn't keep pursuing the archer when Reizo's life might be in danger.

Though he had lost his arm, the archer could still move, and he scampered off like a weasel.

When Daijiro dashed out of the grove, he saw Reizo down on one knee in front of the well. The shadowy shape of a man lay crumpled on the ground, and two more masked men were pointing their blades at Reizo.

Even with an arrow in his chest, Reizo had taken down one man with his short sword and was keeping the others at bay.

'Sensei . . .!' Daijiro ran up to them like the wind. The two men turned from Reizo and attacked Daijiro from both sides.

Daijiro's feet dug into the ground. With blinding speed his blade met the left man's waist, and the man's sword fell to the ground. He collapsed without so much as a groan.

The last assassin gave a shout and swung at Daijiro from the side. The air stirred by the blade whipped Daijiro's face as he took a wide step back on his left foot and slashed the man's throat up to his chin in one swift move.

He didn't even stop to watch the man fall to the ground. He rushed over to Reizo just as Reizo's legs gave way, and his sinewy body fell into Daijiro's arms. The arrow was lodged deep in Reizo's chest.

'Shimaoka Sensei . . .' Daijiro murmured.

Reizo nodded with a grunt. The deepening gloom obscured

the expression on his wrinkled old face, but he seemed to be smiling at Daijiro. 'Farewell,' he said in a clear voice.

That was Reizo's final word.

The farmer's wife must have fainted in shock some time ago; she lay slumped against the back door.

Reizo breathed no more.

VII

Late into the night, Kohei and Daijiro laid Reizo's body in a coffin, with the arrow still protruding from his chest, and loaded it on to a cart. They carried it to Kakimoto's house at the back of Saiko-ji temple.

As they had expected, the young man did not appear at the gate.

Kohei crashed through the closed gate, strode up to the front door and kicked it down.

'Don't let your guard down, Dai,' he said, tying up his sleeves with a leather cord at lightning speed. 'You stay close to Reizo and guard his body.'

'I will.'

Kakimoto emerged from the back room. Brandishing his katana, he shielded himself with a pillar and demanded, 'Say your name.'

'You first. Are you Kakimoto Genshichiro?' Kohei said.

'I am.'

'We come for Shimaoka Reizo, who died from an arrow shot by the dirty coward you sent.'

'What did you say . . .?' Kakimoto stammered.

Kohei and Daijiro exchanged a look. Kakimoto's swollen form staggered out of the darkness; he was gasping in pain.

This . . . is Kakimoto . . .?

Father and son exchanged another look in surprise.

When they brought down the coffin from the cart, and Kakimoto looked at Reizo's body with the fatal arrow, he began to shake as if he were suffering from a raging fever.

'It must have been Sanya . . .' Kakimoto moaned.

'So you *were* behind it,' Daijiro said.

'I wasn't. But – I have no doubt this arrow was fired by my disciple, Ito Sanya.'

With a low murmur, Daijiro put his hand on the hilt of his sword, but Kohei stopped him. Kohei saw that Kakimoto was telling the truth.

'Master Shimaoka,' Kakimoto said to the corpse in a strange, strangled voice. 'Forgive me.' The next moment, he groaned in agony. He had taken his short sword and plunged it into his failing heart.

*

A few days later, Kohei and Daijiro stood in the graveyard of Honsho-ji temple in Asakusa Imado, lighting an offering of incense sticks for Reizo, whom they had buried there for the time being.

Honsho-ji was also the resting place of Daijiro's mother, Otei. Reizo's grave post, made of unpainted wood, marked the mound next to her grave.

'This is just my guess, but I have a feeling the Ito Sanya boy might've taken on the role of Kakimoto's lover, too . . .' Kohei said.

'From what I've heard,' Daijiro said, 'Sanya is the third son of Ito Hikodayu, the steward of the Edo mansion belonging to the Shibata domain. Kakimoto's elder brother still serves there . . .'

'That's probably how Sanya came to take care of Kakimoto. He's still missing, you know. Remember that, and be ready, Dai. He lost his right arm because of you, and on top of that, he lost the master to whom he gave himself. That kind of grudge runs deep.'

Daijiro was silent.

'You chose to be a swordsman yourself,' Kohei said.

'I am aware of that.'

'A swordsman must always shoulder the grudge of others every time he comes out alive from a clash of blades – whether he likes it or not.' Kohei looked long and hard at Reizo's grave post, then turned his gaze to his wife's grave. 'Reizo must've known that Otei is buried here,' he said quietly.

'Yes . . .?' Daijiro gave him a quizzical look.

'I'm sure he came to this temple and paid her a visit, too,' Kohei went on.

'What are you saying?'

'As you know, Otei was the daughter of Yamaguchi Yohei, a wandering ronin from the Kuwana domain in Ise province. She worked as a maid for Hei'emon Sensei.'

'Yes, I know.'

'Back then, both Reizo and I tried to gain her favour. And I won.'

It was the first time Daijiro had heard about any of this. He was stunned.

'And that's when our paths diverged.' Kohei turned his back to Daijiro and started off. 'Now . . . how should we share the news with Reizo's family in Yamato . . .? It might be best if you could take my letter to them yourself. How about it, Daijiro? Would you be willing to go to Yamato . . .?'

After a moment, Daijiro answered, 'I will go.'

'I'm counting on you.'

It was a warm, cloudy day. They heard the rumble of springtime thunder somewhere in the distance.

'But I wonder . . .' Kohei murmured, a hint of sadness in his voice. 'That Kakimoto fellow – he was determined to fulfil his oath to Reizo, fair and square, even when he was so weak from his sickness. He must've been ready to die in the duel, too – just like Reizo.'

Chapter 3
The New Geisha

I

'Not at all, sensei . . . I wouldn't dream of telling anyone else about this – only you . . . So, sensei – you *must* promise me to keep this between you and me.' With this little preface, Omoto, the attendant at Fujiro, filled Kohei's cup with sake and proceeded to tell her story with the urgency of someone who absolutely couldn't rest until she let someone in on her secret. They were sitting in a private guest room at the back of the restaurant in Asakusa Hashiba, where Kohei was a regular.

Three days ago, in the early afternoon, Omoto had been locked in a passionate embrace with Choji, a cook at Fujiro, in the very room Kohei and Omoto were sitting in now.

'Oho . . .' Kohei paused with his cup in mid-air and gave her a look.

'Stop it, sensei. If you look at me like that, I'll keep the rest to myself.'

'Oops, sorry. So tell me, what happened?'

'We heard some guests coming. Oh, I nearly jumped out of my skin.'

'Wish I could've seen the look on Choji's face . . .'

This private room was in an annexe to the main building of the restaurant, connected by a roofed passageway; the annexe consisted of two rooms, one on each floor. Omoto and Choji had bumped into each other in the hallway of the main house, and they'd signalled to each other to slip into the ground-floor room that faced the inner garden. Oblivious to their tryst, another attendant named Okane led a pair of guests to the annexe room.

Though it was only meant to be a brief encounter, Omoto and Choji had been kissing with such abandon that by the time they'd heard the footsteps approaching in the passageway outside, they had no time to run away.

Fujiro had strict policies on this kind of 'behaviour' among the employees. If they were found out, they would be in big trouble.

'H-hurry . . .!' Omoto grabbed Choji's arm without even bothering to straighten her dishevelled kimono and they stole out through the shoji door adjoining the alcove, quickly shutting it behind them.

They had nowhere else to go, though – this door opened to a small dirt-floor pit about the length of two tatami mats, and there was only a private privy on the other side of the pit.

The moment Omoto and Choji crammed into the privy, Okane bustled into the guest room and promptly slid open the shoji doors that faced the inner garden. Okane was a large, middle-aged woman, and she wasn't exactly the sensitive type. If she had been, she would have surely noticed the suggestive odour that still hung in the room.

It was a balmy spring day, and the garden was flooded with light.

Two men walked into the guest room. One of them asked, 'Shall we have the doors closed?' but the other said in a rather easy tone, 'Don't you worry – I say it's always better to have them wide open when you've got something to hide.'

Their voices reached Omoto and Choji, who were holding their breath in the privy. Omoto recognised the second one: a fifty-something-year-old man called Yamada Kansuke, who had been to Fujiro several times before. He was a direct vassal of the Tokugawa clan, though not so high in rank as to have the right to an audience with the Shogun himself.

Among the retainers of the Shogun, Kansuke's stipend was at the lowest tier, worth forty tawara bags of rice per year. He was of the class of samurai who couldn't get a proper position in the shogunate and didn't contribute anything useful to society in this era of peace, yet who still happily received their salary – just like leeches. A respectable samurai was expected to wear a pair of swords in public – the long katana and the short wakizashi – but Kansuke and his sort didn't think twice about going without a katana on their waist, as if to say, 'You expect us to carry around those heavy things? No, thanks!'

Kansuke lived among his ilk at Honjo Mitsume, and for the last thirty years, he had done nothing but tipple and gamble. He had a knack for sniffing out juicy titbits and extorting money from various quarters, with a pack of ruffians from Honjo and Fukagawa at his beck and call. In short, blackmail came as second nature to him.

Whenever he came to Fujiro, he would gorge himself on food and drink without the slightest intention of paying for it; to top it off, he would wring some money from the owner of the restaurant before going home.

In this day and age, there was certainly no shortage of dirty men like him among the vassals of his status.

'But here's the thing, sensei,' Omoto said. 'That fraud Yamada changed sometime around last summer – seemed like he got flush with cash all of a sudden, and he'd actually pay his bill here.'

'Mm-hmm . . .'

'He'd even tip us girls, and he started getting all spiffed up in brand-new clothes.'

'I see.'

'Anyhow, I felt like my heart was in my mouth the whole time I was hiding.'

Clasping each other in their arms, Omoto and Choji had no choice but to stay in the privy. She was so nervous she couldn't make out what the two men were saying exactly, but she could hear them murmuring. After some time, she heard Kansuke announce with a guffaw, 'Believe you me – we're dealing with Ishikawa Kai-no-kami here. He's high up there, closely serving the Shogun's clan. He has to watch his step very carefully now – otherwise, he'll find himself in real big trouble when I bite him.'

'Even so . . .' the other man said hesitantly, 'this is rather—'

'Just leave it to me,' Kansuke cut in. 'We can push a lot higher than a couple of hundred – you'll see.' There wasn't a trace of doubt in his voice.

That was when Okane brought sake for them. Kansuke handed her a tip and asked her to get the bath ready so they could freshen up before dinner.

From that point until the two men left to take a bath, Omoto felt as if she were living on a tightrope – especially after overhearing their clandestine discussion.

When the men left, Omoto and Choji burst out of their hiding place, leaped into the inner garden from the roofed passageway, and scurried off in opposite directions before anyone could find them.

That was the tale Omoto had to tell.

Kohei seemed pensive as he sipped his cold sake. 'The filthy vassal – so he wants to blackmail Ishikawa Kai-no-kami, eh?'

'Do you think Yamada has got something on this Ishikawa what's-his-name?' Omoto asked.

'He wouldn't be plotting something if he hadn't.'

'Well, yes, I suppose so . . .'

'You must be feeling relieved to get it off your chest. Secrets don't stay secrets for long with you women – that's the way you are.'

'Oh, don't tease me . . . I *do* feel lighter, though.'

According to Omoto, who saw the two men leave the restaurant later that evening, the man accompanying Yamada was a younger samurai about twenty-seven or -eight in age, formally dressed in a haori jacket and a hakama over his kimono. His face looked ashen.

'He was so pasty I thought he might have consumption or something,' Omoto recalled.

As he was leaving Fujiro, Kohei told Omoto in all

seriousness, 'Make sure Choji keeps quiet about this. It's not the sort of thing you should babble about. You hear?'

Omoto shuddered, her face turning white.

Kohei reflected on her story as the ferryboat carried him across Ohkawa in the pale twilight of spring.

This is getting interesting, he thought. If a scoundrel like Yamada was scheming to extort money from a high-ranking official like Ishikawa, Yamada must have a sensational secret up his sleeve.

Ishikawa was a member of the Osobashu, who were close aides to the Shogun and acted as a kind of secretary, mediating between the Shogun and the senior officials. The overseer of this unit accompanied the Shogun at all times, and his power in the shogunate was immense. Not even the Council of Elders and Junior Elders could interfere with the overseer's influence.

The famous Lord Tanuma used to hold this position before he was promoted to the circle of roju. Thus Tanuma held some sway over the current overseer, and his unit as well.

Now, Ishikawa Kai-no-kami Sadamasa was a greater hatamoto with 8,000 koku; at this level, he was to all intents and purposes as important as a daimyo.

Lord Ishikawa used to be the chief of one of the units in the Shogun's personal guards: a post with a heavy responsibility. He rose to his current rank last spring at the recommendation of Lord Tanuma.

For Ishikawa, this was a rare opportunity that opened doors to future prosperity; if he was fortunate enough to win the Shogun's favour through his work as a close aide, he might be promoted to the unit's overseer or even a daimyo.

And so it followed that Ishikawa had to guard his reputation at all costs, especially at this juncture in his career. Anyone could see that if the likes of Yamada Kansuke blackmailed Lord Ishikawa, and if this became public knowledge, it would do irreparable damage to his future.

II

A few days had passed since Kohei's visit to Fujiro.

These days, he had got into the habit of asking Oharu to ferry him across Ohkawa after breakfast to visit Honsho-ji and pay his respects to his old friend Reizo's grave; he would also clean up his wife Otei's grave while he was at it, then take an idle walk to Daijiro's dojo nearby, just in case anything was amiss.

After Reizo and Kakimoto's promise for a duel had ended in such tragedy, Daijiro had departed for Reizo's hometown, Shibamura in Yamato, carrying a lock of Reizo's hair and a letter from Kohei to deliver to Reizo's elder brother, Hachiro'emon.

It would have been more appropriate to bring home Reizo's body, but the land of Yamato was far away. Besides, two nights before the day of the duel, Reizo had handed ten gold ryo to Daijiro and told him, 'When I die, you can simply let my family know by letter. I already told my brother before I left. As for my body – use this money to bury me, for old friendship's sake.'

Kohei and Daijiro had decided to follow Reizo's last wishes. But since he had died in such an abnormal turn of events, Daijiro had felt the letter wouldn't be enough. He took a lock of hair from Reizo so that the Shimaoka family could have a small part of him, at least.

They had had to think of a way to deal with Kakimoto's body, too. He was the younger brother of Kakimoto Isaku, who belonged to the Shibata domain, so they couldn't just leave him lying around. Kohei went to the domain's mansion in Edo and told Isaku what had happened.

'My brother was a swordsman, after all,' Isaku said. 'I am sure he has no regrets. I am deeply obliged to you for bringing me the news like this.' With this reasonable response, he went to Kakimoto's house behind Saiko-ji temple to retrieve his brother's body, which Kohei and Daijiro had kept safe.

As for Kakimoto's young pupil – Ito Sanya – he was still missing.

Isaku promised Kohei that he would report the incident to Sanya's father, Hikodayu, who was a fellow retainer of the Shibata domain. Kohei heard nothing in particular after that.

I doubt Sanya is dead, Kohei thought. He himself had wounded or killed a number of opponents in his life. This was the sort of thing that a swordsman had to live with, in one form or another: to be the object of the bitter resentment harboured by the defeated. That was the fate of a samurai. And yet . . .

For every opponent Daijiro defeats, he'll have to bear the weight of more and more enmity . . . As his father, Kohei couldn't help but feel some dismay at the prospect. *They say a young lover's grudge grows deep roots . . .*

Sanya could turn out to be a dangerous enemy. After all, he had hired some ruffians in order to save his beloved master, and – though it had been a disgraceful ambush – he had killed an expert swordsman such as Reizo with only a single arrow.

I can't get it out of my head – the bow and arrow . . . I do hope it won't harm my boy somehow . . . The thought crossed his mind every time he visited the graveyard at Honsho-ji.

With these worries clouding his face, Kohei seemed to be in low spirits these days.

To crown it all, Oharu had started pestering him to marry her with a proper ceremony.

As the swordswoman Mifuyu's feelings for Kohei grew ever more passionate, Oharu became restless. Mifuyu, who appeared at Kohei's door at least once every three days and spent a couple of hours in his company, barely took any notice of Oharu's presence.

Lately, Kohei was beginning to enjoy their idle chats, too. Mifuyu had plenty of interesting themes to offer: stories from Izeki dojo, where she reigned as one of the 'Four Rulers', for instance, or her observations around the city of Edo, and many more besides.

What was more, Mifuyu was a considerable swordswoman, so when they fell to discussing swords they never ran out of things to say, and they would become so animated that Kohei found himself leaning forward with eagerness.

When Mifuyu held Kohei in her gaze – her eyes gleaming with ardour – and when a certain scent of a twenty-year-old maiden wafted in the air, Kohei felt awkward and troubled, but also a little flattered.

'I won't have it. Don't let her come near us any more,' Oharu would cry. She would have a fit, sulk around, and in the end walk out on Kohei, back to her parents' home in Sekiya. Then Kohei would have to go fetch her and coax her into coming back.

'Listen, Oharu,' he would tell her. 'That swordswoman is just an interesting fellow to me, that's all. It's never going to turn into anything you'd have to worry about – I promise.'

'Will you marry me then? I want to be husband and wife, sensei.'

'If we get married, would you be fine with Mifuyu visiting?'

'Oh, yes. Then I won't be bothered.'

And so it happened that Kohei promised Oharu they would have a wedding ceremony once Daijiro returned from Yamato. Kohei had no intention of letting Oharu go. He surprised himself when he realised how much he wished to spend the rest of his days with her.

I'm too old for this . . . Kohei had never imagined he would have two young women pursuing him, at his age.

Preoccupied as he was, he had thought no more of that story he'd heard from Omoto at Fujiro until several more days had gone by.

One afternoon, when a steady drizzle made haze rise over the land, a middle-aged samurai came to Kohei's house.

This was Kishii Jinbei, a pupil of Kohei's from back when he used to run the dojo in Yotsuya. He was a retainer of

Sakai Iwami-no-kami Tadayasu, a daimyo of the Matsuyama domain in Dewa province with 20,000 koku.

Even after Kohei had retired to live near Kanegafuchi, Jinbei never forgot to pay him a visit at least once a year, and he would always bring a little something with him as a gift. Though he had little talent in swords – his years of practice at Kohei's dojo hadn't made any difference in the end – Kohei had once told Daijiro: 'When it comes to character, that man is second to none.'

As always, Jinbei greeted Kohei with a warm smile. 'It's lovely to see you, sensei. I'm sorry I've stayed away for too long,' he said gently. 'I'm happy to see you're as fine as ever.'

'Thanks for coming, Jinbei. Glad to see you're looking well, too,' Kohei said heartily, welcoming him in.

Oharu was out on an errand to get some fresh vegetables from her parents, and Kohei was in the middle of cleaning and oiling his katanas.

Jinbei was essentially a diplomat for the Sakai family: he undertook the crucial role of building relationships and facilitating communication between his own domain and others, as well as the shogunate. Only someone with exceptionally good character and quick intelligence could fulfil such a position.

Because of the nature of his work, he had an ample budget for diplomatic social occasions, so he was also a rather flamboyant figure.

Indeed, it was rare for a man in such a role to practise swordsmanship at a dojo for three whole years.

'My maid will come back soon. For now, I hope you'll

make do with this,' Kohei said, bringing cold sake from the kitchen. They sat in the room facing the garden.

'Sensei. Before I partake of your sake, there is something . . .' Jinbei bowed respectfully, pressing both hands flat on the floor in front of him.

'What is it?'

'To tell you the truth, sensei – I should like to ask for your advice about something, if you would be so kind . . .'

'Hmm . . . What could this be about?'

'Well . . .!'

'Is it a delicate matter that's difficult to broach?'

'Very much so – but I am determined to tell you all and ask for your opinion . . .'

'You think too highly of me.'

'Not at all. Well . . . the fact is . . . I have a cousin called Irie Kin'emon. He serves Lord Ishikawa, a close aide to the Shogun . . .'

'Mm-hmm . . .' Kohei's eyes glinted like needles. The story he'd heard from Omoto about eight days ago came back to him.

Jinbei stayed for about half an hour.

Soon after he left, Oharu returned. As soon as she saw the bowls and small plates that were still left in the room, she asked accusingly, 'Sensei, was that samurai woman here again?'

'Don't be silly. I was just having sake with a different visitor.'

'If you say so . . .'

'You know, Oharu – I was getting a tiny bit worried these days that we're almost hitting the bottom of our money box . . . but something's come up that might just bring us luck.'

'Oh, that's nice. Something with a reward, sensei?'

'If all goes well, yes, maybe. You can look forward to it anyhow.'

III

The sky cleared the next day.

In the afternoon, Kohei crossed Ohkawa on his own boat, steered by Oharu, and from Hashiba he walked to a restaurant in Asakusa Namiki called Tomoe-ya Katsukura. In a private room on the first floor, Jinbei awaited Kohei alongside a refined samurai aged about sixty.

'It is a pleasure to make your acquaintance, sensei. I am the cousin of Kishii Jinbei, Irie Kin'emon,' the man greeted Kohei with the utmost courtesy. 'I would have sent a palanquin to carry you here, but I was told you would rather come on foot. I am much obliged for your trouble indeed.'

His manners were in keeping with his status as the steward of the Ishikawa family, who managed his lord's private affairs.

More than a hundred people served Lord Ishikawa, counting everyone from retainers to maidservants. Besides the domain's main mansion bestowed upon him by the shogunate, he owned a personal mansion as well. The inner workings of these mansions were as elaborate as a daimyo's, with strict boundaries between 'the front' and 'the back'.

While public affairs were dealt with on the front side, the back – or the inner chambers, as it were – was reserved for the world of women, with Lord Ishikawa's official wife presiding over the daughters of the family, the waiting maids, and all other women who belonged to the house.

As the inner steward, Irie was in charge of the general affairs of the interior. His family had borne this weighty responsibility ever since his great-grandfather's generation.

'Jinbei is the son of my maternal aunt,' Irie went on, though at the same time he stole a glance at Jinbei with a somewhat anxious expression. It was a look that seemed to question Jinbei's claim that the old man sitting in front of them could really help them out of their crisis. As far as Irie could tell, Kohei was just a small, skinny old man who appeared to be nothing more than a benevolent grandfather.

Their conversation lasted for about two hours.

When they were done, Irie called a palanquin and went home, leaving Kohei and Jinbei to stay at Tomoe-ya and drink some more.

'From what your cousin said, it sounds like this Lord Ishikawa is a man of character,' Kohei remarked.

'Oh yes, sensei,' Jinbei said, 'I can assure you he is. The circle of roju has great trust in him, the Lord Shogun himself holds him in high esteem, and to top it off, he even has a good name among the ladies of the Ooku, as he's a selfless man who's always just.'

'Somehow those decent, upright men always end up with lousy kids, don't they?'

'I couldn't agree more. Just between you and me, even my cousin Irie is at his wits' end *this* time. That's why I came to you, sensei. You know the ways of the world inside out – I would be so grateful if you could give us a hand . . .'

'I'd say you're the real expert,' Kohei said, chuckling.

'You are too kind . . .'

'But, well, you're a diplomat – the face of the daimyo family. I know you can't move as freely as I.'

'I am in your debt, sensei.'

They discussed a more detailed plan of action over dinner. After nightfall, Kohei crossed the bridge over Ohkawa and returned home in a palanquin.

Already at the height of spring, the air was warm even at night.

'Oh, before I forget,' Kohei said to Oharu later that night, 'would you mind running along to your father in Sekiya tomorrow? I want him to tell Yashichi of Yotsuya to come and see me straight away. Would you do that for me, please?'

In the afternoon the next day, Yashichi hastened from Yotsuya Tenma to Kohei's house as soon as he heard the message from Oharu's father, Iwagoro.

'I'm going to need your help again, Yashichi,' Kohei told him. 'Would you do me a favour?'

'Of course. I'm all ears.'

'This comes from Kishii Jinbei, in fact.'

'From Master Kishii . . .' Yashichi leaned forward eagerly.

Though Yashichi was a goyokiki – essentially a private eye – he had undergone proper training in swordsmanship at Kohei's old dojo in Yotsuya, and he knew Jinbei well as a fellow pupil. The restaurant run by Yashichi's wife, Musashiya, was well known in Yotsuya; since Jinbei often dined with various officials for his diplomatic duties, he was one of Musashi-ya's regular patrons.

When it came to sword fighting, Yashichi was much more competent than Jinbei, so he'd treated Jinbei like a junior pupil back when they were still at the dojo.

'I know your duty is to the Shogun, but do you think you could forget about the lord for this time and work for Kishii's sake? How about it?' Kohei asked.

'I'd be very happy to, sensei.'

'Well, I would've turned him down, depending on the particulars . . . But as it happens, Ishikawa Kai-no-kami seems to be a good man who deserves better. So I've made up my mind to help them out of their trouble.'

'Ishikawa . . . Do you mean Lord Ishikawa in the Osobashu?'

'That's the one.'

'Well, I'll be!'

'Sit tight, Yashichi. I'll tell you the whole story.'

The pair's secret discussion went on for two hours.

Three days later, Yashichi reappeared at Kohei's house, announcing that he'd managed to puzzle out the general sense of things – since his last visit, he had been covertly digging into the affairs of the slippery Yamada Kansuke.

Yashichi had a good reputation among the goyokiki in Edo, so he had a number of private spies in various parts of the city; they gathered intelligence for him, and in return, he looked after them well. These spies did the legwork in investigating criminal matters while holding down their own day jobs as barrel maker, tobacco seller, bar owner, and so on. They all worked for the Shogun, but that didn't mean the Shogun paid them their wages. It fell to their boss, the goyokiki, to take care of them – but even the goyokiki didn't receive a salary from the Shogun. Instead, the goyokiki assisted the low-ranking officers of the city magistrates in their policing duties, and those officers in turn looked after him. But that alone wasn't enough for him to make a living – which is why many goyokiki ended up exploiting their status as servants of the shogunate to reap extra benefits.

Men like Yashichi, who had followed in his father's footsteps to become a goyokiki, and who could boast with a clean conscience that he had never done anything shady in his life, were few and far between. Those who could say so truthfully usually had a wife who ran another business to help provide for the family.

IV

'Here's the thing – I've seen and heard a lot of things in my time, but this one made me raise my eyebrows,' Yashichi began.

According to him, Kansuke had a second house in Asakusa Tawaramachi in addition to the official one in Honjo. One might expect it to house a secret mistress, but that wasn't the case. Kansuke had actually set up an establishment offering entertainment with performing dancers.

Professional dancers appeared some time during the reign of Emperor Higashiyama, between 1688 and 1704. With their art of shamisen music, Joruri singing, and dancing, they performed at dinner parties held by daimyos and samurai families. There is no space here to give a history of dancers, but needless to say, they became an essential presence in entertainment houses all over the city, especially as Edo grew into a metropolis befitting the castle town of the Tokugawa shogun who ruled over Japan – aside from Kyoto, the seat of the Emperor – and as Edo's own kaleidoscopic culture came into full maturity, or was even on the cusp of becoming overripe.

Nowadays, daimyos and samurai families no longer called dancers to attend to dinners at their own mansions, but they didn't need to host such parties any more; as long as they had the money and time, Edo offered them plenty of interesting establishments to choose from.

Apparently, the latest word at the time for such dancers was 'geisha', meaning one who had mastered their art.

'How words do change, huh,' Kohei said with a wry grin. 'Geisha was what we used to call those who were accomplished in martial arts, but now . . . it's a name for dancers. You never realise that a word is shapeshifting until, one day, it hits you in the face.'

So, Yashichi tracked down Kansuke's dancer business, which he had opened in February of the previous year. He had six geishas in total, including his nineteen-year-old daughter, Osato, whom he had given the stage name Hatsuito.

Having hired some scoundrels from Honjo as his henchmen, Kansuke made the geisha in his Asakusa house entertain his customers. He himself was busy going back and forth between his two residences. His wife and one of his daughters had died from an illness five years ago, so Osato was now his only child.

His business was booming. Since every one of his geisha girls was young and beautiful, he had no shortage of invitations from fancy restaurants and teahouses all across town.

'I see . . . What is the world coming to, eh?' Kohei laughed with a hint of bitterness, as if to say, *Though I'm a fine one to talk.*

And what had Yashichi sniffed out about Kansuke's extortion scheme?

Kansuke had lodged this complaint against Lord Ishikawa: 'My daughter, Osato, is with child, and the child's father is Lord Ishikawa's son, Master Gentaro. How do you intend to make amends for this matter?'

It was Horigome Kichitaro – a retainer who worked at the Ishikawa family's second mansion in Nihonbashi Hamacho – who brought Kansuke's demand to the lord.

Gentaro was Ishikawa's eldest son, turning twenty-one this year. Rumour had it that he had been withdrawn from society until mid-December the previous year, convalescing in the family's personal mansion.

In early autumn, Horigome had decided 'a little change of pace' would do Gentaro good and invited Kansuke's geisha to put on a performance at the mansion.

Gentaro's illness was some sort of depression. Kohei would've called it 'a rich boy's self-indulgent malaise'. Since Gentaro was an only son and heir to Ishikawa, he had wanted for nothing all his life, and his mother, Masako, in particular had spoiled him rotten since he was little, never letting him out of her sight.

After Horigome's attempt to lift the young man's spirits with a little diversion, Gentaro's depression had cleared up as if blown away by the wind. From that night on, he became infatuated with Osato and pestered Horigome to invite her to the mansion alone.

Osato returned to the mansion several times between the beginning of autumn and December; no doubt she and Gentaro grew significantly more 'intimate' over the course of these visits.

In December, even after Gentaro moved back to the main mansion in Kojimachi Sanbancho, he visited the other mansion several times to keep up his secret rendezvous with her.

Then, about six months ago, Kansuke had informed Horigome of Osato's pregnancy, and Horigome had brought the matter to the steward Irie's attention.

Irie was astonished and thrown into confusion.

No one could blame him for it – the news had come just as the young master Gentaro's marriage was being arranged with the help of the all-important Lord Tanuma himself.

The intended was the second daughter of Ikoma Chikugo-no-kami, a greater hatamoto worth 7,000 koku.

Before going to his lord or the chief retainer, Irie reported the news to Lady Masako first of all.

'As an inner steward, I am bound to the lady by duty, you see . . .' Irie had explained. Kohei read between the lines: Lady Masako's trust in Irie had to be profound.

Masako ordered him to keep this matter concealed from Gentaro's father. She lost no time in summoning Gentaro and interrogating him – but her son said nothing.

He knew he couldn't claim total innocence.

After she made Gentaro withdraw, she called Irie back. 'Use this to settle the matter,' she said, handing him fifty gold ryo on the spot.

Kansuke, however, had other plans. He demanded a staggering fortune as compensation: no less than a thousand ryo.

Lady Masako, now forty-four, was of noble birth – her father was Abe Settsu-no-kami of the Okabe domain in Musashi province worth 20,250 koku – and she had a certain pride that matched her upbringing. It couldn't be said that her relationship with Lord Ishikawa was warm and affectionate. They had only one child, while he had fathered three illegitimate daughters.

Though a proud woman, she always behaved with the decorum expected of a daimyo's daughter. She treated everything in an even-handed manner, and she did not stir up trouble among the women of the house, since that would only get in her husband's way.

'How outrageous . . .' Masako murmured, a flash of anger crossing her handsome face. 'But I suppose we can't simply do away with this impudent man.' Quelling her rage, she entered into lengthy negotiations with Kansuke through Irie's mediation.

Kansuke went as far as to propose that the Ishikawa family could take Osato as a concubine. But Masako knew that *that* was out of the question – over her dead body. Her husband had only recently been promoted at Lord Tanuma's recommendation, and with the roju's help, they were now so close to finalising a favourable marriage for her precious

Gentaro. How could she allow a geisha girl to become his concubine, especially at such a time? It might threaten his future as the heir of the family.

At this point, Masako had about 120 ryo at hand. She handed over all of it to Irie to hammer out a deal with Kansuke, but Kansuke was adamant.

'It might be best, my Lady, to raise the matter with our lord or the chief retainer . . .' Irie advised Masako. She wouldn't hear of it, however.

She believed Gentaro's misconduct was due to her negligence, as if she were the only one who bore the full responsibility of managing their son's education and behaviour. In any case, she did not wish such a disgrace to be known by anyone except Irie. She had to resolve the issue in absolute secrecy.

Still, a thousand ryo was not the kind of sum one could simply whip up out of thin air. Gradually, anxiety consumed her entire being and she lost her appetite.

'She has grown as thin as a thread,' Irie had said despairingly. Trapped in their quandary, Irie had finally confided in his cousin, Jinbei.

V

Around four in the afternoon, the day after Yashichi had reported to Kohei about his findings, Fujiro's cook Choji came sprinting to Kohei's house, covered in sweat.

'Yamada Kansuke's come back, sir!' he announced. 'And the other man with him is the same one from the other day, no doubt about it.' Kohei had asked Omoto to let him know as soon as possible if Kansuke returned to Fujiro.

'Good. Come with me,' Kohei said, leading him to the little boat moored in the garden as Oharu grabbed her steering pole.

They rushed to Fujiro at top speed, where Omoto was waiting for them in front of the elegant thatched gate. 'They're in the bath now, sensei.'

'All right . . .' Kohei fell silent for a moment, but went on quickly, 'Well then. Take me to the privy where you hid the other day.'

'Are you sure? You can't come out of there once they're back.'

'Leave it to me.'

They entered the annexe through the garden, and Kohei sneaked into the private guest room. He crossed the dirt-floor pit on the other side of the shoji door and hid in the privy.

Just like the other day, Kansuke and his companion had talked for a while in the guest room first, then went to take a bath to freshen up before dinner. After some time, the pair returned. Omoto brought them sake and a range of dishes to go with it, then left.

The two men began to talk over their drinks. Kohei daringly crept out of the privy and crouched on the dirt pit so that he could hear them better through the shoji screen.

At first they spoke in low tones, but soon Kansuke burst into chortles. 'Well, if push comes to shove, I'm going to settle for seven or eight hundred ryo. I have it all planned out.'

'Are you sure about this, Master Yamada?'

'I've been racking up a pretty sum from my new business, but it's nowhere near enough. You see, I've got a debt of more than a hundred ryo from gambling. Now that's something I can't dodge. The people I owe are the sort you wouldn't want to play games with . . . That's why I asked you, my old friend, to help me put on this whole act. If we get a fortune now, we can start a big business when the time comes. On top of that, you can quit that stiff-as-a-board job at the mansion and marry Osato – talk about a happy start, eh?'

'Well, if it goes according to plan, yes . . .'

'No one would ever guess Osato's actually pregnant with *your* child – not even Gentaro himself!'

'D-Do you think so . . .?'

'It's just off by a month. Of course they won't notice.'

'Hmm . . . if you say so . . .'

'You know what I'll do once the gold comes in? I'm going to open up a huge fine-dining restaurant in the entertainment district in Nakazu. Something with a catchy flair that'll make a big splash,' Kansuke babbled on. 'Sorry,' he said, getting to his feet, 'I've got to take a leak.'

Kohei didn't even flinch at hearing this. He stayed put, still crouching on the dirt floor.

The door rattled open.

'Oh . . .' Kansuke gasped and froze in place.

Kohei smirked up at him. 'Who's in trouble now?' he said lightly, as though he were teasing a child.

'Wha—' Kansuke was dumbstruck. *Who the hell is this old geezer? What's he doing here . . .? He must've heard everything we said.*

'Master Yamada? What's going on?' the other man called out from the room, but Kansuke couldn't even find his voice.

Kohei straightened up. To Kansuke, the small frame of this old man seemed to loom over him like a giant.

'Oh . . . uh . . .' Kansuke spluttered, completely cowed by Kohei's presence. He edged backwards as Kohei stepped into the room and slid the door shut behind him.

'Who are *you* . . .?' the other man blurted out, half rising from his seat. He was a spindly young samurai with glistening red lips.

'Y-you weasel . . .!' Kansuke muttered.

'What? That's *my* line,' Kohei said. 'What a disgusting plot you cooked up. And you.' He turned to the younger one. 'You're Lord Ishikawa's retainer, aren't you – Horigome, was it? Looks like I hit the nail on the head . . . No need to tremble like that. Well, well – you've betrayed your master and tried to pass off your own unborn child as the young heir's. What a wily, skinny fox.'

Horigome was shaking all over. He had left his long sword in Fujiro's katana room, so he grabbed the small one on his waist.

With a high-pitched shriek, he sprang at Kohei, but Kohei moved in a blur, and Horigome instantly dropped his weapon and collapsed headfirst on to the floor.

Kansuke whirled around to flee. Kohei picked up a sake bottle from a high tray and threw it straight at the back of his head. He staggered sideways, groaning in pain and clutching his head. Kohei knocked him down and grabbed him by the collar of his kimono.

'Listen closely,' Kohei said, his voice as sharp as a knife. 'I work for the Shogun as a secret agent, going by the name of Harukawa Daigoro. I've heard all I need to know about your crime.'

Kansuke closed his eyes and went as limp as a dead man, completely resigned to his fate.

VI

When Kohei emerged into the hallway in Fujiro, Omoto rushed over to him. 'H-how did it go, sensei?'

'Nothing to worry about. Just give them a bit of time, and they'll go home without a fuss. And Omoto – I'll come back another time to pay you a visit.'

Kohei stepped out of the restaurant, grinning from ear to ear. Omoto gave him a Fujiro lantern so that he could light his way home. He had just reached the ferry crossing at Hashiba when someone called out, 'There you are, sensei! Hurry, hurry . . .!' and Oharu jumped out of a boat with a young samurai.

'What's wrong, Oharu?' Kohei asked.

The samurai cut in before she could answer. 'I am a retainer of Lord Ishikawa named Sato Kazunosuke. Our inner steward Irie ordered me to deliver this letter to you with the utmost urgency, for a grave matter has come upon the family . . .' As he spoke, he handed a letter to Kohei. Sato had hastened to Kohei's house on horseback, so Oharu had taken out the boat for him and they had just reached Hashiba.

Kohei read Irie's letter by the lantern light.

He had clearly scrawled the message in a mad rush.

Lady Masako had suddenly sent for Irie and declared that she wanted to 'meet with that geisha girl, just the two of us, and negotiate with the father directly'. This was a scandalous proposal. Irie was shocked. A lady of her status – the wife of a greater hatamoto – could never and *should* never do such a thing so carelessly.

Of course, Irie tried to stop her. Lady Masako, however, was already prepared to set forth at once. She had donned the kimono of a waiting maid, covered her head and face with a hood, and gathered a handful of servants to arrange the mission.

'If you won't come with me, Irie, I will go by myself,' she said resolutely and made her way to the eastern back gate.

Old Irie judged that nothing could stop her now. He hurriedly prepared himself, wrote a letter to Kohei, thrust it into the hands of Sato, whom he had secretly summoned, and ordered him to make a beeline for Kohei's house.

'Good. Understood,' Kohei said, tucking the letter in the fold of his kimono. 'You can go home now, Oharu. It's all right; there's nothing to worry about.'

'What shall I do, sir?' Sato asked anxiously, oblivious to the circumstances.

'You can go back to the mansion as if nothing happened.' Kohei flashed him a smile, and the next instant he broke into a run.

Oharu and Sato watched him go, wide-eyed. He disappeared into the night like a fierce gust of wind.

He knew that Kansuke's second house was in the first district of Tawaramachi: only a little more than a mile away from Hashiba. He kept running at full speed without even a lantern and reached the house in less than fifteen minutes.

The broad street of Asakusa was still bustling at this time of night. When Kohei shot past the people, they let out cries of alarm.

'What was that?'

'Oh! That gave me a fright. Must have been a street slasher . . .'

Kohei came to the Mishima-myo shrine in Tawaramachi; diagonally across from the street was a large sweet shop called Yamato-ya Kan'emon. There was a narrow alley along the east side of the shop, and Kansuke's second house stood at the end of it. The house used to be a retreat for the owner of Matsumoto-ya, a purveyor of lacquerware in Higashi-nakacho. It had a small garden and an empty plot of nearly four hundred square yards at the back of the house.

Following the alley, Kohei went past this vacant lot and approached the house from the back.

He heard a gut-wrenching scream from inside the house. A loud crash shook the air as shoji doors were knocked down; some men were shouting furiously.

Kohei leaped over the fence into the garden.

Dark shadows were wrestling with each other in the cramped garden. Beyond the broken doors, he could see a hooded woman pinning a younger woman to the floor, about to strike with a dagger.

Kohei immediately pulled out the small dagger attached to the sheath of his short sword and threw it at her.

'Ah!' The dagger hit the hooded woman's raised arm, and she fell backwards, dropping her weapon.

'M-murderer . . .!' The young woman crawled away into the hallway. Kohei deduced that she must be Osato, Kansuke's daughter, but he barely glanced at her.

'Stay out of this!' Lady Masako snapped at Kohei, whom she thought was an intruder.

'You should not tarnish the lord's duty with a despicable act like this!' Kohei rebuked her in a thunderous voice.

Masako shrank back, petrified.

In that instant, four thugs burst into the room from the hallway and the garden, daggers flashing in their hands. They had pummelled Irie and the three servants and broken through their defence.

But they were late by a hair's breadth.

'Fools!' Kohei moved swiftly, and two men keeled over without even knowing what hit them.

'You old codger!'

'What the—?!'

The remaining two men retreated to the hallway to regain their footing, but Kohei pulled out a pair of metal chopsticks from the hot ashes in the ceramic brazier and flung it at them. It hit them straight in the face.

They yelped and scrambled away, covering their faces, and Kohei turned his attention to Irie, who had just tottered in from the garden.

'Come, take Lady Masako home through the empty lot at the back. I'll deal with the rest. Hurry, there's no time to lose... Oh, and here's a letter of apology from Yamada. Everything is taken care of, so you can rest easy. Now, please, go with her...'

*

Seven days later, in the afternoon, Yashichi the goyokiki came to visit Kohei's house again upon his invitation.

Kohei presented to him a bundle wrapped in paper and formally adorned with a decorative knot.

'It's not much, but do take it,' he said. 'The case you helped me with turned out well, and their reward was plenty.'

'I can't take this. It's not right.'

'There's no right or wrong to it. I'm sure you can put it to good use in all manner of ways. If you use it for your duties, it'll be good for the people, too... One thing I'll ask, though – I want you to get something nice for your missus and your little boy. Come on, Yashichi. Just take it – for me.'

'If you're sure... Well, since it comes from you, sensei, I can take it with a good conscience.'

'Good, good. It's yours. Now, I'll have to make a visit to Omoto at Fujiro, too. I'll go there tomorrow.'

As they sipped sake, Kohei told him about the incident from the other night.

'Lady Masako had said she wanted to negotiate, but that was just a front. Blood rushed to her head, and she staged an ambush on Yamada's house all by herself. Imagine the lady of a greater hatamoto with 8,000 koku, and a member of the Osobashu at that.' Kohei chuckled. 'What a big joke. But you know what? Compared to that green gourd of a boy – the young heir who fell head over heels for a dancer when he was supposed to be convalescing and got himself tangled up in a childish scheme – his mother is still better than *that*.'

'So, what happened to Yamada in the end, sensei?'

'Ah, I just left him to his own devices. If I made the matter public, it would've only harmed Lord Ishikawa. And that way, I certainly wouldn't have got any thanks.'

'I see.'

'That scoundrel – I heard he's cleared his second house in Asakusa completely, and now he and his daughter are holed up in his main house, quiet as mice. Well, no wonder. I made him write a letter of apology, *and* he's convinced that I'm a secret agent working for the Shogun, you see. By the way, Yashichi, Jinbei is over the moon about how it all went down. He said he'll pay you a visit soon, too. Hmm? Ah . . . what became of Horigome? He's still working for the Ishikawa family, just as before – so scared that he's always shaking like a leaf, apparently. This should've taught him a lesson, so he won't cause any more trouble.'

The two of them enjoyed a hearty feast of fresh carp; Kohei himself had dressed the fish and turned it into sashimi and a miso-base dish of simmered fillets. Besides the carp, there was a clear soup with whale bone and julienned ginger, among other delicacies.

Thrilled by the windfall, Oharu cheerfully bustled about, cooking up a storm and doing chores around the house.

The scent of young leaves drifted in the gathering twilight, and they heard frogs croaking somewhere in the dark.

'But you know, when you walk into a case like this,' Kohei said, 'it makes me think all the more that a man's got to know how to use a sword, at least the bare bones. I mean the silly young master, too, but you should've seen the steward, Irie. I know he's getting on in years, but still, he's supposed to be a proper samurai. But he let Yamada's henchmen punch and kick him so much he was covered in bumps by the end. I'm telling you, I could barely stand to look at him.'

'It must've been quite a sight . . .' Yashichi laughed quietly.

'Well, Yashichi – in this day and age, when they've taken the name for skilled martial artists and given it to these dancers to sell their outrageous "art", an old man like me has nothing more to say . . .' Kohei clucked his tongue. Then, in a gentle voice, he called out to Oharu for more sake.

Chapter 4

The Four Rulers of Izeki Dojo

I

Oharu had gone out early that morning.

Her older brother Otokichi and his wife, who lived with her parents in Sekiya, had just had their second baby boy. So Kohei had handed her a celebratory gift for the couple and seen her off, saying, 'Stay as long as you like, my dear, and have a good time.'

After a quiet lunch, he stretched himself out on the wooden veranda facing the garden and gazed up at the deep blue sky. Soon he drifted into a comfortable doze.

Sweet flags grew in clusters around the stream that flowed into the garden; their long, round heads of little pale yellow flowers peeked out from between their green blades, giving off a pleasant fragrance.

After a while, a different kind of scent – that of a living creature, with a faint sweet-sour note of perspiration – wafted into Kohei's nostrils.

Hmm . . .? He awoke from his shallow sleep, but he kept his eyes shut.

'Hello . . .? Hello, Akiyama Sensei.'

Kohei opened his eyes and saw Mifuyu leaning down in the garden, dressed in a fresh early-summer outfit for young men.

'Oh . . . How long have you been there?' Kohei asked.

'Just for a little while . . . I had the pleasure of watching you sleep,' she said in a dreamy voice.

Colour rose to her face, which was slightly damp from sweat, without a hint of face powder or rouge. Kohei sat up, unusually flustered. He certainly didn't have any special feelings for Mifuyu, and he was perfectly happy with having one youthful sweetheart in Oharu, but Mifuyu kept making her adoration for him all too clear. He couldn't figure out what to do about it.

Feeling sheepish, he scratched his white-haired head with his little figure and grumbled, 'Who wants to look at an old geezer nodding off? You've got to stop this sort of thing – you're being silly.'

'There is something I would like to ask your opinion about. That's why I came today.' Her expression suddenly stiffened.

'Hmm . . . What could that be?'

'Tanuma – my father – advised me to seek your guidance as well.'

'Lord Tanuma? Indeed . . .?'

'The fact is, sensei, there is a dispute at Izeki dojo . . .'

'Uh-huh. Well, come in then. Oharu's out today – good timing.'

He said the last remark about 'good timing' in a barely audible murmur. Oharu was intent on marrying Kohei as soon as Daijiro returned from his journey; Kohei himself felt he was too old to bother with a wedding, but he had acquiesced for her sake. His promise seemed to have set her worry and jealousy at rest, but even so, whenever Mifuyu came around, Oharu addressed him with exaggerated tenderness.

Mifuyu never batted an eyelid at Oharu's displays, merely casting a look of disdain in her direction.

Although she was a force to be reckoned with in a sword fight, Mifuyu was rather innocent, especially when it came to matters of love. And so, Oharu's hints fell flat, and the thought that Oharu and Kohei might be more intimate than they appeared never even crossed her mind.

Back to the matter at hand . . .

If a dispute arose at Izeki dojo, it was a matter of course that the high-flying Lord Tanuma should intervene. Not only was he Mifuyu's biological father, Tanuma had been a patron to Izeki Tadahachiro, the revered master of the dojo who died two years ago. It was with Tanuma's favour that Izeki had been able to establish such an imposing training hall in Ichigaya Choenjitani in the first place, after he moved to Edo.

Izeki was a consummate swordsman of the Itto-ryu school, but that wasn't all: he was truly a man of character. The retainers of various daimyos and the children of greater hatamotos had flocked to his dojo in no time at all. By the time he died from an illness at fifty-five, his pupils numbered more than two hundred.

After his death, four of his best disciples, including Mifuyu, took on the leadership of the dojo. People called them the Shitenno, or the Four Rulers of Izeki dojo.

Even now, Tanuma gave both material and moral support to the dojo. Kohei had heard about this before from Ushibori, the master of the Okuyama Nen-ryu dojo in Asakusa Mototorigoe.

Therefore, it was only natural that such a significant patron should step in when there was trouble at Izeki dojo.

Though Mifuyu had been cool towards Tanuma so far, deflecting his fatherly love, she apparently had no choice but to consult him about the future of the dojo.

Aha . . . so she's got to see her father now to talk about the dojo . . . Hmm. Good for her, Kohei thought.

If Tanuma had told her to ask Kohei for his opinion, that must mean she had been telling her father something about him.

After drinking the fragrant tea that Kohei had brewed for her, Mifuyu began to speak.

She must have stayed for about four hours.

When she left, Kohei started getting the bath ready.

Oharu came home soon after.

'Guess what, sensei. Pa caught a catfish for us. Shall we have it in the turtle-soup style?'

'Better yet, how about pouring hot water on the dressed fish, then slicing it into thick fillets with the skin on . . . Once you get the slime out, we can get it simmering in dashi shoyu and peck at it straight from the pot.'

'Aye, sounds good to me.' Oharu set to work at once. Though forty years apart in age, they somehow made a well-tuned team, especially of late.

After their meal, Kohei let her take a bath first; when she

came out, he bathed too. The small room with the bathtub was filled with steam mingled with Oharu's scent.

His face involuntarily creased into a smile. The problem of Izeki dojo crossed his mind, but he decided not to think about it that night.

II

The Four Rulers of Izeki dojo consisted of three men and Mifuyu.

The first was Goto Kuhei. At forty, he was in his prime as a swordsman. His age and experience made him a good teacher, and he was known to have a mild temper, too. His master was Todo Izumi-no-kami, the lord of the castle in the Tsu domain in Ise province with more than 323,000 koku. More than twenty retainers of Todo were training at Izeki dojo now, and Goto was popular among the other pupils as well.

The second was Shibutani Torasaburo, thirty-five years old. This one was masterless. No one knew his origins. His late teacher was probably the only person who knew. Shibutani had stayed close by Izeki's side ever since Izeki had settled in the Sagara domain. And after Sagara became Tanuma's territory, and Mifuyu moved there with her adoptive father, Shibutani became Mifuyu's elder disciple.

According to Mifuyu, Shibutani was the strongest of them all. 'If it comes down to it, I believe no one can win against Master Shibutani . . .' she had confessed to Kohei.

But he was a taciturn man. Despite knowing him for

many years, she had never seen him smile, not even once. Apparently an eccentric, he had no wife or child.

Meanwhile, his coaching methods were rigorous and unrelenting to the extreme. No matter who the pupil was, he struck them hard without holding back. He would annihilate them, one after another, without even so much as a word of encouragement, which made their defeat all the more unbearable.

Pupils nowadays despised such practice, so hardly anyone felt any loyalty towards Shibutani.

The third and final ruler was Ozawa Kazue: the second son of Ozawa Iwami-no-kami Toshihide, a greater hatamoto with 5,000 koku, who served as the chief of a unit of the Shogun's personal guards. Though only twenty-six, he was a considerable swordsman.

'I am certainly no match for him,' Mifuyu had said.

Now, there was a widening schism at Izeki dojo. Putting Shibutani aside – he was in a world of his own – the pupils gravitated towards one of the three other leaders until something like factions began to form.

It can be said that this was a natural course of events.

Izeki dojo had come to be one of the most eminent training halls in all of Edo, especially with Tanuma's backing. When such a large body of students – more than two hundred in total – were taught by four people, it couldn't be helped that many of them would lean towards one or the other and make their allegiance known.

Izeki never married, so he had neither heir nor any living kin. This made the dilemma even thornier.

The pupils who flocked to Mifuyu had to be well aware

that she was the daughter of Lord Tanuma, and that he was a patron of the dojo. On top of that, they were more than happy to practise under the instruction of such a beautiful swordswoman.

'Pathetic,' the pupils of other factions would mock them behind their backs. 'They're practically drooling when they get beaten up by her. It's too embarrassing to watch.' But at the same time, they couldn't ignore the presence of the roju behind Mifuyu, either.

In any case, the rift had grown so deep that the dojo was in danger of imploding if they didn't choose a single leader soon.

If they could choose that one person, he or she could take on the name of Izeki and run the dojo as its sole head. This wouldn't have been unheard of; Kohei's own teacher, Tsuji Hei'emon, had taken his teacher's last name when he inherited the Tsuji dojo.

'But, Mifuyu . . .' Tanuma had sighed, when Mifuyu had come to him. 'Leaving you aside, none of the other three stands out.'

Mifuyu herself had no intention of becoming the head of a large dojo; she simply loved the art of sword fighting for its own sake.

And Tanuma had his own wishes: he wanted to find a suitable husband for Mifuyu as soon as possible, so he was not inclined to use his own influence to make her the new leader.

The most appropriate candidate would have been Shibutani under normal circumstances – he was the longest-serving pupil as well as the strongest, after all – but he did not have the charisma to pull along two hundred pupils.

Mifuyu wished she could push for Shibutani as the new leader, for she had known him since she was little, and he had sometimes instructed her himself with strict discipline. If Tanuma listened to her will and pulled a few strings in Shibutani's favour, it was of course possible to make Shibutani the next master.

But if he did so, the other two rulers, Goto and Ozawa, would leave the dojo, taking with them most of the current pupils. Then Izeki dojo would be sure to decline; it might even be the beginning of its downfall.

This narrowed down the choice to Goto or Ozawa.

According to Mifuyu's assessment, Ozawa was the stronger one. But she insisted that if Ozawa were to become the new master, Izeki's name would be sullied. She seemed to loathe Ozawa for some reason.

Ozawa was brimming with ambition. He was more than eager to take over the dojo and make a name for himself as a prominent swordsman here in Edo, the Shogun's own castle town. His father wouldn't hesitate to shower people with gold to help his precious son rise in the world. Upon his honour as a lord with 5,000 koku, he would try every means to line up the key players on his side; in fact, he was already preparing a tremendous sum of gold and other valuables to present to Tanuma, hoping to secure the roju's support.

Besides, the current shogun, Ieharu, was rather fond of Lord Ozawa.

Even Tanuma had to be careful around him.

Thus a dispute within one dojo entailed potential risks of political ramifications.

Goto was just as committed to grasping the title of

dojo master. He was even ready to leave the service of the Todo family: to quit his position as a retainer and focus on running the dojo. With Goto's popularity with the majority of students, Ozawa couldn't exactly turn a blind eye to his intention.

And so, at his wits' end, Tanuma had suggested to Mifuyu, 'Would you go and ask Akiyama Sensei for his opinion?'

III

Early next morning, Kohei stepped out in his typical outfit: an informal kimono with a haori jacket, a wakizashi forged by Horikawa Kunihiro at his waist, and a walking stick made of sakura.

'I'll be gone for a bit,' he told Oharu before setting off.

He walked to Ryogoku and hired a litter from there. It was just after ten in the morning when he reached Izeki dojo in Choenjitani.

This area used to be a big pond, according to local lore. Izeki dojo stood in a hollow of nearly two thousand square yards, across the road from the Choen-ji temple gate. There were merchants' houses and tea shops in the neighbourhood around the gate, but the dojo side was mostly made up of samurai mansions and the shogunate's residences for lower-level officials.

Kohei left the road and descended the stone steps to the front of the dojo. The front wall had a large open window with a vertical lattice, and a handful of children from the neighbourhood were holding on to the bars and peering in at the swords practice.

'Mind if this old man has a peek, too?' Kohei called out cheerfully as he went up to the window. With his height, he could just about look inside if he put both feet on the stone wall right under the window.

Oho . . . They're hard at it. He smiled.

Mifuyu was in the middle of instructing the pupils; she looked brave with her black-lacquered armour over her torso.

It was a fine, spacious dojo.

About thirty students were waiting for their turn. Every time Mifuyu's shrill voice rang out with her strikes, the young pupils nodded to each other in excitement. The ones who had just received a blow from her wooden sword grimaced in pain, but they seemed to be enjoying their beating.

She wore her lacquer-black hair in an adolescent boy's topknot, as usual, and a thin white cloth was tied tightly around her forehead. With her face flushing from the exertion, her elegant eyes gleaming with a penetrating light, she looked more beautiful than ever – so much so that she was spellbinding.

Hmm, I see . . . Kohei understood why the boys were so eager.

At the front of the room was a dais where a middle-aged samurai with an imposing stature sat watching Mifuyu's training session with a broad smile.

Kohei thought this must be Goto, one of the Four Rulers.

Mifuyu flew back and forth across the large dojo, as swift

as a swallow, shouting out instructions to the pupils. Kohei was impressed by how stern and exact her teaching was.

Sparring with one pupil after another, she landed a blow on a young man's arm; he dropped his wooden sword and tottered to the ground.

'Put your back into it!' her spirited voice rang out. 'How can it be that your skills worsen after daily practice?' She grabbed his collar around the nape of his neck, pulled him up, and with a shout, twisted her torso to throw him with only one hand.

The others burst out laughing.

'Quiet!' Mifuyu barked.

So, this is what goes on in dojos nowadays, eh? Looks like it's all fun and games to them. If they think it's amusing to get beaten up by a swordswoman, they won't get very far. Kohei smiled drily. He glanced at the raised platform and noticed that Goto was still grinning from ear to ear instead of joining Mifuyu in admonishing the pupils.

Ah . . . this one's hopeless. In a flash of intuition, Kohei saw right through him. Goto wasn't interested in training his disciples in body and mind through the art of sword fighting; rather, he was a typical example of a dojo master who cared more about furthering his own fame and social standing by selling his swordsmanship.

When Mifuyu withdrew to the back, dripping with sweat, Goto took her place.

As with Mifuyu, the pupils eagerly gathered around and struck out at him one after another. His popularity was obvious.

He deftly dealt with each pupil without breaking a

sweat, and he dished out a good word for everyone, along the lines of 'That's it. You're almost there,' or 'Watch your footwork. Push harder when you lunge forward,' or 'Good. Remember that rhythm in your breathing.' Spurred on by his words, the pupils threw themselves into practice. At first glance, he appeared to be a clever teacher, but this kind of jester-like method based on tricks and flattery only stunted growth. Even students who had the potential to be a *ten* would reach *three* or *four* at best, while they themselves would be under the illusion that they had made great progress.

The other two leaders, Ozawa and Shibutani, were absent again today.

Shibutani lived in a room in the late Izeki's house at the back of the dojo, along with a manservant, but – as Mifuyu had told Kohei – whenever he came out to lead the training, all the pupils would turn tail and leave. These days he mostly stayed out of the dojo, perhaps brooding over this state of affairs.

At noon, there was a break in the practice. Some went home; others ate the bento lunches that they'd brought with them.

Kohei stepped away from the window and started back for home.

He wished he could have watched Shibutani and Ozawa at work, too, but he felt as though he had seen enough to grasp the general picture.

Mifuyu didn't reappear from the back of the dojo. Kohei hadn't told her that he would be watching in secret today.

After paying a visit to the Ichigaya Hachimangu shrine,

he stopped by at a sweets shop to buy a little gift, then headed to the goyokiki Yashichi's house in Yotsuya.

Since Yashichi was out, his wife, Omine, welcomed him into her restaurant, Musashi-ya, and he had a late lunch there. After the meal, he handed the small pack of sweets to their son Itaro, saying, 'Sorry it's not much today, but here's a little something for you,' and to Omine he said, 'I just popped by since I was in the neighbourhood – no reason in particular. Say hello to Yashichi for me.' He took a litter straight back home.

But something happened the next morning.

Mifuyu came to Kohei's house by litter in a great hurry. She was clearly on edge, her face bloodless. 'Sensei,' she called out as soon as she saw him, 'Master Shibutani was murdered.'

'Are you certain?'

'Yes. He was found dead early this morning by a servant at Choen-ji temple who happened to pass by – on a hill called Kurayami-zaka on the west side of the dojo . . .'

'Did he have a sword wound . . .?'

'Yes, a deep thrust to the heart . . . and it seems he was also struck hard on the head with something. I heard he was covered in blood when the servant found him. I just heard the news at home and came here straight away. I thought I should tell you before I go to the dojo . . .'

Mifuyu's tense voice made even Oharu hold her breath.

'You say he was struck on the head . . .?'

'Yes. Sensei – I apologise for burdening you, but would you be willing to inspect Master Shibutani's body?'

'You mean, go with you to the dojo?'

'Yes, please come—'

'No . . . I think it's probably best that I don't. I should stay out of it, for now. But you, Miss Mifuyu, you'll have to go to the dojo and face Shibutani's body. I suppose the funeral will be held at the dojo, of course.'

'Yes.'

'Observe carefully, and tell me what you see. And . . . I'll jot down a brief letter right now – I want you to ask some pupil or other to take it to a restaurant in Yotsuya Tenma called Musashi-ya. Will you do that?'

'Yes, sir . . . but what . . .?'

'I'll entrust you with it,' he said, quickly pulling up his writing box. 'Anyhow, I'd better not show my face to the people at the dojo just yet.'

IV

In Ushigome Haraikatamachi, a stone's throw away from Izeki dojo, there was a diner called Tama-no-O, popular for its rustic, wholesome fare of rice cooked with green leaves and noppei soup with root vegetables.

Shibutani had been a regular at Tama-no-O. He would often go there around sunset and stay for a few hours at least, having his fill of food and drink.

It was likely that he had been ambushed last night on his way home from the diner. In fact, the official investigation confirmed this later.

Kurayami-zaka, or 'Dark Hill', was also known as Gomi-zaka: 'Garbage Hill.' Not so long ago, it had been a dumping ground for the neighbourhood, but after Izeki dojo was established, with Lord Tanuma's patronage, the dump moved to another location at some point, and people took to calling it 'Dark Hill' instead.

The sloping path was just short of 6 feet in width and 120 in length, bordered by samurai mansions on both sides. The tall trees growing inside the mansion walls formed a thick canopy over the hill, and it was a shadowy place even in daytime.

Shibutani was found lying on his back. Though he had been a swordsman of high calibre, he had perished instantly without even a chance to draw his katana. How could it be that he hadn't resisted at all, even as the murderer smashed his head and thrust the fatal blow in his heart?

A crushed lantern, half burned to ashes, lay a few paces away from the body.

After nightfall, Yashichi hurried to Kohei's house.

The area around Ichigaya wasn't part of Yashichi's territory, but it was nearby, so he was familiar with the other private eyes of the neighbourhood and the magistrates' lower-rank officials who came there to investigate from Hacchobori.

Besides these connections, he had the letter from Kohei, so when he had arrived at Izeki dojo and showed it to Mifuyu, she gave him special permission to inspect Shibutani's body as thoroughly as he wished.

The representatives from the magistrates also finished their examination of the corpse, and a wake was to be held at the dojo tonight. Considering how unpopular he had been with the pupils, the gathering would likely be small. The remaining three of the Four Rulers had rushed to the dojo as soon as they had received word of the strange incident and were now watching over Shibutani.

'From what I've seen,' Yashichi told Kohei, 'I reckon Shibutani was drunk when he was walking up that hill, and someone must've thrown a big rock at him from above – a bang on the head. He blacked out before he could even put a hand on his hilt, and the killer finished him off with a dagger to the heart . . .'

'A rock, eh . . . ?'

Yashichi added that the officials were of the same opinion.

'Was a rock like that found near the body?' Kohei asked.

'No, not quite . . .'

On both sides of the slope stood samurai mansions surrounded by tall earthen walls. Yashichi's theory was that the killer had been waiting for Shibutani to pass by, perched on top of the wall or the thick branches that loomed over the path; using the light of Shibutani's lantern to take aim, the killer hurled down a rock the size of a child's head. As Shibutani was drunk, and he wouldn't have imagined that his life was in danger, he would have made a surprisingly easy target, despite his mastery of the sword.

'The servants told me that he left the dojo when it was still light,' Yashichi continued. 'There are two manservants at the dojo; no maids. Both of them have been there since Izeki Sensei's days, and everyone in the neighbourhood says they're honest, hard-working men.'

'Good.' Kohei nodded. 'Could you stay the night here?'

'Of course.'

'Well then, listen closely to what I've got to say. And let's talk about how to move forward with this.' Kohei took out no less than ten gold ryo from a small box and placed it in front of Yashichi. 'War funds,' he said. Then, in a honeyed voice, he called out to Oharu, who was sewing in the next room, 'Oharu, can you bring us some sake?'

The next morning before dawn, Yashichi departed from Kohei's house.

On the afternoon of the following day, Mifuyu came to see him.

It was another clear day.

But Mifuyu looked grim, weighed down by grief and anxiety. 'It really is unsettling – I never would have thought... What do you think of Master Shibutani's death, sensei?'

'He was murdered, that's for sure. Someone might have had a grudge against him, or perhaps...'

'Are you saying it has something to do with the dispute at the dojo?'

'If that's the case, you ought to be careful.'

'Sensei...'

'Did you tell your father about the incident?'

'Not yet.'

'That's good. From now on, if you go to the dojo, make sure you leave early, while it's still bright.'

'You mean, the killer is after...?'

'Just remember that, and you'll be fine. And no matter what happens, you had better stay out of the dojo's affairs. If anyone asks your opinion, just smile back at them without saying a word – and keep up the act, whatever you do.'

'But sensei...'

'I haven't forgotten about what you asked me to do. So, well, just leave it up to this old codger.'

'Yes, sir. I shouldn't have questioned you. I am grateful.'

'Wait here.' Kohei left Mifuyu standing in the garden and withdrew into the house. He came back immediately, holding two wooden swords.

'S-sensei . . .?' Mifuyu murmured, puzzled.

'I want you to come here for the next three days – about four hours each day is all we need. How about it?'

'Of course, I don't mind at all, but—'

'Here.' He handed a sword to Mifuyu and kept one for himself, stepping down to the garden.

Oharu had been frowning at Mifuyu at first, but now she wondered, *What in the world . . .?* When she saw Kohei's unusually tense expression, she held her breath.

'Miss Mifuyu,' Kohei said.

'Yes?'

'What we'll do now is make a kata – we'll choreograph a pattern of attacks and parries in imitation of a fierce duel in which you will in the end defeat me.'

'What . . .?'

'We have to make it believable to the sharpest observer. That's why we have to practise the sequence for three days or so. Does that bother you?'

'Not at all, sensei. It would be such a privilege to learn from you, even if it's just a performance—'

'Fine, fine. Anyhow, let's work out a good pattern.'

'But why would we—'

'No more questions – just follow my lead. Go on, hold your sword at the ready.'

'Yes, sir!' Mifuyu tugged up her hakama so as to move her legs more freely. She sprung back and raised her sword in the middle position, its point aimed at Kohei's eyes. 'Ready!'

That moment, Kohei's hunched back became perfectly straight.

'Oh . . .' Oharu paled and uttered a low cry, grasping a pillar of the veranda.

His piercing eyes gleamed, and he looked intently at the point of Mifuyu's sword, more formidable than she had ever seen him.

Blood drained from Mifuyu's face.

His right hand holding the wooden sword was still hanging loosely at his side. Just as he slowly began to raise the tip of the sword, a swallow which had nested under the eaves of the house shot out like an arrow and crossed right in front of Kohei's eyes, flying away towards the river.

Kohei didn't even blink.

V

It rained that day.

Though it was a little early for the rainy season, Yashichi said, 'Looks like it won't let up for a few days.' He had been out at work since the morning and had come home for lunch. After a light meal, he stretched out on his side and told his wife, 'Maybe I'll call it a day.'

'Yes, you should rest,' said Omine as she made another pot of tea. 'You've been so busy these days.'

'It's a little "favour" for Akiyama Sensei.'

'Oh, that's what you're up to. Then shouldn't you keep going—'

'Not to worry, I've already cast a fishing net. All there is to do is wait.'

Just then, one of Yashichi's familiar informants – Tokujiro with the umbrella shop – came scrambling in through the back door of Musashi-ya.

'Hey, boss. I just saw Ozawa Kazue with two samurai going into Yorozu-ya at Hachiman shrine.'

'Two samurai . . .?'

'They don't seem to be pupils at Izeki dojo.'

'All right. I'll go alone.' Yashichi quickly dressed up for the rain and shot out of the house like a bullet.

Yorozu-ya was a fine-dining restaurant in the precincts of the Ichigaya Hachimangu shrine – a well-known establishment in these parts. To reach the restaurant, one would cross the main entrance and the first torii gate, climb the extremely steep stone steps, veer right from the second torii gate, and pass the house of worship, which stood on a precipice. The restaurant stood below the cliff, surrounded by a thick grove. Its premises stretched over several annexes, all connected by an expansive garden.

Yashichi and the owner of Yorozu-ya, Chobei, knew each other quite well because of Yashichi's line of work as well as his wife also being in the food business.

In less than twenty minutes, Yashichi reached Yorozu-ya.

Chobei came out to greet him. As soon as Yashichi whispered something in his ear, he said with a nod, 'Wait a moment . . .' and summoned an attendant straight away. After hearing which guest room Ozawa and the samurais had been shown to, Chobei himself led Yashichi through the restaurant.

The guest room was an annexe just at the foot of the cliff. There was a roofed passageway that linked it to the main building, but Chobei stepped out into the garden without even fetching an umbrella and guided Yashichi to the back of the annexe. Glancing around to make sure they were alone, Chobei quietly pulled on one of the horizontal planks covering the wall, revealing a gaping hole about three feet wide on all sides.

Yashichi thanked him silently with a light bow, then he stooped down and slipped inside. Chobei returned the board to its place and went back to the main building as if nothing out of the ordinary had occurred.

Though it looked just like the rest of the wall, the covering hid the entrance to a secret room.

It wasn't the case with all restaurants and teahouses, but the more famous a restaurant, the more likely it was to have a few such guest rooms or annexes with a secret chamber attached. This was not for the benefit of the guests, but for the restaurant itself. If an attendant sensed something suspicious or mysterious about the customer, she would show them into a guest room with a secret room and observe them in hiding. If need be, the restaurant could alert the authorities in the hope of nipping any possible calamities in the bud. Yashichi's Musashi-ya had two such rooms as well.

The attendant at Yorozu-ya hadn't guided Ozawa's party to this particular annexe because they looked dubious. It was simply because Ozawa was a frequent visitor at the restaurant, and he preferred the annexe under the cliff whenever he came.

And so, when Yashichi had alerted Chobei that he was investigating Ozawa for work, Chobei had thought, *How convenient*, and brought him straight to the secret room.

Later, Yashichi would tell Kohei, 'I was lucky from start to finish that day. Of all the restaurants he could've gone to, Ozawa chose the place where I know the owner – and to top it off, they went into the annexe with a secret room . . .'

Now, back to the present:

Yashichi crouched in the dark room of about thirty-five square feet and pricked up his ears. He heard Ozawa laughing; an attendant brought them some sake and promptly left the room. The three men were sitting just on the other side of the wall. Yashichi leaned closer to one corner of the wall, where there was a peephole about the size of a soybean. This hole was well hidden in the shadow of the tokonoma alcove on the other side, so the guests would never notice it.

'One down. Well played,' Ozawa said, sipping from his sake cup. 'I have to admit, I didn't expect it to go so well. You know, Yamashita, I wasn't quite convinced by your suggestion in the beginning, but . . . well, you've done an excellent job.'

'Well, young master, if there's one thing I'm good at, it's being light on my feet,' the one called Yamashita said proudly.

'I don't doubt it,' Ozawa said, nodding approvingly, then turned to the other one. 'And you too, Kamiya. You ran out to Shibutani to finish him off as soon as Yamashita threw the rock from his perch on the wall and hit him right on the head – now *that* was a clever move. Bravo.' Ozawa offered to pour sake for the man called Kamiya.

'You're far too kind. Anything for you, young master . . .' Kamiya raised his cup and gratefully received the drink.

Both Kamiya and Yamashita appeared to be young retainers who served Ozawa's father – which meant Ozawa had ordered his trusted men to assassinate Shibutani. Ozawa pulled out two bundles, which presumably held some gold coins, and handed one to each of them.

'I'm sure I'll rely on your services in the future,' Ozawa said.

'Thank you, sir!'

'Now that Shibutani is out of the way, no one at the dojo can beat me. I'm certain I'd win against Goto and Mifuyu.'

'Of course you will, young master.'

'But Shibutani . . . He was the only one I wanted to avoid. And to think a man like that would snuff it just from a single rock . . .'

'Drinking sure is a dangerous thing.'

Ozawa chortled. 'Indeed.'

All three of them laughed, in high spirits.

Yashichi bit his lips as he listened in the dark, trying to suppress his rage.

'I'm planning to have a match with Goto and Mifuyu to decide the next master of the dojo. I'll ask my father to help me steer everything in that direction. Just you wait – when I take over Izeki dojo, you two will face the music.'

'We're trembling in fear, young master.'

'You'll be wallowing in good fortune,' Ozawa chuckled.

'I'll recommend you to my father even more than before, and I will see to it that you rise to success.'

'We are grateful for your generosity,' said one breathlessly.

'We will be truly delighted, sir,' said the other.

Two hours later, Yashichi hired a litter to carry him at top speed across Ryogoku bridge towards Kohei's house.

When Kohei heard the whole story, he couldn't help but slam his fist down on his knee. 'I can't believe it . . .' he growled. 'Shibutani was murdered by such low scum . . .'

He fell silent, his mouth pressed in a tight line. Frustration burned inside him.

Eventually, he said, 'Yashichi – and you too, Oharu – whatever you do, don't speak about this to anyone else. Understand? Good.'

VI

It was three days later, before noon, that Kohei appeared at the threshold of Izeki dojo.

The remaining three leaders of the dojo had carried out Shibutani's funeral, and these days, they never missed a day of practice.

With Shibutani gone, they were no longer the 'Four Rulers', but now the pressure to appoint a new master was beginning to feel stifling.

While Mifuyu stood apart, Goto and Ozawa were busy manoeuvring people to gain an advantage. And they had completely stopped talking to each other.

Ozawa regarded Goto with a hint of a sneer playing on his young, virile face. Ozawa's father had already begun his entreaties to Lord Tanuma to favour his son.

Meanwhile, Goto had no connections to depend on. Of course, his master, Lord Todo, had little interest in backing him; if Goto succeeded in taking over the dojo, that would only mean one less vassal for Todo. Goto's only hope sprung from his confidence that about two thirds of all two hundred pupils were rooting for *him* to be the next master.

When Mifuyu had returned to her house in Negishi the evening before, Goto had been awaiting her.

'I would like to hear your honest thoughts, Miss Mifuyu,' Goto had said. He asked her if she had any intention of taking on the dojo. He used to believe that she didn't, but it appeared to him that her attitude had changed greatly in the past few days. The way she taught the pupils was even more fiery than before, and she seemed to be keen to win over more students to her side. There was every indication that if the three of them were to test their abilities in a match, she would be fully prepared to take part.

If she *was* interested in getting the dojo, neither Goto nor Ozawa could let down their guard, what with Tanuma's powerful presence hovering behind her.

But Ozawa didn't seem ruffled by this at all; to Goto, Ozawa's perfect composure was rather eerie.

Shibutani's murderer was still on the loose.

Knowing what an eccentric he had been, Goto thought it wasn't impossible that he would have had a few enemies – but even so, it was a freakish death, to say the least.

Goto's anxieties had only grown as the days went by.

In response to his question, Mifuyu had given a clear answer: 'My father is against it, but I wish to succeed Izeki Sensei.'

Goto's face had contorted into a taut, torturous kind of smile; her words had clearly shaken him. The smile quickly vanished from his face, and he soon left for home in a grim silence.

Soon after his departure, Yashichi had come to her with a letter from Kohei.

The message was simple: 'We will go ahead with the plan as discussed. Be sure to come to the dojo tomorrow morning.'

And now, it was time: Kohei arrived at the dojo.

'I came upon hearing of the high repute of Miss Sasaki Mifuyu,' he declared to the pupil who came to hear what he wanted. 'I wish to test the strength of my sword against hers. I am called Tsuchida Sei'emon.'

The pupil looked the small old man up and down, apparently nonplussed. 'Well, if you wish . . .' he said, and passed Kohei's challenge to Mifuyu.

She immediately said, 'Interesting. Show him through.'

There were about forty pupils crowding the dojo. A murmur peppered with snickers ran through them as they watched the unexpected visitor shuffle feebly into the room.

Ozawa and Goto were observing the scene from the dais. Even they could sense that the old man was not one to be taken lightly.

Tsuchida was a total stranger to them. Though they had heard of a Mugai-ryu swordsman called Akiyama Kohei, who used to be a formidable presence in the world of swords in Edo some time in the past, they had never actually *seen* him in person.

Kohei stepped forward in front of Mifuyu. 'I am Tsuchida Sei'emon Terusuke of the Nen-ryu school,' he announced.

Her whole face flushed. 'Sasaki Mifuyu, Itto-ryu,' she answered boldly.

No one would have suspected that the two knew each other.

Instead of the casual kimono style that he usually went out in, Kohei was dressed for battle: he wore a karusan-style hakama which wrapped closely around his calves, as well as a thin cloth tied around his forehead and a tasuki cord to hold up his sleeves. He grasped the wooden sword that a pupil of the dojo presented to him and faced Mifuyu.

Mifuyu sprang back and held her wooden sword in the seigan stance: the middle position with the point of the blade aimed at the opponent's eyes. Kohei raised his in the hasso stance, the hilt held high in front of his right shoulder, the blade upright and ready to strike. As they locked eyes, an overwhelming aura of hostility emanated from both of them.

A hush fell over the pupils in an instant. *Is the old man actually . . . ?*

Kohei and Mifuyu edged forward, slowly closing the distance between them.

'Ready!!'

'Come!!'

Their cries seemed to pierce the silence at the same time. They lunged into a torrent of fierce attacks. The way they clashed was so rapid and vehement that not a single man in the room saw through the choreography that Kohei had drilled into Mifuyu over three days.

Mifuyu thrust her sword upwards; Kohei leaped five feet in the air and swung down his sword with the full force of the jump. The pupils who liked Mifuyu screwed up their eyes, thinking it was over, but she dropped to her left knee and parried the blow from below. Kohei dodged her blade by whirling aside like a preternatural bird.

They stood apart, facing each other in the same stances as at the beginning of the match. The tension mounted again, and they closed in on each other at the same time.

The loud clack of wood hitting wood rang out in the dojo. Kohei's sword spun out of his hands and hit the ceiling.

He sprang back, fell to his knees, and bowed down with both hands flat on the floor. 'I admit defeat,' he said.

Both of them were dripping with sweat. Mifuyu's sweat was real, but Kohei's was an act: for a master at his level, it was a simple matter to perspire as little or as much as he wanted.

'Sasaki Sensei – although my bones are old, I implore you to allow me to join the ranks of your pupils,' Kohei said earnestly.

Mifuyu only smiled drily and turned to withdraw to the back of the dojo, but Kohei ran after her, begging her desperately.

'Please, sensei. Please let me enter this dojo and train as your disciple . . .'

VII

Ten days after Kohei and Mifuyu's performance, the time came to hold a tournament to determine the next master of Izeki dojo.

In the time leading up to this event, Goto had tried every means to put the question to a vote instead – for he was sure to have the most number of pupils on his side – but Ozawa insisted on fighting it out in a match. Because Goto had counted on Mifuyu to back him up, he had grown increasingly restless since he'd learned of her wish to inherit the dojo.

Eventually, Lord Tanuma stepped in to deliver his judgement. He proclaimed that the three of them should face each other in a match, and he will 'bestow the name of Izeki and the headship of the dojo on the strongest one'.

He added one condition, however: 'You have been called the Four Rulers and have worked together to protect the dojo until now. I imagine that fighting against such comrades might be painful to you. If that be the case, you shall appoint one of your pupils to enter the match in your stead.'

Goto and Ozawa had no such intention.

Goto was confident that he could defeat Mifuyu, though he was uneasy about facing Ozawa.

Ozawa's conviction that he was the strongest of them all did not waver for a moment.

The day of the match was hot and humid; a thin layer of cloud obscured the sky. Still, more than a hundred pupils gathered at the dojo.

A senior official named Miyoshi Shirobei attended the match as Tanuma's representative. For the judge, Tanuma had appointed Kaneko Sonjuro Nobuto, who headed a prominent dojo of the Itto-ryu school in the fifth district of Yushima. Kaneko was almost sixty years old, and, as one of the most distinguished swordsmen of Edo, he was acquainted with a large circle of daimyos and greater hatamotos – but he had never met Kohei in person.

At around ten in the morning, feeble rays of sunlight escaped through the clouds, falling on the crimson petals of the pomegranate tree that grew within the dojo's gate. The song of an aged bush warbler came drifting in the air from somewhere in the trees above the cliff.

The hour of the match was approaching when Mifuyu, who had been waiting in a side room, suddenly spoke up.

'I cannot give up my wish to keep Izeki Sensei's will alive and follow in his footsteps . . . But even so, it grieves me to fight against Goto and Ozawa,' she said. 'I will have my pupil, Tsuchida Sei'emon, stand in my place. I can't say I have much confidence in him, but if he loses, I will willingly withdraw.' Her voice, filled with sorrow, never faltered.

She speaks like a woman after all, Ozawa thought. He was sure that the old man would be an even easier win than Mifuyu. Goto thought the same.

The first match was between Goto and 'Tsuchida' Kohei.

In each match, the first man to score a point would win.

Everyone at the dojo was already aware that Mifuyu had accepted Tsuchida as her pupil. Though Goto had been stunned by the pair's clash ten days ago, he knew that he himself outmatched Mifuyu by far. As far as he was concerned, this Tsuchida was just a stubborn old man who wasn't even up to Mifuyu's level, so there was nothing to worry about. Ozawa was much more daunting than him.

Brimming with confidence, Goto went to face Tsuchida in the middle of the hall. Following the etiquette, they squatted down on their heels and held their wooden swords so that the points were almost touching. As the tension rose between them, they suddenly stood upright and drew apart to face each other at a distance of about eight yards.

With a piercing cry, Goto slammed his foot down and lunged forward to crush Kohei with one strike. The pupils were startled by his intense animosity: it was worlds apart from his usual demeanour.

Kohei parried his blow and swerved around him, lowering his sword from the upper hasso stance to the lower position.

Now!! Seeing his chance, Goto raised his sword to swing down straight in the middle. But that instant, the tip of Kohei's sword twitched upward ever so slightly.

A murmur of surprise escaped Goto. He stood paralysed with his sword high above his head; he couldn't strike out any more, as if he were nailed to an invisible wall.

What's going on . . .? To Goto, Kohei's blade suddenly felt much more massive than it was, so much so that it seemed to expand and burst through his eyes. *Who the hell is this old geezer? But he lost to Miss Mifuyu . . . This can't be happening . . .*

When such thoughts crossed his mind, it meant the end for Goto.

As much as his sword, Kohei's gleaming eyes seemed to come right up to Goto's face, and as he swung down he seemed to lose grip on his movements. The next thing he knew, Kohei's sword had collided with his torso; the impact made him lurch forward and fall to his knees, Goto's sword clattering to the floor from his limp hand.

'Cease!' The referee's voice rang out.

Goto picked up his sword and, utterly dejected, withdrew to his waiting room. Next up was Ozawa against Kohei. If Ozawa won the match, there would still be another chance for Goto; if Goto could win against Ozawa, he would be allowed a second match against Kohei. But Goto wasn't sure if he could withstand Ozawa's raging blade, full of youthful vigour. He flumped down in the waiting room, and he didn't stir for some time. By all measures, his confidence was in shreds.

None of the pupils on his side came to see him.

Meanwhile, Kohei – who had taken a short break – and Ozawa were about to face off in the dojo.

Ozawa hadn't been watching the first match. He had been sitting in the side room, surrounded by his retainers, Kamiya and Yamashita, as well as his servile pupils. 'Well, you just sit back and watch,' he had said to them. 'I'll show you something interesting.'

Even when he heard of Goto's defeat, he'd merely scoffed. In fact, he had looked down on Goto more than on Mifuyu, often complaining to others that Goto's jester-like teaching style of tricks and flattery would only weaken his pupils.

After Izeki's death, Ozawa visited numerous sword-fighting dojos across Edo, striving to hone his skill. When Mifuyu had told Kohei that she was 'certainly no match for him', she wasn't being modest: it was the truth.

Who in that dojo, then, would have imagined that a swordsman such as Ozawa would be destroyed by the little old man even more quickly than Goto had been?

The moment Ozawa and Kohei straightened up and faced each other, eight yards apart, Kohei slowly raised his wooden sword from the middle position to the hasso stance with the blade upright; he stooped a little and, peering up at Ozawa, he actually grinned.

Ozawa didn't even know what hit him. As if pulled forward by that grin, Ozawa charged at Kohei with an air-rending shriek. It was a powerful thrust aimed at Kohei's throat, but Kohei dodged it with ease.

Ozawa took a few steps too far from the momentum of his attack, but he planted his foot firmly on the floor and pivoted around to face Kohei again without losing his balance at all. He was no common swordsman.

Expecting Kohei's counterattack, Ozawa drew back his left foot and readied his sword in the middle stance.

Just as he did so, Kohei moved as light as a breeze and, without uttering a sound, he struck Ozawa's sword with his own.

Sharp gasps went up in the room.

Kohei's wooden sword had split Ozawa's in two; the broken tip spun in the air and arced into the crowd of pupils at the south end of the hall. At the same time, Kohei hit Ozawa's right wrist, and Kaneko the referee called, 'Cease!' in amazement.

Everything was over.

Tsuchida had won the tournament. Mifuyu – who was stronger than Tsuchida and was his teacher – was now the head of Izeki dojo, and she would change her name to Izeki Mifuyu.

After the last match, Kaneko asked Mifuyu, 'Where is that elderly man from? I have never seen him before . . . I'd like to have a long chat with him.'

'He is from the countryside, and he isn't good with words, so he doesn't like to meet people. Please excuse him,' Mifuyu answered courteously.

Later that day, soon after Kohei got home, Yashichi appeared at his door.

'I had a peek at your matches today,' Yashichi said.

'You were there? Hmm . . .'

'I've never seen a thing like *that* before . . .'

'Like what, eh?'

'You broke a wooden sword in two, just with a tap. I was blown away.'

Kohei laughed quietly.

'So, sensei – what would you like me to do now?'

'About what?'

'I heard every word Ozawa and his men said about Shibutani's murder with my own ears. They deserve punishment from the Shogun . . .'

'You'll capture them, you mean?'

'Yes.'

'I wouldn't do that. Just let them be.'

'But, sensei, their crime—'

'If the truth about Shibutani's death came to light, it would only bring shame on the dead. Just think – the great Izeki Sensei's oldest and best disciple got himself so drunk that he let someone hit him with a rock from above and dropped dead without even drawing his sword. It'd be a disgrace. Izeki Sensei would be humiliated in his grave.'

'Well, you're right, but—'

'Pay them no mind. They'll get what's coming to them before long.'

Now, about half a month after Mifuyu became the new leader of Izeki dojo, she called on all the pupils to gather. Ozawa and Goto didn't attend the meeting; more than seventy students had quit the dojo to follow them.

To everyone's surprise, Mifuyu announced that she would dissolve Izeki dojo. 'I am certain that I do not have to tell you what an exceptional man and teacher Izeki Sensei was,' she said. 'After his death, the four of us were dubbed the Four Rulers, and we kept the dojo running. All four of us aspired to carry on Izeki Sensei's high virtue and the spirit of his Itto-ryu, and to impart his teachings to a wider circle of people . . . In retrospect, I am only filled with shame at my foolish hubris in thinking that I was capable of such a thing.

'If one of us did indeed have the calibre to stand in Izeki Sensei's place without sullying his name, it would of course have been a fine deed for this person to inherit the dojo. However, none of us even come close to our late master's standard. There are few misfortunes greater than such meagre disciples dishonouring their noble teacher's name together. I trust that every one of you who has observed the course of recent events has come to understand this very well.

'I would also add that, even if we fall short of our late master, we can each live in our own ways. It is my sincere hope that we will all go forth without clinging to the name of Izeki dojo and devote ourselves to our training, to shape our body and mind to uphold our integrity and tranquillity, so that one day we will be good enough to establish our own school of sword fighting. That is how we can make Izeki Sensei proud.

'I encourage each one of you to seek out your own path and press on with dignity.'

A good number of pupils tried to persuade her not to close the dojo, but Mifuyu was resolute.

The next day, Mifuyu visited Kohei and told him everything.

'This conclusion was possible only because I followed your instructions, Akiyama Sensei. I am deeply grateful,' she said in a tearful voice, bowing with both her hands on the floor.

'How do you feel? "Good riddance", eh?'

'Yes, it's like a cloud has lifted. My father, Tanuma, is eager to meet with you and thank you in person . . .'

'That's all right. But I suppose we'll run into each other at some point.'

*

Now, there was something that happened a year later, in the summer of 1779 . . .

One evening, Ozawa – who, by that time, had opened his own dojo near the Shohei bridge in Kanda with the support of his father – went out to a fancy restaurant called Inaya in Nakazu with his father's retainer, Kamiya Shinzo. It was late at night when they left the restaurant.

That was as far as anyone knew.

The next morning, Ozawa and Kamiya were found dead. The wife of a tofu maker in Tomimatsu discovered their corpses lying around by the foot of a wall encircling a mansion of administrative officials, which faced Yanagiwara, the dirt bank along Kanda River.

Each of them had a single wound. Ozawa had died instantly from a slit on his carotid artery; Kamiya from one thrust to the heart.

The official who examined their corpses was astonished by the cuts, saying, 'I've never seen such mastery.'

The next day around sunset, Yashichi came to Kohei's house with the news.

'Oho. Is that so?' Kohei said. 'Didn't I tell you, Yashichi? Like I said that time last year, they got the punishment they deserved.'

Yashichi nodded. He shrank back a little and peered up at Kohei. 'Sensei, I wonder – who could've handed out that punishment?'

Kohei's thin eyes flashed. 'A god.'

'Eh . . .?'

'Divine retribution from the god of swords.' Kohei's face hardened in stern lines for a moment, but soon his usual affectionate smile spread over it like ripples across water. 'Terrifying, eh? What gods can do.'

'Y-yes, sensei . . . It sure is.' Yashichi kept his face down, unable to look at his old teacher.

Chapter 5
River Suzuka in the Rain

I

Before Kohei resolved the conflict at Izeki dojo in Edo, his son Daijiro chanced upon a case of his own.

Daijiro had journeyed to the village of Shibamura in the Shiki district of Yamato province, taking with him a lock of hair which had belonged to the late Shimaoka Reizo. He arrived at the mansion of Reizo's elder brother, Hachiro'emon, who was head of all the local village chiefs. He took the news of his sibling's death with composure.

'I see . . . If you were by his side in his final hour, Master Daijiro, I am sure he was content,' he said calmly. Though he seemed to be in his seventies, he was firm and self-possessed; he was the brother of a master swordsman, after all.

Both Hachiro'emon and the rest of the Shimaoka family warmly invited Daijiro to stay as long as he liked, but Daijiro departed after two days.

Things were different from his younger days; Daijiro had his own dojo now, albeit without a pupil. He was the lord of his castle. He knew that in his absence, his father would come around to the dojo occasionally to make sure everything was in order, but he felt responsible for it. *I mustn't leave it vacant for too long*, he thought.

Still, when he left Shibamura, he kept going through Nara, then Kyoto, and finally reached the small village of Ohara in the Otagi district of Yamashiro province. There, he revisited the now vacant house of his late master, Tsuji Hei'emon, where he had trained for five years. He spent three days seeing his old acquaintances and paying a visit to his teacher's grave.

Since he had spent his formative years training with Reizo under the aged master, he felt deeply moved to be back in this small settlement nestled in the mountains.

The vibrant beauty of new leaves that glittered in the breeze as spring passed into summer; the mystical stillness of moonless twilight before the sun rose over the mountains; the stirrings of wild creatures that could be heard from the depths of the dark night.

These things were missing from the Shogun's great city of Edo.

I wouldn't mind staying here and settling down . . .

Daijiro wished he didn't have to leave Ohara. But when he thought of how his ageing father had helped him build his own dojo and begin to establish his position in the world of swords in Edo, he checked himself. *I shouldn't be selfish.*

He said farewell to the village and went on his way. From Kyoto, he followed the Tokaido road towards Edo.

He was swift-footed. Two days after departing from Kyoto, he had already climbed over the Suzuka pass and entered the town of Seki, a resting point for travellers.

Crossing the pass meant crossing into Ise province. He

had been planning to stay the night in the castle town of Kameyama, which was still more than a league away from Seki, but just as he was taking a break at a tea shop at the foot of the pass, dark clouds started to gather over him. By the time he entered Seki, rain was pouring down, so he took refuge in a hatago inn called Oumi-ya Tahei.

For his journey, he wore a short-sleeved kimono which hung down to his knees and a pair of momohiki trousers over that, with cloth gaiters, tabi socks and straw shoes. Kohei had taught him that this outfit afforded maximum agility.

His small bundle of belongings was strung across his back, and he wore a shallow hat of dark wickerwork.

Soon after he had sat down in the downstairs guest room at the back of Oumi-ya, he heard footsteps coming down the hallway and entering the room next door.

Apparently, a guest who had arrived before Daijiro had just come back from the bath, and a woman's voice greeted him.

A husband and wife, it seems . . . Daijiro thought indifferently. But the next moment, the voices hushed.

In the silence, there was the slightest shift in the air on the other side of the fusuma doors which separated the guest rooms.

Though an ordinary person wouldn't have noticed it, a skilled swordsman such as Daijiro, with his keen sense of hearing, could not but detect it.

The fusuma slid open in perfect quiet, forming a hairline chink.

Daijiro sensed that the stranger next door was eyeing

him through the gap, but he went on sipping his tea without even turning around. After a few moments, he said, 'Do you wish to speak to me?'

Silence followed.

Eventually, he clearly heard the woman say, 'I *told* you it's not him.'

So they mistook me for someone else . . . Something tells me there's a long story behind this . . . Though the thought crossed his mind, Daijiro didn't think any more of it. He took a bath and, back in his room, he sat down for dinner.

The middle-aged woman who served his meal dropped hints about the places in Seki where he could find some unofficial 'entertainment'. It was widely known that certain women who worked at the inns of this post town engaged in that line of work.

Daijiro showed no reaction.

From the sound of it, the guests next door were having dinner, too. They seemed to be talking to each other, but he couldn't pick out anything in particular from their low murmurs, and he didn't feel curious enough to try to listen in more attentively.

When he had finished eating, he went straight to bed.

Sleep early, rise early. No better way to quicken one's journey.

Once he had lain down, the sound of the rain filled the darkness.

The inn had a narrow frontage but plenty of depth; yet there seemed to be very few guests staying that night.

Daijiro intended to start early in the morning, despite the weather. He believed that, whether in rain or snow, an arduous journey offered only an opportunity for him to train his body and mind, and so it didn't bother him in the slightest.

There was, however, an altogether different hardship awaiting him that night.

He settled into a deep sleep. But it didn't last long. The intimacy of the couple next door had grown altogether too intense.

At first, the woman protested – in fact, she rebuked the man – saying, 'We must not,' and, 'No, not again – what excuse would you give to your elder brother? He would be turning in his grave.'

It was her voice that stirred Daijiro. The man said nothing; he merely groaned wolfishly, and soon the woman stopped resisting. He seemed to have pinned her down completely, having as much of her as he wanted.

Daijiro covered his head with his duvet and clicked his tongue. At twenty-five, he had never known a woman, but this was from his own volition. Both his late master and his father had always said, 'If you wish to live by the sword, don't distract yourself with women when you're young.' Besides, all the energy pulsing in his youthful body went into his harsh training and was converted into something worthwhile, a store for future days.

In youth, anything was possible – even abstinence. And the abstinence of a young, healthy man with a fixed purpose was certain to yield a rich harvest.

Nevertheless, Daijiro was no unworldly hermit nor stony man devoid of feeling: it was torture having to listen to the two lovers, separated only by a thin door made of paper.

Despite her protests in the beginning, the woman's moans grew louder as she became wild and unrestrained.

Daijiro couldn't take it any more. He got up, thinking he might while away the time in the hallway, but then he heard the woman cry out in ecstasy, and the man snarled at her:

'That name again! How could you, sister . . .? Still pining for our enemy . . .' Even as he reproached her, he seemed to be greedily consuming every inch of her body.

Evidently, the lovers hated each other, but were abandoning themselves to the pleasures of the body, drowning in desire.

A woman who sleeps with a man she doesn't like and calls out the name of an enemy . . . Hmm . . .? Daijiro couldn't make head nor tail of it.

Either way, he decided it was none of his business. He stepped out into the hallway and gazed at the rain misting over the courtyard. The sheet of rain shimmered white in the dark.

It was a warm night in late spring.

Daijiro crouched there for a long time. But even he got tired of waiting and went back inside. No sound came from next door.

In the morning, the sky was clear.

Daijiro saw the couple leave before him. His shoji door was wide open, and they walked right past it down the hallway, dressed in travelling attire.

The pale, downcast face of the slender woman was beautiful. She looked to be about twenty-three or -four.

The man was young, too. Though he was short, he had

a muscular build; his tough, square face was covered in pockmarks.

The woman hurried ahead without a glance at Daijiro, but the man threw a cold look at him, tightening his grip on his long sword and pulling back his shoulders, before going on his way.

He doesn't look like a wandering ronin . . . but he did mention an enemy last night. Could they be hunting down a man to take revenge? Daijiro wondered.

By the time he left Oumi-ya behind, however, he had forgotten all about the enigmatic pair.

II

Seki was a stage station town on the north bank of the River Suzuka. The mountain ranges of Suzuka stretched out to the west, and the town lay on the paths connecting Oumi to Kyoto, Osaka and Iga, as well as Edo to the east through the Tokaido road. It was also an important resting point for travellers on a pilgrimage to Ise shrine.

It had a long history, and it was one of the most thriving towns in these parts after Kameyama. The town had a long, narrow shape – only a little more than a mile across – but more than twenty hatago inns lined the streets. In fact, there were more than sixty, if one counted the inns with meal-serving women who doubled as unofficial prostitutes.

When Daijiro stepped out of Oumi-ya, a group of pilgrims bound for Ise emerged from an inn higher up the road and walked ahead of him, dissolving into the morning mist.

It was a crisp, refreshing day after the night of rain.

A little way down the Tokaido road, a temple housing a Jizo bodhisattva appeared on the right. This was the Kyu-kanzan Jizo-in Hozo-ji temple, said to have been established by the famous priest, Gyoki. The ancient Jizo statue was so admired that there was even a popular song that went: 'Put a fancy kimono on the Jizo in Seki, she'll take the Great Buddha in Nara for a groom.'

Daijiro entered the temple grounds and bowed low in front of the main hall. There were no gates or walls separating the precincts from the road.

Since some travellers started early and, like Daijiro, stopped by at the temple to pray in front of the main building, the tea shop facing the road opened for business from first thing in the morning, even when it was still dark. They offered not only tea, but also a variety of goods, such as hats, walking sticks, rain cloaks, and even straw shoes.

A middle-aged ronin had strolled into this shop to buy a wickerwork hat made of sedge and ordered a cup of hot tea while he was at it; he was just sipping the tea when Daijiro stepped out of the temple's precincts.

Their eyes met by chance.

'Hey, Daijiro!' the traveller called out.

'Oh . . . Master Inoue!'

They ran up to each other and grasped hands.

'It's been a while,' the ronin said.

'Long time no see,' Daijiro said at the same time.

The ronin's name was Inoue Hachiro.

He hailed from the Hikone domain of Oumi province, and back when Daijiro had been training under Tsuji Hei'emon in Ohara, Inoue was living in Kyoto. He used to visit Ohara for about ten days each month to spar with Reizo day and night.

Inoue had been around forty years old at the time, so he would be fifty or so now.

He was a little chubby, and the beard on his chin had a bit of grey in it; most of his features were far from handsome, except for his sharp and prominent nose.

The old master, Tsuji Sensei, often used to say, 'That proud nose of his is a sign of his short temper.'

When Inoue was thirty-five, he had had a quarrel with a superior samurai of Hikone and broke the man's arm. For that offence, he was expelled from the domain.

Inoue had some connection to Tsuji Sensei – something about a distant relative on his mother's side – and they had been exchanging letters from before. So, when the old master retired to Ohara, he showed up straight away. Back then, Inoue lived in Kyoto with his wife. He had no children.

The Inoue family was punished with a cut in their salary, but Inoue's younger brother Kyujiro, the new head of their family, regularly sent Hachiro a portion of what little money they had. Luckily for Hachiro, he could enjoy an easy-going life in honest poverty.

'The old master's gone, Shimaoka Sensei has gone back to Yamato, now you're in Edo . . . and my wife passed away from an illness last summer. I've been down in the dumps ever since.' Inoue said all this in one breath.

'I had no idea . . .' Daijiro said.

'Is your worthy father doing well down in Edo?'
'Yes. But there's something I have to tell you, Master Inoue . . .'
'What's that?'
'Shimaoka Sensei has passed away . . .'
'What?!'
Daijiro recounted Reizo's violent death.
'I see . . . What a shock. Only last summer, I popped over to Yamato to see him. He was just as usual then – I'd never have imagined we'd lose him so soon.'
Absorbed in their conversation, the two of them had sat down on a bench at the tea shop.
'Well, well . . .' Inoue murmured. 'Hmm . . . So that's how it was, eh . . .'
'By the way, Master Inoue – where are you headed?'
'Eh? Oh, me . . . Well . . .' Still lamenting his old friend's death, Inoue said, 'There's a little something that I'm duty-bound to see to, and I'm on my way to Kuwana.'
'Then let us go together. I was thinking of staying at Kuwana myself tonight.'
'It's a bit rough, but with your legs, it should be a breeze. I'm not sure if I can go that fast now.'
'In any case, we can get started.'
'Sure.'
Daijiro paid for the tea. Inoue didn't object.
Inoue's attire was outright shabby: he wore a faded, scruffy kimono, with its hems tucked into his obi sash, and straw shoes over bare feet. The contents of his money bag weren't faring much better, by the looks of things.
Daijiro found out later that Inoue had been drowning

his sorrows ever since he lost his wife and using up all the money that his younger brother sent him from Hikone.

'It's pathetic, I know,' Inoue told Daijiro with a dry laugh. 'You're young – you don't know how painful it is for a man to outlive a good woman.'

They left Seki and passed through Kameyama, Wadano and Kawai. When they had crossed the bridge over Kawaigawa, Daijiro asked, 'Will you be staying in Kuwana for long?'

'Well . . .' Inoue murmured, then fell silent. A few steps later, he said, 'I have to protect someone. That's why I'm staying sober now.'

'Protect someone . . .?'

'He used to be a Hikone samurai – the same domain I served in the past, you know – but he killed a superior and fled. A bit like me, though I didn't kill anybody. So, the wife of the man who died and his younger brother are looking all over for him to take revenge.'

'I see . . .' As soon as he nodded, Daijiro remembered the mysterious couple at the inn last night and what he had overheard. The man had been angry at the woman for speaking the name of 'our enemy'.

Daijiro couldn't help but wonder, *Could they have been . . .?* But he kept quiet, listening to Inoue.

'So you see, Daijiro . . . if push comes to shove, I'll have to join in the skirmish with my own sword and guard the man who's being hunted down. There's a good reason why I have to follow through, too – it's a long story . . .'

Inoue let out a somewhat abashed chuckle.

III

Inoue had become the patriarch of his family at twenty years old when his father, Kaname, died. Four years later, he had been ordered to serve at the Kyoto mansion of the Hikone domain.

'*That* was when things went wrong,' Inoue often used to say back when he'd come to Ohara to practise swords. When he'd moved to Kyoto, he already had a wife, but once he'd got a taste of the women and sake of Kyoto, he simply couldn't stop.

At the time, he had been tasked with looking after the daimyo's store of clothing, furniture and other valuables in the Kyoto mansion, which meant he would often handle the domain's public money. And so, when he had used up his own money for his own amusement, he couldn't resist dipping into the domain's funds.

He had taken about seventy ryo over time, but eventually, he got caught. His superior, Goto Yohei, summoned him and thoroughly grilled him.

Goto was an elderly man, nearly sixty in age, but he berated Inoue severely. In the end, he stressed, 'Never do it again,' and covered up the incident for Inoue, restoring the seventy ryo from his own pocket. If Inoue's transgression had become known to the upper officials of the domain, Inoue would have been ordered to perform the ritual of seppuku and disembowel himself, or at best, he would have been expelled and his family abolished.

He managed to repay Goto the seventy ryo over four

years, but he never forgot the old man's kindness. Not many superiors would have gone that far to protect their subordinate.

Goto died from an illness the year Inoue had cleared his debt to him. A man named Makino Jonosuke came from Hikone to take Goto's place.

'I just couldn't get along with the new fellow,' Inoue said. 'A different sort altogether from Master Goto. At one point, we'd had a little too much to drink and got into a row. I ended up breaking his arm.'

Because of this history, Inoue was on his way to come to the aid of Goto Iori, son of Goto Yohei.

In early summer last year, Iori had killed his superior, Amano Hanbei, with his sword and fled from the Hikone domain's mansion in Edo. Both Amano and Iori had been stationed in this mansion at the time.

A few months before the fatal incident, Amano had suddenly begun to bully Iori for no apparent reason. Amano kept picking on him for every little thing, no matter how trivial. Many of their colleagues witnessed Amano frequently lambasting Iori.

Whatever fault might have lain with Amano, the fact remained that Iori had committed murder and fled the domain; Amano's family couldn't let him get off scot-free.

Amano's younger brother, Hyoma, was one of the strongest disciples of Muragaki Mondo, who ran a Nen-ryu dojo outside the Kandabashi gate. As soon as he heard the news of his brother's murder, Hyoma set out in pursuit of Iori, accompanied by his brother's widow, Chiyo.

Chiyo sought to avenge her husband; Hyoma his elder brother.

Their relative in Hikone, Suetaka Gohei, received permission from the lord of the domain, Ii Kamon-no-kami Naohide, to assist Chiyo and Hyoma in their hunt. He departed from the castle town of Hikone in November last year with two retainers and a low-rank servant.

And so, these two parties from the Amano side had been searching everywhere for Iori, keeping each other informed by using two vassals of the Amano family.

In contrast, not a single one of Iori's relatives had come forward to support him.

'They want nothing to do with it,' Inoue told Daijiro. 'I for one had no idea that this was even happening. But just the other day – about seven days ago now – the head clerk at an oil seller in Kuwana called Hirano-ya Sohei came to see me with a letter from Master Iori.'

'Hmm . . .'

'And that's how I found out about his troubles. Imagine my surprise. But he's the son of the man who saved my life. I made up my mind that I'd be doing a disservice to Master Goto's memory if I didn't help his son at a time of crisis. So, that's why I came out here.'

Like Inoue, Hirano-ya was sheltering Iori because of their ties to his late father. Besides their shop in Kuwana, they had a branch in Kyoto, too; they used to do business with the Hikone domain's Kyoto mansion back when Goto Yohei was still alive. The owner of the Kyoto branch, Hikosuke, had been friendly with Yohei. This Hikosuke was the younger brother of Sohei, the owner of the Kuwana shop.

In his letter to Inoue, Iori wrote: 'I have been hiding in Hirano-ya for about half a year, but my enemies seem to have tracked me down recently, and I fear for my life. My only hope of survival is you, Master Inoue. My kin are too afraid to extend a hand to me. I lack the strength to stand up against Hyoma and the rest by myself. Would you be willing to keep me company even if only for half a year, or perhaps a year?'

When he read such an appeal, Inoue couldn't forsake Iori.

In the present age, the daimyos ruled over their territories autonomously under the overarching command of the Tokugawa shogun. Hence when a murderer fled to another province, the authorities of the criminal's original domain could not pursue them.

For this reason, it was an unwritten rule of the samurai era that the blood relations of the victim could go after the murderer themselves to avenge their kin as well as inflict punishment for the crime. If the act of revenge was justified, the lord of the domain issued a special licence valid across Japan, which allowed the avenger to kill the offender with impunity, and, of course, an official notice was given to the shogunate as well.

Therefore, in this samurai society, a man could not inherit the position of authority in his family unless he avenged his father or elder brother first.

In Amano Hyoma's case, he wouldn't be allowed to inherit his late brother's place unless he took down the murderer, Iori. This added fuel to the fire, making him all the more desperate to hunt for Iori, and his kin spared no effort in assisting him.

'You know, Daijiro,' Inoue said thoughtfully, 'I'm all

alone now without my wife, and it's no use going on like this, wasting my brother's money on sake every day . . . If I die protecting the son of the man I'm indebted to, that's not a bad way to go, I think.'

Without realising how far they had gone, the two of them were fast approaching another post town, Ishiyakushi.

The sun gave off a weak glow through the gloomy, low-hanging clouds.

A white butterfly fluttered past the two of them as they walked down the road.

Just before entering the town, Ishiyakushi-ji appeared on their left. This ancient temple – dedicated to Yakushi Nyorai, the Buddha of healing and medicine – was surrounded by groves of bamboo and trees. A stone wall enclosed the precincts, which were wrapped in silence.

The pair hadn't seen any travellers for a while, but as they passed by the temple gate, Daijiro's eyes glinted from beneath his deep-brimmed hat.

He saw the couple who had been staying in the room next door standing under the roofed gate of the temple. There was a third man, who looked to be a vassal dressed for a journey; he and the young samurai were putting their heads together in a serious discussion. The woman stood a little apart from them, half inside the gate, with her back turned.

When Daijiro and Inoue walked past them, the young samurai glanced their way. But Daijiro's face was hidden under his hat, and now that he was dressed in his full travelling attire, the man didn't seem to recognise him. He turned his attention back to his companion immediately and they resumed their talk.

Daijiro and Inoue went on at a steady pace and entered the post town.

Inoue didn't seem to have paid any heed to the three travellers at the temple gate.

They stopped to rest at a tea shop called Yaoya Sahei. As they ate their lunch, Daijiro asked in a deliberately casual tone, 'Say, Master Inoue – do you know what Amano Hyoma and the others look like?'

Inoue shook his head. 'No, actually. The Amano family has always been stationed in Edo over generations, so I've never seen Hanbei, his wife, or Hyoma. But I do know their relative who's supposed to be helping them with the hunt – the fellow by the name of Suetaka Gohei. Hanbei and Hyoma's uncle, if I recall correctly. He's a top cavalryman – a proud, stubborn old man.'

Just then, they saw the three travellers hurrying down the road in front of the tea shop. Daijiro saw them as well as Inoue. But no sign of recognition crossed Inoue's face.

IV

The journey from Seki to Kuwana was about twenty-five miles, but Daijiro and Inoue hastened on and reached Kuwana while it was still light.

They never saw the three travellers again. Had they been going down the same Tokaido road, Daijiro and Inoue would surely have caught up with them.

Kuwana was located near the mouth of a river called Ibigawa. It was a castle town under the rule of Matsudaira

Shimousa-no-kami worth 100,000 koku. Travellers on the Tokaido road could sail about seventeen miles across Ise bay from the harbour of Kuwana to Miya-juku in Owari province and continue on the road from there. Being in such an important location, Kuwana naturally prospered as a stage station town.

Daijiro and Inoue crossed the canal on the outskirts of the town, then made their way through the Tenma and Shinmachi districts. Kuwana Castle loomed ahead to their right; mansions of samurai families stood beyond the moat, and merchant houses jostled the neighbourhoods on the west side of the outer moat.

They veered away from the Tokaido road to the west and reached Hirano-ya, the oil seller, in the Aburamachi district.

Sohei, the owner of the shop, was a short elderly man with surprisingly steady nerves. He took good care of Iori, saying, 'Your respected father was very kind to my younger brother in Kyoto – so I am ready to do anything to be of service.'

When they had arrived in Kuwana, Inoue had said, 'If you're staying in Kuwana anyway, why don't you come to Hirano-ya with me, Daijiro? We've got a lot more to catch up on.'

'May I?'

'Of course.'

Since Daijiro still hadn't said a word about the three travellers to Inoue, he was reluctant to leave him.

What would Father do in my shoes . . .? This thought had been circling in Daijiro's head ever since they had passed Ishiyakushi.

Iori was eagerly awaiting Inoue at Hirano-ya.

Though he was twenty-seven in age, he looked at least five years older. He was rather handsome, but he looked gaunt from the strain of recent months. Daijiro couldn't believe that such a man would kill his superior.

He was living in hiding on the first floor of a storehouse with thick walls of hardened mud, which faced the back garden of Hirano-ya.

Since Inoue said, 'It's all right. Come along,' Daijiro accompanied him to the upper floor of the storehouse. They were greeted with a hearty meal prepared by Hirano-ya.

'This is Master Akiyama Daijiro – he trained for a long time under the old master in Ohara, you know,' Inoue explained to Iori. 'You don't have to worry about anything with him.'

Iori took Inoue's word for it and began to recount the whole story in Daijiro's presence.

It had been around last spring that Iori's superior, Amano Hanbei, had started to bully him in front of his fellows. Amano would harangue him for being weak and pathetic, and ignorant of martial arts; he would scour the account books for any errors and blame Iori for all of them. It was unbearable, but Iori put up with Amano's behaviour without complaint.

When summer came, however, Amano levelled a strange accusation at him. That time, it was just the two of them.

'You've meddled with my wife before, haven't you? Speak the truth,' Amano demanded in a low threatening growl.

Iori had no idea what he was talking about.

Of course, Iori had exchanged a word or two with Chiyo when they had both been in Kyoto. Chiyo was the daughter of Kiuchi Sanza'emon, who worked at the domain's Kyoto mansion, and before her marriage, she had been living in the nagaya row house inside the mansion grounds. Because of his father's station in Kyoto, Iori had lived in the same part of the mansion until his father's death, at which point he was posted to Edo.

'But we never spoke more than a few words. I can't understand where he'd got the idea . . .' Iori murmured regretfully. Daijiro could see that he was telling the truth.

Four years after Iori's move to Edo, Chiyo became Amano's wife in an arranged marriage. Since she came to live with Amano in the row house inside the Edo mansion, she and Iori crossed paths once again.

'But the row house I lived in was far from hers, and besides, she is a married woman. I didn't particularly want to see her either, so I'm sure we spoke only a couple of times in Edo . . .'

Both of Iori's parents were dead, and he lived an easy life by himself with four servants. In a bustling city like Edo, all he had to do was step outside when he was off duty, and he had no shortage of entertainment.

'I'm not so foolish as to make advances to a married woman,' he added.

'Hmm. I see,' Inoue said.

'About ten days later after that encounter, Amano summoned me again at night – this time, to the riding grounds inside the mansion.'

'And he accused you again?'

'Yes. He kept going on and on about his wife – he was desperate. When I said I didn't know what he was talking about, he grabbed me by the collar and started punching me. I took quite a few blows.

'I had so much frustration built up in me from before, and I just couldn't take it any more. I snapped, and . . . I don't quite remember what happened. Before I knew it, we'd fallen on the ground, and I was on top of him with my short sword pressed into his stomach . . . He was already dead.'

Iori was thrown into a panic.

The first thought that struck him was: *I don't want to die*.

The only way he could hope to live was to escape from the domain's Edo mansion.

Iori ran back to his row house, called out to his old manservant, Ichisuke, who had been serving his family since his father's generation. He told Ichisuke about his plight.

'Run for your life, master,' Ichisuke said immediately. 'Your Ichisuke knows full well that you would never do such a wicked thing. Come, let us flee together.'

While Ichisuke hid Amano's corpse in the shadow of trees, Iori took all the money he had in the house and ran out with only the clothes on his back. He climbed over the wall of the mansion grounds with Ichisuke, who had been waiting for him there, and they fled.

They had wandered around in hiding for a while, but they knew they were in danger. So, Ichisuke left Iori in an inn in the castle town of Nagoya in Owari and came to Kuwana by himself. To his immense relief, when he told everything to Hirano-ya Sohei, Sohei said, 'Bring him here at once.'

Now that Iori had found shelter at Hirano-ya, Ichisuke went back to his hometown, Minakuchi, in Oumi province for the time being.

Minakuchi was about seven miles away from Kuwana over the Suzuka pass. It was also a castle town under the rule of Kato Etchu-no-kami, worth 25,000 koku. Ichisuke's younger brother, Naogoro, lived there, making his famous tobacco pipes. Ichisuke went to stay with him, and Naogoro's son – named Shokichi – acted as messenger between Iori and Ichisuke, as well as Iori's elder sister, Mura, who lived in Edo.

Mura was the wife of Masui Zenbei, a retainer of Mori Yamashiro-no-kami – lord of the Ako domain in Harima province worth 20,000 koku – and the couple lived with their three children in the domain's mansion in Shibashinmei in Edo.

Since she was very fond of her little brother, Mura wanted to hear every scrap of news about Iori, and she also sent him money, clothes and other necessities. It was Shokichi's job to deliver their letters and bundles.

At this point in Iori's story, a servant carried in a dish of rice cooked with hamaguri clams, which was a local speciality in Kuwana. Sohei explained that these clams had been dug up in early spring and stewed for preservation, since clams were best had before the spawning season, not least because it was forbidden to harvest them then.

When they had finished the rice, Daijiro finally broached the subject. 'Actually, Master Inoue . . .' he said quietly, 'I have been keeping it to myself until now, but I have a feeling that I saw this younger brother and wife of Amano today and yesterday.'

'What did you say . . .?' Inoue stammered, wide-eyed.

Colour drained from Iori's face.

V

As Daijiro told them about the two travellers he had encountered at the inn in Seki, Iori became increasingly agitated. When Daijiro had related everything he had seen, Inoue turned to Iori.

'What do you make of it?' Inoue asked.

'There's no doubt about it . . .' Iori's whisper was barely audible.

'You mean they were Amano Hyoma and Chiyo?'

'It must be them. Their appearance and everything else fit too well.'

According to Iori, a suspicious traveller had been seen lingering in the neighbourhood lately. He seemed to be trying to ferret out what was happening inside Hirano-ya.

'I have been told that a stranger is going around the houses and bars nearby, asking about me,' Sohei confirmed.

Apparently, Hyoma and his uncle seemed to have picked up Iori's scent from the old manservant, Ichisuke. Though Ichisuke rarely stepped outside, it was natural that they would investigate his background. Since he had been serving the Goto house for nearly thirty years, he was as good as family, regardless of their difference in class.

If the Amano side had got hold of the fact that Ichisuke was from Minakuchi in Oumi, they would of course have kept a close eye on his family's house. A spy might have seen Shokichi carrying a message from Ichisuke to Iori in Kuwana. Or Shokichi might have been tailed when he was bringing a letter from Mura, Iori's sister in Edo.

They had numbers on their side, after all.

Iori, on the other hand, was all alone.

Sohei was a merchant, not a samurai; Iori didn't want to drag him into a violent clash if it should come to that. Besides, Hirano-ya would be far from a fortress if his enemies were to barge in with swords drawn. Iori's fear and anxiety from sitting for so long on such thin ice was what had made him reach out to Inoue for help.

'Hmm . . . Looks like things are coming to a head,' Inoue groaned, crossing his arms.

Daijiro stayed at Hirano-ya that night, as well as the next. And the next night, again . . .

Why am I still here . . . ? His own actions were a mystery to him. If he had to spell it out, it might have been because he was moved by his old friend Inoue's determination to remain loyal to his past benefactor, stepping forward to assist the son at the risk of his own life, upholding the old-fashioned sense of duty rooted in gratitude. *Perhaps I can't just look away from his noble decision . . . Am I leaning towards staying to help them – not for Goto Iori's sake, but for Master Inoue's?*

When Inoue asked, 'I'm thankful that you're staying with us, Daijiro . . . but don't you have to go back to Edo?' Daijiro smiled and gave him a vague answer:

'Hmm . . . Well . . . Just a little longer . . .'

Inoue's face brightened up. 'All right, all right,' he said, grinning from ear to ear and stroking his beard. 'Kuwana's got good food, and good sake, too. Well, if you're not in a particular hurry, then . . .' He chattered on cheerily, perhaps to hide his slight embarrassment.

Though Inoue was an accomplished swordsman, he knew that he was no match for Daijiro if they were to cross blades. So, it heartened him to have Daijiro close by.

Meanwhile, Inoue and Sohei were busy devising a strategy. They sent Hirano-ya's most trusted servants all across Kuwana to search for anyone that matched the description of Hyoma and the others.

Next, they started preparing for Iori's escape from Hirano-ya to a safer refuge.

Daijiro consciously stayed out of their discussion.

Inoue didn't try to pull him in, either, since he was a stranger to Iori. Yet at the same time, he worried about the prospect of Daijiro leaving at some point for Edo.

Several days passed.

Daijiro remained at Hirano-ya.

He kept asking himself, *What would Father do?* He had the feeling that his father would have solved a problem like this in a trice, as if it were nothing.

With many years behind him, Kohei had attained the level of maturity in which he had full control of his mind and spirit. He could instantly judge what was good for him to do and what he didn't have to do, then promptly put it into action.

'When you grow older, you can't move your arms and legs as you used to,' Kohei had told Daijiro once. 'But in exchange, your eyes become sure and steady when you look at the world, and you don't waver or lose your way as you do when you're young. That's what they call the wisdom of age—brings you a sort of ease that you could never imagine when you were still green.'

On their seventh day in Kuwana, Inoue came to Daijiro's room in the main building of Hirano-ya in the middle of the night.

When Daijiro stirred, Inoue said, 'Sorry to wake you,' and sat up straight beside the pillow. 'Can I talk to you about something, Daijiro . . .?'

'What is it?'

'About the house that the old master in Ohara used to live in . . .'

'You're thinking of hiding Master Iori in Ohara, is that it?' Daijiro asked without missing a beat.

'Well . . .' Inoue's eyes widened. 'Y-yes, exactly. Do you know who lives there now?'

'It's vacant.'

'I-indeed . . .?'

'It will make the perfect hiding place.'

'Yes . . . Hmm . . . Will I be able to rent it, do you think?'

'I think if we ask the elder of the village, it should be fine. Our old master did buy that house, after all – and right now, the village is simply making sure it doesn't fall into disrepair.'

'Iori should be able to offer them an adequate sum in thanks.'

'I will go with you to Ohara. It would be better if I speak to the elder myself.'

'W-will you do that for us? Are you sure?' Inoue seemed ready to dance for joy.

Daijiro himself was surprised that his mind, at this very moment, had finally settled on a course of action.

VI

Two days later, in the small hours of the night, a peculiar party emerged from the back of Hirano-ya.

A merchant-like man in travelling attire came first, then an itinerant monk, followed by Inoue and Daijiro. The latter two were dressed in similar clothes to those they had worn when they had come down the Tokaido road.

The young man leading the group was a servant at Hirano-ya called Matsunosuke, a native of Shimagahara in Iga, who had been helping Iori in a number of ways during his stay.

Iori, disguised as a journeying monk, walked about twenty yards behind Matsunosuke. With his staff and large wickerwork hat, he looked just as monkish as they hoped, as long as he kept his face well hidden beneath the hat.

Inoue followed close behind Iori. Then, keeping a distance of about ten yards, Daijiro brought up the rear.

There was still quite a long time until daybreak. Their plan was to leave Kuwana behind and go all the way up to the post town of Shono before the sun rose.

From Kuwana to Shono, going past Ishiyakushi, it was about seventeen miles. They would reach Shono while it was still dark and keep out of sight during the day. Shono was a small stage station, almost like a village, so travellers on the Tokaido road rarely stayed there.

One of the three hatago inns in Shono, Iwami-ya Kihei, was run by a distant relation of Hirano-ya Sohei. Sohei had sent a messenger the day before, asking them to take good care of Iori's party.

Once they were safely in Shono, they would get plenty of sleep while the sun was out, then set off again after midnight, avoiding the Tokaido road and taking a minor path instead. In less than ten miles, they would reach Seki.

They would keep going past Seki under the cover of the darkness before dawn, veering off from the Tokaido road once more, and make their way towards Iga province.

From Ueno in Iga, they would go to Matsunosuke's hometown, Shimagahara, and take shelter at his family's home for a couple of days while keeping an eye on the roads. If the coast was clear, they would go to Nara, then from Nara to Kyoto, and finally, from Kyoto to the village of Ohara.

They would be taking as roundabout a way as one could go, but they decided that this would be the safest route.

The risky part was the twenty-seven miles or so until they reached Seki. But these days, they had seen no sign of the strangers who had been sniffing around Hirano-ya, so they took the chance.

It was an overcast night, without any stars or wind. The darkness held a gentle warmth.

Using Matsunosuke's lantern as a guiding light, the party crept through the narrow alleys of Kuwana and soon left the town behind.

Just as they had crossed Yokkaichi and were approaching Shono, dawn broke.

Looks like rain, Daijiro thought.

Inoue walked ahead of him, his broad shoulders

swaying with every step. He could see Iori in the monk's garb and, even further down the road, Matsunosuke going at a quick pace.

The four walked in such a way that a passer-by would never suspect that they were travelling together. None of them glanced behind, let alone called out to each other.

When they reached Tsuetsuki-zaka, a hill just before Ishiyakushi, rain began to fall.

They passed other journeyers who had left the post town and were going down the road in the opposite direction.

The rain gave them an advantage; there would be fewer travellers coming and going on the road. But at the same time, it meant the four of them would stand out. With this in mind, Daijiro kept a sharp eye on their surroundings from beneath his hat.

Once they climbed to the top of the hill, they came to a field of grass called Marigahara. They were very close to Ishiyakushi now.

A traveller on horseback came up the hill and overtook them. The horse was drawn by a packhorse driver, and on its back sat a merchant, tilting his hat to keep the rain off his face, his shoulders hunched under his rain cloak. He seemed to be an old man.

Daijiro and the others observed the rider, but since there had already been several other men and women of various ages who had passed them on the road, they judged him to be harmless, too.

However, this traveller was none other than Ito Hikoroku, who served Suetaka, the Amano brothers' uncle.

The Amano side had, in fact, never left Kuwana and

instead had been keeping a close watch on Hirano-ya the whole time. In a cunning move, they had over the last few days only feigned their silence: they were drawing Iori out of his hiding place.

The crisis came before long.

VII

The rain shrouded the land in fog.

Iori and the others walked straight on through Ishi-yakushi without even stopping to eat or put on their rain cloaks. It was only about two miles until their first destination: Shono.

As the road approached Shono along the River Suzuka, it gained a slight incline.

Bamboo grew in thick groves around this area, and the road was completely deserted.

Suddenly, the rain intensified.

Matsunosuke at the front pulled out his rain cloak without slowing his pace; as he was throwing it on, he looked behind him for the first time, as if to say, *Watch out for the rain – you better take out your cloaks, too.*

That instant, a figure darted out from the bamboo grove on their right and ran up to Matsunosuke from behind.

A blade flashed, and Matsunosuke's shriek tore the silence.

Three men, who had been lying in wait below the left bank of the road sprang up and raced towards the others, swords drawn.

With a cry of alarm, Iori turned and started sprinting back, desperately outstretching his arms towards Inoue. Inoue and Daijiro had already flung aside their hats and were racing towards Iori.

Daijiro heard footsteps approaching from behind and glanced back. Two men dressed for battle were charging at him with swords in the air.

He lowered his body and slashed out at lightning speed.

The man leading the attack took the blow on his knees before he could bring down his sword, and he toppled over, his face distorted in pain.

Daijiro drew back.

The next samurai lunged at him with a roar, but the upward swing of the blade simply sliced through the air above Daijiro's head as he ducked and pulled back his right foot; holding his sword in only one hand, he cut a sweeping arc at the man's legs.

The man screamed, dropping his sword and pitching forward on to the ground.

Daijiro had no intention of killing them. As long as he gave them a deep enough wound on their legs, they would be immobile and useless in battle.

He turned sharply to look into the distance.

Inoue and Iori were running down the bank to the dry riverbed along Suzukagawa.

Five samurai circled around them.

He recognised one of them: it was the very same man who had stayed next door to him at the inn in Seki. This had to be Amano Hyoma.

The old man who held his sword at the ready next to Hyoma was likely the uncle, Suetaka Gohei.

The other three were probably Gohei's men, Amano's kin, or their servants. They all looked brawny.

When they saw Daijiro running down the bank towards them, they changed their formation.

'Oh . . .!' Hyoma gasped when he recognised Daijiro from Seki.

Inoue and Daijiro stood in front of Iori, who was deathly pale and trembling all over. They faced the five assailants with the river behind them.

Rain was beating down on them now.

Inoue held his long sword in the middle stance: it was the hiraseigan position, with the blade tilted at a slight angle.

'Forget the revenge you're here for,' he declared in a ringing voice. 'Now it's *us* picking a fight with *you*. Get that into your head and come at us!!'

'Cross the river and run for it, Master Goto,' Daijiro said to Iori under his breath. 'We'll take care of the rest.'

*

It was about a month later when Daijiro returned to Edo and reported this incident to his father.

The rainy season had come upon Edo.

'Hmm. Well, well . . .' Kohei said when he had heard the story. 'So, you wounded four men out of five right in the legs?'

'Yes.'

'Huh. Nicely done . . .'

'Thank you.'

'And . . . what about the duel between that Amano Hyoma and Inoue Hachiro?'

'It was very intense. Master Inoue was wounded on his left shoulder and right chest, but in the end . . . in the end, he took Hyoma down with a cut of his sword.'

'Bravo.'

'Yes, it was quite a sight – he fought with everything he had.'

'Mm-hmm . . . And the woman . . .?'

'She never appeared that day . . . I don't understand, Father. What was that Chiyo woman after . . .?'

'Hmm. I'd say she was secretly in love with Goto Iori, but Iori paid her no attention. So she resigned herself to a marriage that her parents had arranged and became Amano Hanbei's wife . . . but she could never forget the good-looking Iori. She probably cried out his name while Hanbei was in bed with her.'

'And yet she lay with her brother-in-law while seeking revenge . . .'

'Well, that's passion for you.'

'It's chilling.'

'Oh yes. It's more difficult than sword fighting.'

'Hmm . . .'

'So, are Inoue and Iori safe in Ohara?'

'Yes. I went with them and talked to the villagers . . .'

'That's all right then. But they shouldn't let their guard down. Those men whose legs you cut – they won't let this pass.'

'Both of them are prepared for it.'

'Good, good . . . For the rest, I'm sure they'll do whatever they see fit.'

'Yes. But Father . . .'

'What is it?'

'Did I do the right thing?'

'Hmm . . .' Kohei cocked his head a little and, stuffing a pipe with tobacco, he said, 'Well, sounds about right.'

'I see . . . I'm relieved to hear that.'

'Anyhow, there's a pressing matter I have to talk to you about . . .'

'Yes?'

'You know Oharu – she's over in the kitchen now, getting sake ready . . . To tell you the truth, I need to ask for your permission . . .'

'For what?'

'I want to marry her. What do you think? Would you approve?'

'W-well . . . You can do whatever you like, Father . . .'

'That's a yes then – what a relief. Oharu! Happy news. Daijiro just gave us his blessing.'

Oharu flew out of the kitchen, plonked down in front of Daijiro, and planted her hands on the floor in front of her in a deep bow.

'Thank you *so* much, young master,' she said, blushing bright red.

Daijiro was at a loss for words.

The call of frogs rang out in the pouring rain.

Chapter 6
Kinchan of the Painted Brows

I

It was well into the rainy season.

There seemed to be no end to the soft rain, day after day, but on that particular morning, there was a rare lull in the rain, and little patches of blue even appeared in the sky around noon.

But the rain came back at sunset.

Ushibori Kumanosuke – the master of the Okuyama Nen-ryu dojo in Asakusa Mototorigoe – was enjoying a tipple before supper as he gazed at the misty drizzle.

His favourite was a famous sake called Kame-no-Izumi, or the Spring of the Tortoise, which he procured from a nearby sake shop called Yorozu-ya. He liked to have it cold in a small bowl, whether in winter or in summer.

He was turning forty-one this year. Kohei had visited him last winter to ask about the swordswoman, Sasaki Mifuyu, when she was in danger. Since then, the two men had become much closer.

Small white flowers tinged with soft yellow speckled the persimmon tree in the garden.

Kumanosuke was from Kuragano in Kozuke province, the second son of a village headman; he had never married, devoting his entire life to the way of the sword and paving his own path as a swordsman. Though his dojo was small, many of his pupils came from distinguished families.

'Sensei . . .' An old manservant named Gonbei spoke up as he brought a bowl of stewed whole aubergines and a relish of miso mixed with buckwheat. 'The oddball's come to see you again,' he said, crinkling his face into a scowl. Gonbei was from Kuragano, too, and he had been looking after Kumanosuke ever since he was little.

'The oddball . . . Who is it?'

'The girly boy – Miura.'

Kumanosuke clicked his tongue. 'You told him I'm here?'

'Yup.'

'Fool. You could've said I'm out . . .'

'But you know there's nothin' I hate more than lies. I know *you* don't like 'em, either.' Gonbei could be as stubborn as a mule about any number of things.

'What does he want?'

'It's somethin' important, or so he says.'

'Fine. There's no way out of it. Show him in.'

'Righto.'

Soon after Gonbei left, Miura Kintaro, 'the oddball', stepped in. A faint whiff of white face powder wafted into Kumanosuke's living room. The scent came from Miura's ears.

Miura was a tall, slender man dressed in a stylish, dark blue Echigo kimono. Gonbei, who had a sharp tongue, dubbed him 'the sponge gourd freak'. He had a peculiar mien: an oblong face with a soft, round jawline, and two beady eyes that resembled soybeans. There was something crooked about his nose. He was a bachelor at twenty-eight years old.

'Hiya, Ushibori Sensei. It's been a while. Ah, is that stewed aubergine you're having with cold sake? Excellent choice,' he prattled on in a ringing, high-pitched voice as he stooped a little to cross the threshold. He licked his crimson lips, the tip of his tongue flicking in and out. He seemed to be wearing rouge on his lips, and his eyebrows were painted, too.

In short, that was why Gonbei called him names: Miura dabbed his earlobes with face powder, coloured his lips, and drew his eyebrows, despite this usually being the habit of women.

His eccentric appearance aside, Miura's skill in sword fighting was impressive. His father was said to be a ronin who had deserted the Honda family worth 50,000 koku in Okazaki domain of Mikawa province. But how and why Kintaro himself had set upon the path of the sword remained a mystery even to Kumanosuke.

In any case, Miura was strong. He had a natural flair for the blade.

Though he was a ronin swordsman without a master to serve, and it wasn't exactly clear what he did for a living, he was a well-known face among various dojos, and he apparently had his own ways of bringing in money. He always dressed in a smart outfit, and if somebody asked about his face powder, he would say with a chuckle, 'You'd be surprised how a little dab of powder on the back of your ears can make the women in the Okabasho brothels go wild . . .'

Before he had moved to his present home in Fukagawa, he had suddenly turned up at Ushibori dojo and had stayed for about half a year as a temporary instructor. So far, none of the pupils were a match for him.

'Please do forgive me, Ushibori Sensei. I've come on an unexpected errand today, so I haven't brought anything for you . . .'

'Never mind that. So, what do you want?' Kumanosuke drained his sake bowl without even offering a cup to his visitor.

'Could I have a little sip from your bowl, sensei?'

Kumanosuke gave a reluctant grunt and was about to call Gonbei for a new one, but Miura reached over and plucked the bowl out of Kumanosuke's hand.

'This will do just fine,' Miura said. When Kumanosuke poured him some sake, he thanked him, put his glistening red lips to the bowl, and tossed down the drink with visible pleasure.

'What do you want, Miura?' Kumanosuke asked with a frown.

Miura put down the bowl and edged forward on his knees. 'I hear you've lately become close friends with the old master, Akiyama Kohei Sensei,' he said.

'Indeed. I'm surprised you're aware of it.'

'Well, I may not look it, but I'm rather well versed in the comings and goings of swordsmen in Edo. Oh yes, I do keep my finger right on the pulse, and—'

'All right, all right, you've made your point. And? What about it?'

'His son, Master Daijiro, is supposed to have his own dojo near Masaki Inari . . .'

'Yes, so I've heard. His performance at Lord Tanuma's mansion last year is said to have been admirable.'

'Hmm . . .'

'What about him?'

'Well . . .'

'Well what?'

'Actually . . . to tell you the truth . . . his life seems to be in danger.'

'Wh-what did you say?'

'Someone wants him dead.'

'Is that true?'

'Yes.'

'Tell me everything.'

'I'm afraid I'm not at liberty to give you *all* the details. I wish I could, but, well, I must tread carefully – I have my own position to keep, you see.'

Kumanosuke's eyes began to change colour. 'Are you sure that Master Daijiro is truly at risk?' he asked.

'I don't know anything about how good he is with the sword . . . but yes, I'd say so. A bit shaky.'

II

Kumanosuke hurried to Kohei's house on foot and arrived at around eight that night.

That day, Kohei and Oharu's marriage ceremony had been underway since sunset. It was a long-awaited moment for Oharu. Even Kohei was rather embarrassed by the wedding between a sixty-year-old groom and a twenty-year-old bride, but he had promised her that he would marry her once Daijiro returned to Edo, so he couldn't back out now.

His only condition was that the ceremony would be a modest affair. On Kohei's side, Daijiro was in attendance; on Oharu's, her parents from Sekiya village, Iwagoro and Osaki. The five of them performed a simple rite by sharing a cup of sake.

That was all Oharu needed to be perfectly happy. She had no particular wish to dress up as a bride.

Her parents, of course, were delighted.

After the ritual, they enjoyed their dinner with sake, and it wasn't long after the parents and Daijiro had gone their separate ways when Kumanosuke appeared at the door.

'Glad to see you, Master Ushibori,' Kohei said. 'We have plenty of food to go with sake tonight. Stay as long as you like.' He invited Kumanosuke to sit down in the living room, and Oharu busied herself in the kitchen, getting the drink ready for them.

'Thanks for coming all this way in the rain—' Kohei began, but paused when he saw the look on Kumanosuke's face. 'What is it? Something urgent?'

Kumanosuke nodded. 'Could we please speak in private . . .?' he asked.

'This is private enough . . .'

'No, please – I'd like to make sure this stays between you and me . . .'

'She's as good as family, so you can talk about anything in front of her . . . but if you insist . . .' Kohei went to the kitchen, asked Oharu not to come in until she was called, and came back to the living room.

'Master Akiyama – I once told you about Miura Kintaro, who used to be at my dojo, if you recall,' Kumanosuke said.

'Ah, I remember. You mean "Kinchan of the Painted Brows".' Kohei brought up Miura's nickname at once.

'Yes, that's the one . . . He came to see me a short while ago.'

'Mm-hmm?'

'According to him, certain swordsmen are plotting to murder your son.'

'Murder Daijiro . . .?'

'Indeed.'

Miura's story began with an incident at a gambling den from two nights earlier.

Miura had gone out to the chugen servants' quarters at the third mansion of Matsudaira Izumi-no-kami in Fukagawa Man'nen, which transformed into a gambling den almost every night.

Miura's lodging was at a small temple, Saiho-ji, which stood on the outskirts of a nearby district called Hamaguri. So whenever he had the chance, he went to try his luck at the Matsudaira mansion. As the third home of a daimyo was like a holiday villa of sorts, the temporary servants who worked there were often a bunch of scoundrels. They passed a bit of hush money to the lord's retainers who were stationed there and transformed their quarters into a gambling house come nightfall.

Kumanosuke had once told Kohei: 'Miura's a swordsman sure enough, but who knows what he gets up to behind the scenes? He really is a peculiar fellow.'

Still, he didn't seem to be crossing any serious lines.

'Ushibori Sensei,' he had said at one point, 'I can get by fine just with gambling . . . and I have plenty of women who would feed me even without my asking, but, as fate would have it, I'm hooked on sword fighting, so I end up chasing two rabbits, which isn't good for either.'

That particular night, Miura had had a losing streak at the gambling den. Just as he gave up and was about to go home for the night, a ronin slunk up to him.

'It's been a while, Master Miura,' the ronin said. He was a bulky man in his thirties called Uchiyama Mataheita. Hailing from Numata domain in Kozuke province, he was also a considerable swordsman like Miura.

Uchiyama was a familiar presence at the Nen-ryu dojo outside the Kandabashi gate, which was led by Muragaki Mondo – perhaps because Muragaki was also a native of Kozuke.

Muragaki dojo was one of the most thriving training halls in Edo. As a swordsman, Muragaki had 'a rather clever way of getting along in the world', to borrow Miura's words.

Since Muragaki was free with his money, Miura also frequented the dojo, staying for a week or two at a time and teaching the pupils in exchange for room and board. Uchiyama did the same – in fact, he slept there most nights.

'I thought I'd find you here,' Uchiyama said to Miura. 'I went to Saiho-ji just now, but they told me you were out.'

'What's going on, Master Uchiyama?'

'Your sweat's making your eyebrows run.' Uchiyama had meant to tease him, but Miura was unfazed.

'Gambling is harder work than sword fighting,' Miura said. 'Cold sweat.'

'Hmm. By the way, could we step out for a minute? There's something I want to tell you.'

'Something that'll bring in money?'

'Exactly why I've come looking for you.'

'Huh. Well, well, that's good news. Give me a moment.' Miura gave a tip to one of the mansion's servants and made him fetch a hot towel. After wiping his face and the nape of his neck with it, he pulled out a thin brush and a small paper envelope containing his eyebrow ink and smoothly drew his brows without even looking at a mirror.

Miura had been born with unusually sparse eyebrows.

Uchiyama watched this procedure with his mouth pursed into an awkward smile. The other gamblers in the room had seen Miura paint himself so often that they barely noticed.

Then, Miura led Uchiyama to a boathouse on the south end of Chidori bridge, which hung over Aburabori. Miura was a regular there, and they went to a private guest room on the first floor.

Uchiyama broached the subject as they sipped sake. 'There's a swordsman by the name of Akiyama Daijiro, who has a small dojo on the outskirts of Hashiba in Asakusa. He's young, but rumour has it he gave a solid fight at Lord Tanuma's tournament last year.'

'Uh-huh . . .' Miura nodded, thinking, *He doesn't know that Daijiro is the son of Akiyama Kohei Sensei.*

Of course, Miura himself only knew Kohei's name from Kumanosuke. In Edo's world of swords, men like Miura and Uchiyama were already of a very different generation from Kohei.

Miura popped by at Kumanosuke's about once a month, and on one of those recent visits, Kumanosuke had told him about the father and son.

'You know, when I look at Master Akiyama, it makes me want to step away from sword fighting,' Kumanosuke had said. 'But I can never be like him. He's as free as a bird; nothing binds him. He's far, far ahead of me . . . and seeing as I can't reach his level, there's no other way for me but to keep going further on the path that I'm already on.'

When Miura had urged Kumanosuke to introduce him to Kohei, Kumanosuke grimaced as if he'd bit into a smelly insect. 'If you want to meet him, go and wash those paints off your face,' he spat out.

Facing Uchiyama now, Miura feigned ignorance. 'So. What about this Akiyama fellow?' he asked.

'He's got to be killed!'

'By whom?'

'The two of us.'

'Hmm . . .'

'Kill him, and we walk away with fifty gold ryo.'

'Hmm . . .'

'Not a bad job, I'd say.'

'You're right. But why kill him?'

'Don't know. But I'm told he's a bad egg.'

'Hmm. And where will the money come from?'

'Don't know. Well, I can't tell you that.'

'But if you did away with him on your own, you'd get all the money to yourself, wouldn't you?'

'Well . . . but I have to make sure I can kill him. There's no room for error. That's why I'm asking for your help. How about we take home twenty-five ryo each?'

Uchiyama refused to tell him the name of the employer. Miura simply said he would think about it for a few days and went home.

The next day, Miura mulled over it all day long and went to see Kumanosuke. 'I don't know why, but I like you, Ushibori Sensei,' he said then, 'and I started feeling like I couldn't keep this a secret from you any more. I'm fond of you, you're fond of Akiyama Sensei, and it's about his son, so here I am . . .'

Before leaving, Miura said he was thinking of declining the offer.

Now, when Kumanosuke finished his tale, he asked, 'What do you think of all this, Master Akiyama?'

'Well, my deepest thanks to you for going out of your way to warn me. Your kindness warms my heart. But, Master Ushibori, this is Daijiro's business. If he wants to be a full-fledged swordsman, he'll have to overcome threats like this with his own strength, one at a time . . . And if he dies in the attempt, perhaps there's nothing to be done about that.'

Kumanosuke didn't know what to say.

After his visitor left, Kohei went to bed, but his nerves were strangely on edge. Oharu soon joined him, having preened herself to look her best for their wedding night.

'Sensei . . . What's wrong? Tell me . . .' she pressed him eagerly, but he only said, 'It's no go tonight, Oharu.'

'Why? Sensei . . . How come?'

'Just think about it. Your groom is sixty. Sometimes it just doesn't work.' There was nothing more he could say.

Oharu turned her back to him in a sulk – but all Kohei could see floating in the darkness of the room was not Oharu's but his son Daijiro's youthful face.

III

The next morning, the rain let up again.

Kohei tried to act calm, but he couldn't help feeling restless. At breakfast, he might as well have been chewing on sand for all he could taste.

'I'm thinking of popping over to my boy's place – could you get the boat out, Oharu?'

'Sure thing,' Oharu said. She had no way of knowing what was weighing on his mind. 'I really hope you'll be ready for me tonight, sensei. I'll be waiting . . .'

'Mm-hmm.'

'Promise, sensei—'

'Weren't you saying you'd want to drop the "sensei" and call me "dear" or "darling" or something like that once we're married?'

'No, no, it's too soon. You're making me blush.' She was still the same honest girl.

She untied the boat while Kohei got ready to leave. Just as he came out of the house, Mifuyu strode into the yard in her usual dashing way.

'Oh hello. Welcome,' Oharu greeted her brightly, so

different from her usual manner around Mifuyu. Becoming Kohei's official wife had given her a great deal of confidence.

All this was unknown to Mifuyu. She merely glanced in Oharu's direction and gave her a small nod, but Oharu didn't seem to mind at all.

'I haven't seen you in a while, Akiyama Sensei. I'm sorry for not coming sooner,' Mifuyu said.

'I can say the same,' Kohei replied amiably.

'Are you going out somewhere?'

'Just dropping in at my son's place.'

'You have a son?' Mifuyu looked surprised. Come to think of it, he had never mentioned Daijiro to her before.

'The young master has his very own dojo at the back of Masaki shrine,' Oharu told her proudly.

'A dojo . . . for sword fighting?'

'Indeed it is,' Kohei said. 'You came right in time. How about I introduce you to Daijiro? He's just returned from a journey.'

'I had no idea. I would be happy to accompany you.'

Oharu docked the boat at Hashiba and unloaded her passengers; then she turned the boat around and guided it back across Ohkawa, smiling ear to ear as she handled the pole. Mifuyu stared in bewilderment at her sudden transformation.

Kohei was already heading to Daijiro's dojo; Mifuyu hurried after him.

They didn't find Daijiro there.

The neighbouring farmer's wife, Oko, who was doing laundry by the well, told Kohei with silent gestures that the young master had gone out.

Kohei retraced his steps.

He stopped by at Honsho-ji temple in Imado, thinking that Daijiro might be paying a visit to the graves of his mother and Shimaoka Reizo, but he was nowhere to be seen.

Back outside the temple gate, Kohei gazed up at the leaden sky; a heavy sigh escaped him.

'Is anything the matter, sensei?' Mifuyu asked.

'No . . . nothing in particular . . .'

'Is something troubling you . . .? Please let me hear it. I would be glad to be of service to you, no matter what the problem is.' She circled around him to look him in the face. Her eager eyes were glowing with passion. Apparently, her feelings for Kohei hadn't changed at all.

Kohei looked away. 'Ah, Miss Mifuyu, it's only that . . .'

'Yes?'

'I was merely thinking how I've become a doddering old man.'

'How can you say such a thing? I can only see how youthful you are, sensei.'

Kohei laughed wistfully. 'Look at me, fretting over my son, who's already flown the nest – the same one that *I* prodded to fly away . . . It's the most ridiculous thing. I thought I was better than that.'

Mifuyu didn't understand. She saw the melancholy look on Kohei's face – a look that seemed to draw an invisible line between them that she could not cross. She swallowed back her words, hanging her head.

Just around that time, Miura appeared again at the Ushibori dojo in Asakusa Mototorigoe.

A fierce practice session was underway in the dojo. Kumanosuke sat on the dais, keeping a sharp eye on his pupils, but he was distracted by the old manservant, Gonbei, who crept up to him from behind and whispered, 'Sensei – the oddball's back again. This time he can hear all the bamboo swords bangin' in here, so I can't just tell 'im you've gone off somewhere. Besides, he says if I tell you that he's come to see you, you'll surely meet with 'im.'

As Miura had predicted, Kumanosuke ran down the passageway to his living quarters, where his visitor awaited him.

'Hullo, sensei. I'm sorry about my lack of manners last night . . .'

'No matter.'

'Did you get a chance to tell Akiyama Kohei Sensei about it?'

'Yes. I did.'

'What did he say?'

Kumanosuke repeated Kohei's words from the night before. 'Of course, it's expected of a swordsman, but I was a little taken aback by his sternness.'

'Well, well . . .'

'"Well, well" what?'

'I see.'

'You see *what*? Spell it out, will you?'

'I am genuinely impressed. But, Ushibori Sensei – if that's how *he* sees it, I suppose that changes the picture, doesn't it? I'm free to step in and help Uchiyama with the kill.'

Kumanosuke pierced Miura with a look.

'I mean, pose as if I'm helping,' Miura added with a

mischievous grin. 'I'll get twenty-five ryo out of it. I'll simply sit back and watch them fight it out. How does that sound?'

Kumanosuke didn't answer. He stared at Miura for a long time. The colour of his eyes deepened, and a hard glint came into them.

Without so much as a flinch, Miura met his gaze.

The soft patter of rain began seeping into the room.

Kumanosuke broke the silence at last. 'If you agree to help this Uchiyama fellow . . . you'll hear everything about his movements, won't you . . .?'

'Of course.'

'Will you pass on any news to me in secret?'

'Of course.'

'Hmm . . . and you're sure that you'll only be putting on a front?'

'I'm happy as long as I can swindle him out of his money . . . But sensei – if Uchiyama succeeds in taking Daijiro out by himself, that's none of my concern.'

'Understood.' Finally, the grim creases on Kumanosuke's face seemed to soften a little.

IV

That night, Miura met with Uchiyama at the same boat-house by Chidori bridge in Fukagawa.

'What say you, Master Miura? Have you decided?'

'Does your employer know that I will be helping you in the ambush?'

'No. I won't tell anyone about you. I'm supposed to be

getting the job done by myself. But as I said before, there's no room for error. That's why I'm asking you, just to be sure.'

'All right. I'm in.'

'I owe you one.' Uchiyama's thick nostrils twitched. A bloodthirsty gleam entered his eyes; he hastily pulled out thirteen gold coins from the fold of his kimono and put them down in front of Miura. 'That's thirteen ryo out of your half of the bounty. I'll give you the rest once we finish off Daijiro. Agreed?'

'Too bad, I figured I'd get twenty-five up front.'

'You must be joking,' Uchiyama said with a smirk. 'This is how it's done with jobs like this.'

'Huh. Then you're used to taking on jobs like this?'

Uchiyama's face grew sinister, and he fell silent.

'So, when will we do it?' Miura asked.

'We can go tonight,' Uchiyama said, even before Miura had finished his question. 'Let's ambush him in his dojo.'

'No, tonight won't work,' Miura said, tucking away the money. 'I want to have a look at his house first. How about the day after tomorrow?'

'Fine.' Uchiyama summoned an attendant and made her bring a writing box. He drew a rough map of the area around Daijiro's dojo and handed it to Miura. 'I've already seen the place. You'd better go alone.'

'Did you see Daijiro?'

'I caught a glimpse of him a couple of times when he stepped out.'

'How did he look?'

'Well . . . to be honest . . . I thought it was a good idea I asked for your help,' Uchiyama groaned. While spying on Daijiro from the shadows of the grove, he seemed to have sensed that Daijiro would be a formidable opponent.

It wasn't long after this exchange that Uchiyama left Hyotan-ya. Miura saw him off and stayed behind.

'Hey, Yonekichi,' he called to a young boatman he knew well who was standing by the entrance on the dirt-floor pit. When the boatman ran up to him, Miura slipped him some money and murmured, 'Follow that samurai who just left and watch where he goes. Don't let him see you.'

Yonekichi nodded, grabbed a rain cloak and rushed out of the door.

He returned after about two hours.

Miura was still waiting for him at the boathouse. 'You didn't give yourself away, did you?' he asked Yonekichi.

'No, I was fine, sensei.'

According to Yonekichi, Uchiyama went straight to Muragaki Mondo's dojo by Kandabashi. Since Uchiyama was lodging at the dojo, there was nothing unusual about this, but Miura fell deep in thought.

If Uchiyama had been truthful when he'd said he wouldn't tell his employer about Miura, then there was nothing to it. However, it would be a different matter altogether if his real intention was to do just the opposite.

In the latter case, Miura was certain that Uchiyama would report to his employer straight away. In other words, there was now a possibility that Muragaki dojo, or Muragaki Mondo himself, might have something to do with whoever it was that was behind this assassination plot.

Miura left the boathouse soon afterwards.

The rain was pouring down, as usual.

It must have been past ten at night when Miura reached the small gate outside Ushibori dojo.

He was about to knock on the door of the gate, but he stopped himself. Instead, he tossed his umbrella and tall wooden clogs over the wall, then climbed in himself. He was as nimble as a wild monkey.

He crossed the garden without hesitation and came right up to the sliding shutter outside Kumanosuke's room. He tapped on it quietly and said, 'Sensei. Sensei, it's me, Miura Kintaro. Could you please open?'

Kumanosuke got up immediately and came to open the shutters. 'Has something happened?' he asked.

'Yes . . .'

'Come in. You could've knocked on the gate . . .'

Kumanosuke's attitude to Miura was starting to change. When he thought about how Daijiro was the only son of the man he admired, he found himself determined to do whatever he could to help Daijiro – and all the more so because Kohei's own stance seemed cold to him.

Meanwhile, Uchiyama was having a clandestine discussion with Muragaki Mondo in Mondo's room at the dojo.

'Good, good. All according to plan,' Mondo said. 'With Miura Kintaro's help, we are sure to succeed. Even Akiyama Daijiro won't stand a chance against the two of you. Everything will go swimmingly. I'm sure of it.' Mondo's face split into a wide grin.

Mondo was past fifty; his hair hung down to his shoulders, and he was wearing a summer haori jacket. He cut a rather imposing figure, with an air of dignity that befitted his status as the master of a large dojo attended by more than three hundred pupils.

He had just returned from his mistress's house in Umanokura Alley in Kanda. The word was that he had three children by his young mistress, on top of the six children he had by his wife.

'Here's a small token of gratitude from me to you. It's not much, but take it,' Mondo said, putting five gold ryo on a piece of paper and sliding it towards Uchiyama.

'There's no need for that, sensei . . .'

'It's all right. Just take it.'

'Yessir . . . Thank you very much . . .'

'In return, be sure to finish off Daijiro.'

'I will. But sensei . . .'

'What's the matter?'

'Well . . . where exactly does this assignment come from?'

'Don't ask!'

'Yessir . . .'

'It should have been my duty to do away with this fellow called Akiyama Daijiro. But as it is, I don't have the freedom of doing so. I am well acquainted with a number of daimyos, and I am responsible for all my pupils. If anything should leak out, there would be trouble.'

'I fully understand.'

'I'm counting on you. When will you do it?'

'The day after tomorrow, late at night . . .'

'I know you will be careful, but make sure you carry it through . . .'

'I assure you, it will be done.'

'Go and get some sleep, then. I'll have a maid bring you sake.'

'I am much obliged.'

'I'll send that young one – Miyo, was it? Feel free to do what you like with her.' Mondo chuckled.

V

The next morning, Kohei and Oharu were still asleep when Kumanosuke knocked on their front door and called out, 'Hello. I'm sorry to disturb you.'

Kohei's eyes snapped open. He leaped to his feet like a toy with a coil spring and ran to the door. But he paused on the dirt-floor pit just inside it and steadied his breathing.

'Is that you, Master Ushibori?' he asked, doing his best to keep his voice calm.

'Yes.'

'I'll open the door.'

Oharu stayed in bed. Ever since their wedding night, Kohei hadn't touched her. Despite her youthfulness, he had come to think of her as a real wife; he somehow couldn't help being himself in front of her, letting her see his sullen or anxious moods that he wouldn't reveal to others.

She was angry at him for not fulfilling his duties to her as a husband.

Kohei invited Kumanosuke in and made tea for his guest himself.

'Miura came to see me late last night,' Kumanosuke said.

'Kinchan of the Painted Brows . . .'

'Yes. According to him . . .' Kumanosuke related everything that Miura had said. 'What do you make of it, Master Akiyama?'

'What do you mean . . .?'

'Don't you think there's something between Uchiyama and Muragaki Mondo in connection to this matter?'

'Muragaki, eh . . . That man knows what he's doing. You've got to be like him to get by in the samurai business nowadays. He's not only good with his sword, but he's worldly-wise and shrewd with his money. His affairs run deep. I've heard he's even an extortionate moneylender.'

'Is that true?' Kumanosuke stammered.

'He's worlds apart from you, Master Ushibori.'

'What could be his link to your son? Does anything come to mind?'

'Well . . . I don't know anything about my son's matters. But I really am grateful for your kindness . . .' Maintaining his mask of composure, Kohei touched the floor with both palms and bowed to Kumanosuke.

'I keep worrying about your son.'

'I'm sorry it troubles you. But Master Ushibori, I'd like you to let it be. My son must overcome a thing like this if he is to stand on his own feet.'

'Yes . . . well . . .'

'I trust *you* would understand.'

'Yes . . .'

At such insistence, Kumanosuke had no choice but to withdraw. He stood up and said, 'Uchiyama and Miura will ambush your son in his dojo tomorrow. But Miura won't lend a hand. That's all I'm going to say.'

'Yes . . . Thank you.' Kohei's hands were still pressed against the floor.

When Kumanosuke left, Kohei's shoulders slumped down.

As Oharu finally trudged out of the bedroom, Kohei shouted, 'Oharu. I'm going to Daijiro's. Get ready.'

She paled, her eyes wide open. She had never seen him so angry before. 'Um . . . but what about breakfast, sensei . . .?'

'No need. I said get ready! Now!'

Kohei didn't say a word to Oharu on the boat ride; he stared hard at the surface of the water the whole way until they reached the dock at Hashiba.

As he set off towards Daijiro's house, Oharu pushed the boat out into the river and shook the pole at his retreating figure, muttering, 'You're awful, sensei . . .'

Her eyes brimmed with tears.

Daijiro was splashing water on himself at the well when Kohei reached his house. The smell of miso soup wafted from the kitchen. It must be the farmer's wife getting breakfast ready.

'Oh, Father . . .' Daijiro looked surprised to see Kohei so early in the morning. He pulled up his kimono over his shoulders and said, 'Please come in.'

'No, we can talk here.'

The rain had ceased, but dense grey clouds covered the sky; it was as dark as if night were already falling.

A damselfly flitted past, tracing an unsteady path between the father and son as they locked eyes.

'Tell me, Dai. You know Muragaki Mondo by the Kandabashi gate, don't you?'

'Yes.'

'Have you ever met him?'

'No, I've only heard of him.'

'Then . . . there's nothing between you and him?'

'With Muragaki Sensei . . .? No, there's nothing.'

'I see. Hmm . . . Right. What about his pupils, then?'

'I don't know anyone there . . . Why do you ask such a thing, Father?'

'Oh, no reason . . .' Kohei fell silent and looked up at the sky. He seemed to be brooding over something. Daijiro had never seen his father like this in his life.

'Father . . .'

'You see, Dai . . .'

'Yes?'

'Ah . . . never mind. All right, good. That's all I wanted to know.'

Kohei turned his back on Daijiro and walked away. He seemed to stumble over his own feet.

Daijiro watched him go, stunned. *What on earth . . .?* He couldn't fathom what had happened to his father. He thought long and hard, but nothing came to him.

Kohei, in the meantime, roamed the streets without knowing where he had come from or where he was going.

Eventually, he found himself sitting in a daze on a bench in a tea shop within the precincts of Senso-ji temple.

Uchiyama and Miura were supposed to strike tomorrow night.

It's not too late . . . Kohei thought. Even if he were to stay out of the skirmish, he could still alert Daijiro to the ambush; then his son would be ready for it, at least. Daijiro could take every possible means to counter their attack, and he wouldn't be caught off guard.

But in the end, Kohei hadn't told Daijiro.

He must get through this by his own strength alone.

Was it Kohei's principles as a swordsman that had made him hold his tongue? Or was it out of his love for his son? Or was it, in fact, out of his own affectation, or the stubbornness of old age?

He couldn't make sense of himself any more. He put down some change for the tea and wandered off again.

By the time he reached the gate of Kandabashi, the sun's timid rays were starting to tinge the clouds. It seemed the rain would hold off for the rest of the day.

Muragaki dojo stood on a corner lot in the first district of Mikawa: a prime location that looked out on the moat of Edo Castle across a wide street.

Kohei walked down this street along the moat from north to south, retracing his steps to and fro a few times.

It was crowded with people who were out to make the most of this rare dry spell in the rainy season. Out of the corner of his eye, Kohei watched the pupils coming in and out of the dojo's front gates.

What's got into me . . . ?

He couldn't make himself out. If he had to pin down a reason for his present actions, he supposed he wanted to know why Muragaki was after Daijiro's life.

But even so, it was pointless to keep watch in broad daylight like this. Everything he did now seemed utterly foolish and immature compared to his usual self.

Turns out I'm thoroughly flustered . . .

Feeling dejected, he came to a halt on the edge of the moat. Just then, Muragaki emerged from the dojo with several pupils seeing him off.

Kohei hastily turned to face the other way.

Muragaki walked south along the moat at a leisurely pace without any attendants. He was holding a wickerwork hat in his hand, which he put on when he crossed to the other side of Ryukan bridge.

Kohei tailed him. All of a sudden, heat rose in his old body; his pulse seemed to quicken.

Eventually, Muragaki entered a fine-dining restaurant called Sakura-ya in Horie Rokkencho. A well-known establishment around these parts, it stood on the eastern side of Shian bridge, where Nihonbashi River met the man-made waterway stretching to the east of Edo bridge. Kohei had been there a couple of times before.

A short while after Muragaki went inside, Kohei followed suit. He asked to be shown into a small private room, and as soon as he was seated, he told the attendant, 'Could you bring me some sake? And something good to go with it.' He sounded like himself again.

When a plump, friendly woman came with his sake, he was quick to dish out some compliments and tuck into her kimono a generous tip wrapped in paper.

'My, that's too much . . .' she said.

'Never mind, it's all right. Now, could you pour some sake for me?'

'Sure.'

'By the way, you saw the man who came in just before

me – the fine-looking samurai. He's an acquaintance of mine, Muragaki Mondo Sensei. He's quite a swordsman.'

'Ah, you know him well then.'

'Who's he sitting with, eh? A pretty woman like you?' Kohei asked with a chuckle.

'Oh, not at all – he's meeting with Master Ito Hikodayu, the steward of Lord Mizoguchi from Echigo.'

'Huh. Is that so?' he said with a nonchalant smile, but his heart was roaring.

Ito Hikodayu – the steward of Mizoguchi Shuzen-no-kami who ruled over the Shibata domain in Echigo province worth 50,000 koku – was none other than the father of Ito Sanya, whose arm Daijiro had cut off with his sword to protect his old teacher, Reizo.

'I hear Master Muragaki goes to Lord Mizoguchi's first mansion all the time, teaching swords to the people of the house,' the woman went on.

'Ah . . . that's right, I remember. So he comes here often to see Master Ito?'

'Oh yes. Especially these days.'

'I see.' He then changed the subject so she wouldn't suspect anything.

That incident with Ito Sanya had occurred in early spring this year.

Shimaoka Reizo – who was like a second teacher to Daijiro – had returned to Edo for a final duel with Kakimoto Genshichiro, but around sunset on the evening before, the nineteen-year-old Sanya had ambushed Shimaoka with his bow and arrows, driven by his concern for Kakimoto's ailing condition. Sanya had been Kakimoto's disciple as well as his lover.

Reizo had died from Sanya's arrow, and Daijiro had slashed off Sanya's right arm on the spot. Sanya had fled and had been missing ever since.

When Kakimoto learned what Sanya had done, he ended his own life to atone for his own ignorance that had sullied his oath with Reizo.

Reader, I trust this tragedy is still fresh in your memory.

This means Ito Sanya's father might be harbouring him, Kohei thought. *And perhaps Hikodayu hates Daijiro so much that he hired some assassins . . . Or even if he doesn't know where Sanya is, Hikodayu might be acting purely on his own grudge to do away with Daijiro . . .*

Kohei was convinced that the truth must lie in either theory.

After Ito and Muragaki had left the restaurant separately, each covering his face under his wickerwork hat, Kohei departed as well.

VI

It rained again the next day.

Kohei stayed on his futon the entire day, listening to the drips and drops.

Oharu tiptoed around the house doing chores; she was afraid of disturbing him.

He had barely spoken to her since the morning, but she could sense that something about him was different today.

He lay still on his back, just gazing at the ceiling, but as the day wore on, she noticed a vivid light starting to gleam in his eyes.

Around four in the afternoon, he slowly got up without a word. He washed himself with cold water in the bath shack and had a couple of bowls of plain rice porridge with umeboshi and pickled gourds on the side, which he'd asked Oharu to prepare.

'Sorry to make you go out in the rain, Oharu – could you take out the boat?' he asked.

Since he spoke in the same gentle tone as he always had, Oharu sprang into action and happily got ready to go.

Kohei put on a rain cloak and a wickerwork hat, folded up the hem of his kimono, and wore straw shoes over bare feet. He also took a paper umbrella and, as usual, his Horikawa Kunihiro wakizashi – the short sword with a blade of nearly eighteen inches – on his waist.

Oharu expertly guided the boat across Ohkawa in the rain and ferried Kohei to Hashiba.

'I might be late, but I'll be back – I promise. Don't worry about me.'

'Aye,' Oharu said with a carefree nod. She seemed to have perked up with renewed cheer. 'I'll have sake ready for you.'

'Ah, good idea. Thanks, Oharu.'

He watched her drift back over the river, then started walking.

About an hour later, he was hiding in a grove on the east side of Daijiro's dojo. He was sitting on two rush mats that he'd bought in town in Hashiba, and instead of his hat, which he'd taken off, he shielded himself from rain with the umbrella. The zelkovas and sawtooth oaks around him cast dense shadows; only his eyes glowed white in the gloom.

So, here I am. I've come out here after all.

A wry smile crossed his face.

The moment he had discovered the furtive meeting between Muragaki Mondo and Ito Hikodayu, Kohei had suddenly realised what he had to do.

If that's how it is, who knows what kind of tricks they might have up their sleeves?

Even though Miura had claimed that he wouldn't pitch in, it was conceivable that Muragaki would send another assassin just to be sure.

If they try anything underhand, I can step in, too, he'd decided.

That was how he had reasoned it out, but all in all, he might have only been giving himself an excuse.

The urge that he had been desperately suppressing until then had burst out, provoked by his new knowledge, and it had found its own justification on the way.

The farmer's wife, Oko, came out from the kitchen – having prepared Daijiro's supper – and headed back home.

After that, the hours slipped by.

Hour after hour, Kohei sat in the rain, perfectly still. Once in a while he sipped from a bottle of sake that he had bought in Hashiba, and he waited.

Daijiro seemed to have gone to sleep.

All Kohei could hear was the patter of rain on his umbrella.

They're here . . .

His sharp eyes, now accustomed to the darkness, caught sight of two figures emerging from the grove on the other side of Daijiro's house.

Daijiro probably hadn't barred the doors, as usual.

The two shadows stood by the stone well and whispered to each other. The next moment, their swords glinted in the night.

They split up: apparently, one was going to storm in through the front door of the dojo, and the other from the kitchen. Both of their faces were covered with black masks, so Kohei couldn't make out which one was Miura.

One of them slid open the door to the kitchen and crept in.

Kohei couldn't see the other one who had gone round to the dojo side. He darted out of the grove and hid in the shadow of the well.

He was itching to burst in, but it seemed that the enemy were only two men.

If Daijiro should be taken by an ambush of this level, then there's nothing to be done. All right then, I'll keep guard here and watch out for other attackers, he told himself, but of course, he could hardly stay still.

Argh, I don't care any more. He pulled out his short sword and was about to shoot into the kitchen door when he heard an ear-splitting shriek from inside the house.

Some tumbling noises followed, then silence.

One dark figure staggered out of the kitchen door, emitting guttural groans, and after a few feeble steps, collapsed on the mud. It wasn't Daijiro.

Daijiro appeared at the threshold, holding a long sword.

Good, good. Well done. But what about the other one . . .?
Kohei almost stepped forward when a voice called out from the dark.

'Master Akiyama Daijiro.'

Daijiro turned sharply to the direction of the voice.

'I came with the man that you cut down just now. I wasn't planning on assisting him . . . but I've changed my mind. I saw it all – you were sleeping, but when that man thrust his blade at you, you dodged it, then drew your sword and dealt him a fatal cut all in one motion. Extraordinary. Simply extraordinary.'

The speaker emerged from the veil of darkness, revealing his tall figure. He tore off his mask.

'I am called Miura Kintaro,' he said in an exhilarated voice. 'Though I am an unknown swordsman – but precisely because I am as yet unknown – I am overcome by the desire to fight a duel with you. Will you accept? What do you say?'

'As you wish.'

Daijiro's voice was perfectly calm.

A shiver ran through Kohei as he watched from his hiding place.

'Then let's begin,' Miura said, leaping down. No sooner had he set his sword in the lower position than Daijiro strode towards him without any hesitation, simply carrying his sword by his side.

He moved as naturally as if he were a body of water gliding over the ground.

Even Kohei was startled at this, and he half rose without thinking.

Miura was unsettled, too. He had never experienced such an audacious yet unhurried advance from an opponent.

In the blink of an eye, Daijiro had closed the distance between them.

Now there was no turning back – nowhere to run.

Miura was cornered. With a fierce howl, he thrust his sword at Daijiro.

The night was riven by the shrill clang of blade hitting blade. The two men drew apart, but without a moment's pause, they struck out at each other once more.

There was a muffled moan.

Miura dropped his sword and crumpled to the ground.

Daijiro stood apart and watched him fall.

'Well done!!'

Kohei was about to leap out, but another man had raised his voice before he could utter a sound.

'I am Ushibori Kumanosuke, a friend of Akiyama Kohei Sensei.'

Kumanosuke appeared out of nowhere. Like Kohei, he must have been watching over the fight from the shadows.

Kohei swallowed back his cry of 'well done', ducked his head, and hurried back into the cover of the trees.

Kumanosuke and Daijiro quickly carried Miura, who was still breathing, into the house.

Kumanosuke tried to treat his wound, but Miura stopped him.

'It's no use, Ushibori Sensei,' Miura murmured. 'Well, I've turned myself into a bore now. No more women or sake for me . . . But sensei – turns out, the swordsman's soul is what really runs through my blood, after all.'

The lashing rain had washed away his painted brows and the rouge from his lips; his gourd-shaped face was as white as a sheet.

'This man, though . . . Akiyama Daijiro. What a fellow.' Miura grinned up at Daijiro. 'Maybe you'll be like your father before long,' he said in an oddly gentle voice.

His breath seemed to catch in his throat, and the shadow of death took over his face.

'Ushibori Sensei – I have a small envelope with my eyebrow ink inside my collar. Please – take it out for me.'

'All right . . . This one?'

'Yes. There's a small brush in there. Could you wet it and put plenty of ink on it – and hand it to me . . .?'

'Here . . . Like this? Is this good?'

'Yes . . . Please wipe my face.'

'Of course.'

Kumanosuke took a face cloth and wiped him clean. Miura slowly raised his hand holding the thin brush. But just as the tip was almost touching his faint brow, the brush fell from his hand.

*

The next morning, when Daijiro came to his father's house in the quiet drizzle, Kohei was stretched out on the engawa veranda, his white head propped on Oharu's lap while she cleaned his ear.

A dreamy smile played on his rosy face as he stroked her knee.

'Father . . .'

'Oh, Daijiro. Any news?'

'Yes, I have a little something to tell you about . . .'

'Hmm. Did something happen?'

'Yes.'

'Hmm. Well, stay a while. I'll be done soon. Then we can sit down with some tea, and I'll listen to whatever you have to say – we have all the time in the world.'

'Yes.'

'Oharu – I feel better than ever.'

Oharu hummed in answer.

The scent of gardenias wafted in the air from somewhere in the distance.

Chapter 7

Assassination by Poison

I

When the swordswoman Sasaki Mifuyu left her home in Negishi, the sky was a brilliant blue that promised the end of the rainy season. But by the time she had passed Sakamoto Kuruma-zaka, gone down the main street of Asakusa and reached the gate of Shitaya Kotoku-ji temple, the rain started pouring again.

In the blink of an eye, it turned into a terrible torrent that pounded against the ground.

Mifuyu was wearing a summer hakama over a short-sleeved kimono made of white linen, and a pair of silk-strapped sandals over her bare feet; she looked dashing with her hair freshly arranged in her usual wakashu-wage topknot, a style reserved for adolescent boys.

'This won't do,' she murmured to herself, and rushed into a tea shop covered by reed blinds which stood next to the large torii gate of Shitaya Inari shrine on the south side of the street.

When the people in the tea shop saw her come in, they held their breath. They couldn't believe their eyes: here was a beautiful young maiden who was dressed like a boy and carried herself with the brisk, supple gestures of one well trained in swords.

Mifuyu took her slender katana off her waist and called out, 'Hello. I'd like a cup of tea.'

Her voice had a clear, bold ring to it, and everyone in the shop, including the owner, looked at her in admiration, as if she were a mysterious creature.

A clap of thunder tore through the sky, and they were cut off from the outside world by a screen of white rain. But in a matter of seconds, the rain ceased, as if the sky had been merely playing a trick.

A blazing shaft of summer sunlight was already breaking through the clouds.

Still, Mifuyu sat on the bench, leisurely sipping her tea.

She was glad that, with Kohei's help, she had been able to quell the conflict at Izeki dojo in Ichigaya and close its doors for good – but now, she didn't know what to do with herself.

When she had been one of the Four Rulers of the dojo, not a day had passed without her going to the training hall and teaching the many pupils there after the old master had died. Thinking that she would lose her touch if she didn't find another dojo, she began to train at the dojo led by Kaneko Sonjuro Nobuto – one of the most respected schools of sword fighting in Edo – which was in the fifth district of Yushima.

But on this particular day, she had other plans: she was going to visit Kohei's house for the first time in a while.

Kohei Sensei's son, Master Daijiro, owns a dojo near Hashiba. When I went with Kohei Sensei the other day, he was out, but . . .

oh, I know! I'll ask Kohei Sensei to introduce me to him – it'll be interesting to try my hand against him.

Having made up her mind, she had finished an early lunch and was on her way to Kohei's house near Kanegafuchi.

'This is for the tea,' she said, putting down some change, and glanced outside. 'Ah . . .' Her lips curled into a grin.

She spotted a familiar face among the crowd of people who were spilling into the street, having waited out the rain under any available roof: a vassal of her father called Iida Heisuke.

Heisuke was a low-rank vassal with an income worth forty tawara bags of rice per year, and he was a member of the Gozenban, who oversaw all the meals of the lord.

This unit was responsible for closely examining every single piece of food that was to reach Lord Tanuma's mouth. Mifuyu knew who Heisuke was because his son Kumetaro used to attend Izeki dojo.

The people of the Tanuma house called Heisuke 'Toothless Tanuki'.

Indeed, he did look exactly like a toothless raccoon dog. He was a little man with the face of a small tanuki and a short snip of a salt-and-pepper topknot sitting on his head. All his front teeth were gone, which made him look a couple of decades older than he really was.

Now, as Heisuke was walking past Shitaya Inari shrine, a young man dressed like a merchant appeared from behind the corner of the high walls of a samurai mansion on the west side of the street. The moment they passed each other, the man snatched something from Heisuke's kimono.

No one in the jostling crowd noticed this.

But since Mifuyu had been watching Heisuke, she had seen everything.

Oops . . . Tough luck for that Tanuki. She stifled a laugh.

Heisuke hurried on towards Ueno without realising anything was amiss.

Mifuyu let him go on his way and decided to stalk the pickpocket, who was trotting off in the direction of Asakusa.

II

The pickpocket made a beeline towards Asakusa through Shinteramachi, where the streets were lined with small and large temples on both sides. Soon he veered north on to a street that continued between Togaku-ji and Saiko-ji temples.

He was a short, thin man, and he didn't look at all like a thief. He wore his kimono stiff and proper with a wide obi sash neatly tied around his waist and white tabi socks on his feet.

He kept going north on this street, which was also bordered by temples, heading towards the Iriya rice fields.

He glanced behind him a couple of times, but he didn't see anyone chasing him.

The midday sun shone bright on the empty white street.

He slowed his pace and stuck his hands into the folds of his kimono. He was about to take the coins from the purse he'd stolen and toss the rest when he heard a voice.

'Stop.' Mifuyu stepped out from behind the wall of

Seiko'in temple. She had circled ahead of him. 'I was watching you,' she said with an ominous chuckle.

The man felt a jolt, but when he saw that he was only up against a gentle-looking adolescent – unaware that she was actually a girl – he seemed relieved, apparently thinking he could deal with her without breaking a sweat.

He threw a backward glance to check that the street was still empty, then without uttering a word, unsheathed a dagger hidden in his kimono and lunged at her.

Of course, Mifuyu didn't let him touch her. She dodged his blade with ease, lowered her body a little, then the next thing he knew, he was swept off his feet and thrown against the ground. 'There!' she said.

The thief groaned in pain, lying face down. He seemed to have fallen on a bad spot, and he could barely breathe, let alone move.

Mifuyu closed in on him and pulled out Heisuke's purse from his kimono and tucked it into her own.

'Hey. I'll make sure you can never do mischief again,' she said. She grabbed his right hand.

He let out a high-pitched shriek.

Mifuyu had broken two of his fingers.

With a satisfied laugh, Mifuyu turned her back on him and strolled away. This was a day in the life of this twenty-year-old maiden.

Soon afterwards, Mifuyu sat down at a tea shop in the precincts of Higashi Hongan-ji temple nearby and examined the contents of Heisuke's purse.

She had it in mind to go to her father's mansion inside the Kandabashi gate, call up Heisuke, and tease him by saying something along the lines of 'Didn't you get into a pickle yesterday? Hmm?' But when she saw what was in the purse, a strange light came into her eyes.

The purse held ten gold ryo. It was unthinkable for someone of Heisuke's status to be carrying around such a large sum.

What was even more puzzling was the small object carefully wrapped in oiled paper.

What could this be? Mifuyu unfolded it out of curiosity and almost gasped.

It was a packet of medicine.

When she opened it, she found a small quantity of white powder inside: less than a teaspoon. A very faint trace of pale crimson swirled in the white. It was almost odourless.

What kind of medicine is this . . .?

It seemed exceedingly strange to keep an ordinary dose of medication wrapped up like this.

She closed the packet, wrapped it up again in the same oiled paper, put it back in the purse and tucked it safely into her kimono. Her face looked a little pale.

She sat there, perfectly still.

The noisy hiss of the cicadas seemed to shake the trees around the temple.

Despite her fearless spirit, which never faltered before any man, beads of cold sweat broke out on her wan forehead.

Some time after that, Mifuyu appeared at Kohei's house.

Kohei was indulging in a nap all by himself.

Oharu was away, perhaps off to Sekiya to see her parents and get some vegetables.

When Mifuyu presented the purse and the packet

of medicine to Kohei, he stared at it silently for a rather long time.

'S-sensei – do you think this could be a poison?' Mifuyu asked when she couldn't wait any longer.

'What makes you think so, Miss Mifuyu?'

'Well . . .'

'Don't worry. Just tell me what you think.'

'The owner of that purse, Iida Heisuke, is one of the Gozenban who are in charge of my father's meals.'

'So his duty is to inspect everything Lord Tanuma eats, is that it?'

'Yes, sir.'

'And this man was carrying a single packet of a mysterious medicine in his purse – and very carefully wrapped in oiled paper, at that . . .'

'Y-yes, exactly. I wonder if someone asked Heisuke to poison my father . . .'

'And he had ten ryo on him, too . . .'

'It's suspicious. He shouldn't have so much money on him, with his level of income.'

'I agree with you on all points, Miss Mifuyu.'

'Then you also think this is . . .?'

'Let me hold on to this powder and the purse. I'll have someone examine it for me in confidence. Well, just leave it to me.'

'Thank you for your counsel.'

'Now, you can go to Lord Tanuma's mansion, but act as if everything is as usual. Stay there until a messenger comes from me. Not to worry, I'll send someone by tomorrow.'

'I will do so.'

'And you'd better keep an eye on what Heisuke does without saying a word about it. Well then, shall we set off together?'

Kohei jotted down 'Out for a bit' on a piece of paper and left it on the table in the living room.

These days, Kohei had been teaching Oharu how to read, so she could read a little now.

Kohei got ready and stepped out without even closing the doors.

'What does this Iida Heisuke fellow look like?' he asked Mifuyu.

'Everyone at the mansion calls him "Toothless Tanuki".'

'A toothless tanuki, eh . . .? Hmm.'

III

Kohei and Mifuyu parted ways on the east side of Ryogoku bridge: she crossed to the west side, and, after seeing her off, he paid a visit to a town doctor named Ogawa Sotetsu, who lived in Honjo Kamezawa.

Kohei's friendship with Sotetsu went back fifteen years.

Sotetsu had an excellent reputation around the neighbourhood. He gave his full attention and the best treatment to every patient, no matter how high or low their social class.

Fortunately, Sotetsu was home.

'Well, hello there, Master Kohei. Anything the matter?' the doctor asked. Though over seventy, he had rosy cheeks, and his voice rang out loud and clear.

'Sotetsu Sensei – would you mind doing me a favour without asking any questions?'

'Oh, no problem,' Sotetsu readily replied.

'Could we please speak in private?'

'Sure thing.'

Sotetsu saw to it that no one would disturb them, and the two of them sat down in a room at the back of the house.

'I'd like you to examine this medicine,' Kohei said.

'Let me see . . .' Sotetsu took the packet and sniffed the powder with a look of concentration. After a moment, he said, 'This is poison.'

'I thought it might be . . .'

'You were right.'

'Do you smell it?'

'The nose of a doctor is something else, Master Kohei.'

'What kind of poison is it?'

'You're better off not knowing. It's not from Japan – I'll leave it at that.'

'I see . . .'

'But how did you come to – ah, never mind, I promised I wouldn't ask anything.'

'I appreciate it.'

'You're very welcome.'

'Well, if you'll excuse me . . .'

'Leaving already? I was hoping we might have a game of Go. It's been a while since the last time we played . . .'

'I'm in a bit of a hurry . . .'

'No wonder – when you've got a deadly thing like that on your hands.'

'Actually, Sotetsu Sensei – could you call a litter here, please?'

'Easily.'

Sotetsu clapped his hands to call a maid and told her to fetch a litter with bearers from the nearest shop.

Soon Kohei was in the townsfolk's litter, heading towards the private eye Yashichi's place in Yotsuya Tenma.

When he arrived at Musashi-ya, the restaurant run by Yashichi's wife, Omine, she greeted him warmly. 'Oh hello, sensei – Yashichi's out at the moment, I'm afraid.'

'Mrs Omine – would you mind if I wait here till he gets back?'

'Please, feel free to stay. We've got some nice fresh ayu today, if you fancy some fish?'

'Sounds great. I'd like some sake, too. Ah, I didn't realise the sun's going down already. I'm starving.'

Omine whipped up a special dinner for Kohei, and he was eating and drinking in a private room on the first floor of the restaurant when Yashichi came back.

'Good to see you, sensei. Time flies – I'm sorry I didn't come to visit you in the rainy season.'

'Don't worry, Yashichi, I'm just as guilty. Well, whenever I show up like this, I always bring you trouble. I'm sorry about that – I really am.'

'Not at all, nothing to be sorry about. So, please, tell me whatever you've come to say.'

'This time, it's something that's in line with your work: something that's of great consequence to the Shogun himself.'

'Indeed . . .?' Yashichi tensed.

'Before I start talking, can you make sure no one comes in?'

'Of course.' Yashichi left the room and returned at once. 'What in the world is this about, sensei?'

'This is strictly between you and me, Yashichi. I have a feeling that this case stretches far and wide – much more than meets the eye.'

'Yes . . .?'

'What I want you to investigate is a toothless tanuki . . .'

'A *what*?'

'A man with the face of a tanuki, I mean. He looks just like a raccoon dog, apparently.'

'Phew, you scared me.'

'Now, listen carefully. I know I can trust you, so I'll lay it all out. But Yashichi – from now on, I need you to keep me informed about everything you do. It's a bother, I know, but I have to be aware of every move. I mean to say, that's how grave this affair seems to be, you see.'

'Yes, sir, crystal clear.'

'Here, have a drink . . .'

IV

Tanuma Okitsugu's primary mansion stood inside the gate at Kandabashi. This side of the bridge was enclosed by the outer and inner moats of Edo Castle, and the daimyos who had their official residences there were all high officials of the shogunate.

Having parted from Kohei, Mifuyu arrived at the

Tanuma mansion and went straight into a room called 'Keyaki no Ma' that she always used whenever she visited.

In a daimyo's residence, there was a clear distinction between 'the front' and 'the back': none of the women of the house, from the wife to the waiting maids, ever set foot in the front chambers, which were reserved for conducting official duties. Mifuyu, however, was an exception. She looked perfectly natural in her male attire, and when she was in her father's mansion, she thought of herself as a man.

Tanuma had noticed that, ever since they had worked together to resolve the dispute at Izeki dojo, Mifuyu visited his residence more frequently, and she was more willing to meet with him.

'Mifuyu has changed a great deal since she met Akiyama Kohei Sensei and started receiving his guidance. It's a good thing – I am very glad to see it,' Tanuma had confessed to his steward, Ikushima Jirodayu.

Now, having rested for a while, Mifuyu came out of her room.

The hanging lamps in the hallway were already lit.

She walked down the long hallway and nonchalantly wandered into the waiting room of the Gozenban, which was right next to the room where all the meals for her father were prepared. She found Mogami Ikugoro, another member of the unit and Heisuke's colleague, studying an account book.

Mogami saw Mifuyu and prostrated himself before her.

'Is Iida Heisuke here?' she asked.

'No, miss. He's not on duty today . . .'

'Oh, right . . .'

'I will send for him if you need him . . .'

'No, that's fine. I wanted to ask how his son Kumetaro is doing, that's all.'

'I see . . .'

Mogami knew that Heisuke's fifteen-year-old son used to go to Izeki dojo and receive lessons from Mifuyu.

'Hmm. All right. I'd like to see Kumetaro – it's been a while. I shall go to Heisuke's house directly. Could you get someone to show me the way?'

'I would be happy to.'

Heisuke's family lived in a four-room unit in one of the row houses for the retainers who were lower down in the pecking order. The long, one-storey building stretched along the northern wall of the mansion grounds.

Once she had sent away the low-rank samurai who had guided her there, Mifuyu opened Heisuke's door and called, 'It's Sasaki Mifuyu. Is Kumetaro home?'

Heisuke's wife, Yone, and Kumetaro rushed out to greet her.

'Oh . . . sensei!'

'You look well, Kumetaro. Just you wait – sooner or later, I'll find a good dojo where you can practise again . . .'

'Thank you very much.'

'It's a bit messy in here, but please come in, miss,' Yone said.

'Hmm . . . Where is your husband?'

'Since he's off duty, he has been away since the morning. He did say he'll come home before it gets dark . . .'

'But he's still out?'

'Yes. Did you need him for something?'

'No, not in particular . . .'

Speak of the devil – Heisuke himself came tottering down the stone-paved path towards the back gate. In the deepening gloom, his dark figure crossed the small gate with faltering steps and approached the doorway. As soon as he saw Mifuyu, he stopped dead, his eyes as big as saucers.

'Oh dear, what's wrong?' Yone called out.

'You look pale. Has anything happened?' Mifuyu asked casually.

'Oh, no, it's just . . . why, thank you for – for coming all this way . . .' he croaked. He tried to greet Mifuyu, but he could barely speak. He hung his head in a bow so deep that he looked like he was reeling, and there he remained, hunched over.

'Are you unwell?' Mifuyu asked.

'Ah, it seems – I have pain in my stomach all of a sudden . . . So . . . please do forgive me.'

'I don't mind. Go inside and rest. Say, Kumetaro – come and visit me in Negishi sometime.' With that, Mifuyu turned around and left Heisuke's house.

Heisuke must have realised he'd lost his purse somewhere on the way, she thought. *I bet he turned around in a panic and looked everywhere for it. But where could he have been going when I spotted him in front of Shitaya shrine . . .? He looked like he'd come from Asakusa, judging from the direction. If that packet of powder was really a poison, he might've got it from someone around Asakusa and was on the way back to the mansion . . .*

The more she thought about it, the more nervous she grew.

It was too early to draw any conclusions, but she couldn't help suspecting that that poison was meant to kill her father. After all, Heisuke was responsible for inspecting every meal and drink that touched Lord Tanuma's mouth.

She couldn't simply let it pass.

Though she used to detest her father, circumstances had brought her into his company more often this year, and Kohei had also spoken to her about Lord Tanuma on more than one occasion. So, little by little, she was starting to understand and appreciate her father as a politician who held sway in the shogunate without flaunting his authority.

That night, she stayed at the Tanuma mansion.

Her father was delighted to have her company, but when they had finished their dinner, he said, 'Sorry, I'm a little busy tonight. Hope you'll forgive me, Mifuyu,' and withdrew to his room by himself.

His work seemed to follow him wherever he went, even to his own mansion late at night.

The next morning, Heisuke was supposed to be on duty, but he did not present himself. He had taken the day off on account of a sudden illness.

Around noon, a young samurai came to see Mifuyu at the Tanuma mansion.

The sturdily built man told the guard at the gate: 'I come as a messenger for Akiyama Kohei. I would like to speak to Miss Sasaki Mifuyu. My name is Akiyama Daijiro.'

V

Soon, Daijiro was led to Keyaki no Ma and met Mifuyu there.

'Ah . . .! You're the one I passed back when . . .' Daijiro said in surprise.

'Oh . . . Please excuse my rudeness that time.' Mifuyu's face reddened.

One day in the spring, they had run into each other on the dirt bank near Kohei's house. Daijiro had stared at her male beauty in wonder, and she'd snapped at him – 'What do you want?' – before striding away.

Once she had read Kohei's letter, which Daijiro had delivered, they became engrossed in a discussion on the way of the sword. They talked for about an hour, then he left.

In the letter, Kohei informed her that the powder in the packet was indeed poison and added: 'From now on, I will send my son, Daijiro, whenever I have anything to tell you. I suggest you stay at Lord Tanuma's mansion for the moment and secretly keep your father from harm.'

Mifuyu also wrote down what had transpired since the evening before and entrusted the letter to Daijiro.

Waiting until it was close to sundown, Mifuyu summoned Kumetaro.

'I've found a good teacher for you, Kumetaro,' she told him.

'Truly?'

'A man named Akiyama Daijiro of the Mugai-ryu school,

who has a dojo at the back of Masaki Inari shrine near Hashiba in Asakusa.'

'I see . . .'

'He came to see me earlier, so I asked him to take good care of you.'

'Thank you very much.'

'You don't look very happy.'

'Oh . . . yes, I am . . .'

'He may be unknown now, but he is far above me in skill.'

'Yes, miss.'

'I am thinking of visiting his dojo sometimes to practise with him.'

'Is that true?'

'There, now you're smiling. Are you so fond of me?'

Kumetaro blushed and looked down. His childlike affection for her was obvious.

'You're sweet, Kumetaro. By the way . . .'

'Yes?'

'I heard your father came down with a sickness. How is he?'

'He's staying in bed. He hasn't had a bite to eat since this morning. Mother urged him to see a doctor, but he refused.'

'He wouldn't let her call a doctor?'

'No. He took some medicine that we had at home. He doesn't seem so bad. But he looks exhausted; it might be the hot weather getting to him.'

'Maybe so . . .'

'Whatever it is, he hasn't been very well lately. He hardly ever says anything when he gets home from work now . . .'

'Hmm. Has he been like that for a long time?'

'No, just from the spring, I think – he suddenly got a lot quieter, and I've often noticed him sitting by himself, lost in thought. Mother is worried about him, too.'

Under normal circumstances, the child of a low-rank retainer wouldn't be allowed to talk so freely to Mifuyu, the daughter of the lord. But because Mifuyu had taught him sword fighting and looked after him with tender care, Kumetaro couldn't help opening up to his favourite teacher once he started talking. Mifuyu found this endearing.

After Kumetaro went home, Mifuyu dropped by the waiting room of the Gozenban. There were three members in this unit, and they took turns reporting for duty. Everything seemed to be running as usual.

It seems we're safe as long as Heisuke stays home . . . she thought, but of course, she knew she couldn't let down her guard.

The next day, Heisuke slipped out of the mansion without Mifuyu realising. He said he was going to see a doctor he knew, and since it was his day off, no one in the mansion thought anything of it.

When Heisuke stepped out of the Kandabashi gate and walked off somewhere, Yashichi spotted him immediately from his stake-out point in a tea shop by the moat.

I see what they mean by 'Toothless Tanuki', he thought as he started shadowing his target.

Since Kohei had told him, 'It'll be hard work, but I want you to do everything by yourself,' he couldn't use any of the civilian informants he usually worked with, like Tokujiro.

'If anyone needs me, tell them I've gone off to Odawara for a little while,' he'd said to his wife before leaving home. He had relatives in Odawara in Sagami province.

It was yet another bright, clear day; the heat seemed to be mounting with each passing day.

Late into the night, Yashichi appeared at Kohei's house.

As soon as Kohei caught sight of him, he said, 'You'd better wash off your sweat first. The bath will be ready in no time. And after that, you can sit back and tell me the whole story.'

He asked Oharu to draw a bath and went to the kitchen himself to prepare the food and drink.

VI

It was 1772 when Heisuke began serving the Tanuma family, so he had been in his current position for almost seven years.

He was originally from Ueda in Shinano province, but he had become a ronin and had come to Edo when he was nearing thirty. This was soon after his first and only son, Kumetaro, was born.

About two years later, Heisuke was hired by the Hitotsubashi family through someone's recommendation. Needless to say, he was of low rank.

The history of the Hitotsubashi house began when the eighth shogun, Tokugawa Yoshimune, bestowed upon his fourth child, Munetada, a piece of land within the precincts of Edo Castle which lay inside the gate at Hitotsubashi bridge.

The Shogun Yoshimune also bid another child, Munetake, to establish the Tayasu family.

Later, the current shogun, Ieharu, gave his younger brother, Shigeyoshi, a piece of land inside the Shimizu gate, which became the foundation of the Shimizu family. Hence these three houses – Hitotsubashi, Tayasu and Shimizu – came to be called the Gosankyo, or the Three Lords, of the Tokugawa clan.

The Three Lords all held the rank of Jusanmi Chunagon, and each house received 100,000 koku from the shogunate to cover their expenses. The status of the Three Lords was second highest after the three noble daimyos ruling over Owari, Kii and Mito, who were called the Gosanke, or the Three Houses, of Tokugawa.

In the Hitotsubashi family, as with the other two families, the operation of the house was managed by a retainer of the Shogun.

Tanuma Okitsugu's younger brother, Okinobu – who died five years ago – had entered into the service of the Hitotsubashi house and had been promoted to karo, the house elder.

As Okitsugu's influence swelled ever more with the favour of the Shogun, Okinobu's standing in the Hitotsubashi family had risen with it.

Now, Okitsugu was making every effort to persuade various parties so that his younger brother's son, Okimune, could rise to the same stature: *How I wish to see him named karo of the Hitotsubashi family, just like my late brother*, he thought.

Okimune, the nephew, currently worked as an inspector

for what could be called the Shogun's intelligence agency. But considering how much political power his uncle held, everyone assumed it was only a matter of time before Okimune became the house elder of the Hitotsubashi family.

In other words, as long as the Hitotsubashi house was managed by the shogunate, it was a simple matter for Tanuma Okitsugu – the most influential man under the Shogun – to have his own nephew appointed as the karo of the house.

Okitsugu, however, was loath to parade his own authority and force his will upon others. Since his brother's death, he had worked on the Shogun and the high officials of the shogunate over five years to gain their sympathy for his nephew in a way that made them all feel fully satisfied. In addition, he had successfully secured the consent of Tokugawa Harusada, the head of the Hitotsubashi family.

Only the other day, Okitsugu had finally told his nephew with a relieved expression on his face: 'I believe His Highness the Shogun will announce his approval of your appointment shortly. Once you have become the karo of the Hitotsubashi house, I expect you to fulfil your duties in such a manner as to honour your late father's name.' His words were spoken in great earnest.

Such was the shape of the relations between Tanuma Okitsugu and the Hitotsubashi family.

As our story evolves with the passing of time, how this relationship between the two families will touch upon the lives not only of Okitsugu, but also of Mifuyu, Kohei and

Daijiro is yet to be seen – and that is something I myself am looking forward to discovering.

Now, the year Heisuke transferred from the Hitotsubashi house to Tanuma was the same year in which Okitsugu's income was increased by 30,000 koku, and he was officially appointed to his current position of roju.

With his promotion, the scale of his political activities broadened more than ever, and he needed more retainers in his service. He promoted a selection of his men to higher posts, which lead to a shortage of staff, especially among the lower ranks.

In contrast, the Hitotsubashi family had too many retainers. So it was arranged for thirty-odd samurai, including those of the lowest rank, to move to the Tanuma family. Heisuke was one of them.

Let us go back to Yashichi, who had turned up at Kohei's home after shadowing Heisuke: he reported his findings over cups of sake, and the two of them devised a detailed plan for their next move. The following morning at the Tanuma mansion, Heisuke presented himself at work.

He looked somewhat revived.

Perhaps he had met with someone in the city the day before, and, as a result, his anxieties were somewhat assuaged.

Kumetaro came to see Mifuyu. 'Father's gone to work today. He looks much better,' he told her.

'Hmm . . . so he's back. Glad to hear it.'

'I am sorry he made you worry . . .'

Kumetaro had no inkling of his father's secret. He was a lively teen who still wore his hair with a fringe – he hadn't come of age yet – and whose face retained traces of sweet boyishness.

Soon after Kumetaro left, Daijiro came.

He handed her a letter from Kohei along with Heisuke's purse, which Kohei had kept. 'My father says he will return this to you.'

Mifuyu took the items and read through the letter. 'Everything is clear,' she said.

'I will leave you then.'

'Master Daijiro.'

'Yes?'

'I have a favour to ask of you, so I will visit you sometime in the near future.'

'What is this about?'

'I would like you to accept a pupil.'

'I see,' he answered calmly.

When he was gone, Mifuyu went out of her room and traced the hallways to the Gozenban's waiting room.

The retainers who caught sight of her gossiped among themselves:

'Well, this is unusual.'

'Miss Mifuyu never stays this long . . .'

'The lord is very happy, I hear.'

'But apparently, he's so busy at the moment, he barely has the time to talk to her properly.'

As Mifuyu entered the Gozenban's room, Heisuke looked up from checking the account book.

'Miss Mifuyu . . .' he said, bowing with both hands on the floor.

'Are you better now?' she asked.

'Yes. I am all better . . .'

'I see . . .' She took a step closer to him and looked around to make sure no one else was present. 'Heisuke.'

'Yes?'

'You forgot something,' she said, putting down his purse in front of him.

The utter shock on Heisuke's face in that moment was indescribable. He froze where he sat, his mouth hanging open.

Mifuyu quickly rose to her feet and left him without even a backward glance.

The purse still contained the ten gold ryo, but the packet of poison was in Kohei's hands.

VII

Who knows what went on in Iida Heisuke's mind as he spent the rest of the day?

Mifuyu left the Tanuma mansion immediately after seeing Heisuke.

The next day, Heisuke was off duty.

His face looked pasty when he awoke.

His wife, Yone, and Kumetaro were worried about him.

'I don't feel well. I'll go and see the doctor again,' Heisuke said, leaving the Tanuma mansion around ten in the morning.

He was gone the entire day, and he hadn't come home even at sunset.

Yone and Kumetaro grew increasingly restless.

A short while earlier, Mifuyu had returned to the Tanuma mansion.

Her father had also retired from the Castle and was present at home.

'I would like to see my father – at once,' Mifuyu told the steward, Ikushima.

'I'm busy. Can't it wait until tomorrow?' Okitsugu said to Ikushima, who relayed his response to her, but she wouldn't take no for an answer.

'It can't wait until tomorrow; that's why I said *at once*. Please go back and tell him so.'

Okitsugu reluctantly invited her into his study: a room called Kaede no Ma.

'What on earth is this about, Mifuyu . . .?' he asked.

'I'm sorry for putting a strain on you when you are so hard-pressed, but this is an urgent matter . . .'

'Tell me, what is it?'

'Could we please talk in complete seclusion?'

Okitsugu looked perplexed.

'Please, I beg you . . .' She looked straight into her father's eyes.

He ordered his page to ensure privacy. Ikushima, who had been presenting a number of documents to Okitsugu, also withdrew from the room.

'Now we are alone. Will you tell me what's the matter?'

Despite the disruption, Okitsugu was happy that his dearest Mifuyu – whom he cherished, even though she was illegitimate – had come to him with such a grave secret.

Okitsugu was a thin, smallish man, and not at all impressive; his appearance betrayed no hint of the authority or stately dignity that one would expect of a roju in his prime. He looked just as plain when he was conducting his duties at the Castle. He was far from ostentatious, and he carried himself with quiet composure at all times.

As Mifuyu went on with her account, the smile on his face faded.

But by the time she had finished telling him everything – and there had been quite a lot to tell – his cheeks lifted again in a smile.

'You've done me a good turn by letting me know. Thank you.' He took his daughter's hands and raised them towards his forehead in respectful gratitude. He felt it from the bottom of his heart.

At the same time, he didn't show any surprise or anger at the news that Iida Heisuke – the very man who was supposed to ensure that his meals were safe to consume – had possessed a deadly poison.

I never realised . . . Mifuyu thought. Her father had more backbone than she'd imagined.

'I will have to be very cautious from now on,' he said solemnly.

'What will you do, Father?'

'Let me see . . .'

'I believe Akiyama Kohei Sensei will take measures on his side to help us . . .'

'Indeed . . . we're always causing trouble for Akiyama Sensei, aren't we?'

'Yes. He said I should leave all the decisions in this mansion up to you – and if there is anything you would like to tell him, I can pass it on.'

'I see . . .'

Okitsugu and Mifuyu spoke of the matter for some time, then she went home without even having dinner.

Soon afterwards, Okitsugu's dinner was carried to his room on a tray, but he turned it away immediately, and entered into a confidential discussion with Ikushima.

The steward was Okitsugu's trusted right-hand man.

If Okitsugu brought the matter to the house elders or other high-ranked counsels, it would blow up into a terrible commotion. Thus he spoke privately with Ikushima to keep the situation under control.

Their meeting didn't take long.

When they had finished, Okitsugu immediately ordered his men to prepare for a night-time procession, left the mansion without eating anything, and made his way to his secondary residence in Nihonbashi Hamacho.

He sent a notice to the shogunate to the effect that he had been struck by a sudden illness and would rest for three days in his secondary mansion.

'What's going on?' his retainers murmured to one another.

'The lord was fine just a minute ago.'

'I saw him, too. This is so bizarre . . .'

They looked mystified, like some fox had just played a trick on them.

Meanwhile, Heisuke was still missing.

Too anxious to wait for him at home any longer, his wife and son had gone to ask his colleague, Mogami, for guidance. Mogami ran to his superior to inform him, and just as they were arguing about what they should do, it was suddenly announced that the lord was moving to the secondary mansion, and the household broke into a flurry of activity, which wiped the trivial question of Heisuke's disappearance clean from their minds for the time being.

VIII

Where could Heisuke have been around that hour?

There was a canal called Shinborigawa in Asakusa.

It drew its water from Ohkawa on the south side of the shogunate's rice storehouse. It flowed northward from Torigoe past the district of Abekawa, then on the west side of Higashi Hongan-ji temple, and into the Asakusa rice paddies.

When there was a rising tide from Ohkawa, boats could travel on this canal, and it was possible to channel any leftover water in the Shakujii reservoir into it.

On this stretch of rice fields in Asakusa, in a corner bordering the canal, there stood a single mansion hemmed in by a grove. It wasn't such a large building, but it belonged to the Hitotsubashi family as one of their reserve houses.

It might have been around ten in the evening when the back gate of this mansion opened without a sound and spewed out five shadows.

The wind had died away, and the hot, humid air of the summer night hung heavy and still.

On the other side of the mansion across the canal, Kohei, Daijiro and Yashichi were hiding amidst the trees.

When Yashichi had followed Heisuke from the Tanuma

mansion the other day, he had seen Heisuke enter this reserve mansion, come back out before sundown, hire a litter at Tawaramachi and head home.

And tonight, too – Yashichi had been keeping watch outside the Kandabashi gate and shadowed Heisuke as he made his way to this mansion in Asakusa yet again. Yashichi had alerted Daijiro, and Daijiro had run to Kohei immediately with the news.

'All right . . . Mm-hmm. It's almost time for the finale,' Kohei had said. He got ready to leave in no time, and together with Daijiro, he rode Oharu's boat up to the bank of Yama-no-shuku, then hastened to the grove where Yashichi was waiting for them, spying on the house.

After that, hours crawled by as they watched for Heisuke to emerge from the gate.

'I wonder . . .' Kohei murmured. 'They might've killed Heisuke in there already.'

'Then shall we try going in quietly? What do you think, Father?'

'Well, I don't think we have to go that far. This is all within the bounds of Lord Tanuma's affairs, after all.'

'Yes.'

'But stay vigilant.'

'I will.'

Meanwhile, Yashichi had left their hiding place and was now exchanging intelligence with Mifuyu, who had come out of the Tanuma mansion right after her meeting with her father. Having spoken to her outside the Kandabashi gate, he sprinted back to the grove and recounted her news to Kohei.

'So, Lord Tanuma is on his way to his secondary mansion?' Kohei asked.

'Exactly.'

'I see – good. Did you tell Miss Mifuyu to go back to her place in Negishi and wait to see how things turn out?'

'Of course.'

'Perfect. All good.'

'Sensei – I bought a chilled gourd in front of the temple. Would you like some?'

'Ah, that'll be a real feast. Could you slice it up?'

'Right away.'

It was about two hours later when the five silhouettes slipped out of the house.

'There they are. Hope Heisuke's one of them . . .' Kohei murmured.

The five figures went around to the south side of the mansion, where the canal pooled into a large pond.

The bank protruded into this reservoir, forming a small island of sorts which was covered by a dense copse.

Two of the five figures held paper lanterns, but they blew out the light before entering the copse.

One of them cried out, 'Wh-what are you—!' His voice was cut off.

It was Heisuke.

Now the situation was clear: four samurai were dragging Heisuke into the thicket on the islet.

'Go on. Hurry up . . .' one of them ordered the others. The large man held Heisuke from behind, clasping his hands over the captive's throat and mouth. Another man gripped Heisuke's right arm from the side. 'Come on . . . Get on with it.'

'I'll do it.' The third man went around to face Heisuke and drew his long sword.

Just as he was about to thrust the blade into Heisuke's stomach, a stone flew out from the darkness and struck the man straight in the face.

The man yelped and dropped his sword, staggering back. 'Wh-what was that?' he spluttered, covering his face.

'What's wrong, Ohzawa?' the other three asked in alarm.

Heisuke saw his chance and wrenched himself free from the men's grip. He scrambled away as fast as he could.

'Damn.'

'Go after him!'

'Which way?'

'This way!'

All four of them pulled out their swords to pursue Heisuke, who fled towards the reservoir bank, but a small shadow rose in their path, as if it had oozed out from subterranean depths.

'Ah . . .!' One rammed into this small figure in the dark and crumpled to the ground with a sharp cry.

'Wh-what is it, Yamada?'

'Hey, who the hell is that?' The others finally noticed the stranger barring their way.

'Watch out.'

'Doesn't matter – just kill him.'

'All right. I'll go after Iida.'

'Fine, go.'

One samurai turned around and broke into a run, but the small man paid him no mind. 'Hmph . . . you can't cut me like *that*,' he said, leaning forward to bring his face closer to the tips of their blades.

Only Kohei could have pulled this off.

'You little . . .!' The men were startled by this reckless move and raised their swords at the same time.

Kohei leaped forward while their blades were still high in the air. Without even using the short sword on his waist, he struck one man's flank with his fist. The man slumped to his knees and fell sideways, where he writhed in pain before passing out.

The remaining samurai was paralysed with fear by this sudden attack. In a total panic, he thrashed his sword around at random, backing away from Kohei. As he retreated between the trees, he stumbled on a root. He shrieked and took to his heels, scampering off to the mansion without a backward glance. Kohei hadn't even touched him.

He left the two samurai lying there, still unconscious, and came out of the thicket to the edge of the pond.

There, the man who had gone after Heisuke was sprawled on the ground in a faint.

Kohei traced the path along the edge of the water to the other side of the pond, where he found Daijiro and Yashichi waiting for him.

No, not just them – there was another one: Heisuke, soaked from head to toe, was drooped over Yashichi's shoulder.

'Is Heisuke all right?' Kohei asked.

'I caught him when he crawled out of the pond and struck him unconscious,' Daijiro said.

'Good work,' said Kohei. 'Come, let's hurry. The

Hitotsubashi men might come after us in greater numbers. It's Lord Tanuma's wish to keep this affair under wraps, so we should avoid any big clashes if we can help it – let's go home while it's still quiet.'

Kohei led the way westwards along the narrow path through the Iriya rice fields, as swift and sure-footed as if he were walking in the light of day.

IX

About ten days passed.

That afternoon, Kohei was indulging in a nap, which had become something of a daily habit for him in the summer heat.

The oleander tree at the back of his secluded house was in full bloom, with sprays of vibrant red petals.

After lunch, Oharu had set off to get some vegetables from her parents' farm in Sekiya.

Kohei had spread a cool mat woven from bulrush on the engawa veranda and stretched himself out on top of it without a care in the world.

The breeze carried the somewhat melancholy sound of water lapping against the scull of a boat going down Ohkawa.

A pack of horses was coming closer on the raised dirt bank at the back of the house. The clop of their hooves stirred Kohei from his shallow sleep.

Sounds like some samurai are riding out on a journey in this baking-hot sun. Hard work, that is, he thought. He was drifting back into a dream when a voice came from the garden.

'Hello, Akiyama Sensei. This is Sasaki Mifuyu.'

'Oh . . . well, hello, thanks for coming out in this hot weather.' Kohei sat up and saw a small, elderly samurai approaching behind Mifuyu. *Is that Lord Tanuma . . .?*

Indeed it was.

Okitsugu had gathered Mifuyu and a dozen men on horseback to pay Kohei a visit.

'Pleasure to meet you, Master Akiyama Kohei. I am Tanuma Tonomo-no-kami,' he said cordially.

'My my . . .' Kohei said, getting to his feet. 'Please do come in . . .'

'That's all right, I'm happy to sit here.' Okitsugu casually sat down on the edge of the veranda. Of course, this had to be easier for him, since he was dressed for a long journey: a wickerwork hat with an upturned brim and a special hakama for horse riding, and straw sandals tied on to his feet.

The samurai who were escorting him had fastened their horses to the foot of the bank and were waiting somewhere a little way off.

'One moment, please . . .' Kohei said, going out from the kitchen to the back of the house.

There were some shiratama dumplings cooling in a bamboo basket in the well water.

Kohei remembered what Oharu had told him as she left the house: 'There's a little snack for you in the well to keep it cool – you can have it when you wake up.'

She had kneaded rice flour into a soft dough, rolled it into small balls, and boiled them until they were smooth and chewy. He served the shiratama on three plates with plenty of white sugar sprinkled over them, then poured hot sencha into three cups. He carried these to the veranda on a tray.

'I wonder if such a simple snack would suit your taste, Lord Tanuma . . .'

As soon as Okitsugu saw the dumplings, his face creased into a warm smile. 'It's been a long time since I had them last, but shiratama is a big favourite of mine. My mother used to make it often for me, once upon a time.'

'I'm very glad to hear that.'

'Mm. Delicious. It's nice and cool.'

'Thank you.'

They ate shiratama, sipped tea, and looked at each other in amiable serenity.

'Well, Akiyama Sensei,' Okitsugu said.

'Yes?'

'I should have thanked you sooner. All that you have done for us in recent days – I don't take it lightly. I am deeply grateful.'

'Oh, it was nothing . . . So, what has become of Iida Heisuke?'

That night, Kohei and Daijiro had returned the unconscious Heisuke to the primary Tanuma mansion. Kohei had told the guard at the Kandabashi gate that they had come across him suffering from a sudden illness, done what they could to revive him, and asked for his name and position, which had enabled them to deliver him there.

Kohei had handed over Heisuke, nodded to Daijiro, and promptly left them to it.

The people of the mansion never suspected Heisuke of anything.

So, he was back at work the very next day.

Three days later, Okitsugu reported his full recovery to the shogunate and returned to his Kandabashi mansion.

It was in the small hours of that same night that Heisuke killed himself.

Even when Okitsugu had returned to his main residence, he hadn't summoned Heisuke or conducted any interrogations.

'Then you were going to let him keep working for you as before?' Kohei asked.

'Yes.'

'Hmm . . .' Even Kohei was surprised by the roju's magnanimity, and he later told Daijiro: 'I didn't expect him to have that much mettle.'

Okitsugu told Kohei that Heisuke had hanged himself.

Both his wife, Yone, and Kumetaro were in the dark as to his motives.

'Still, you would have to be quite wary from now on . . .' Kohei said.

'Well, Akiyama Sensei – I told Mifuyu the same thing, but if I were to be assassinated by poison at some point in the future, it would be a poor return for all that you and Mifuyu have done for me this time around.'

'Indeed it would.'

'But Father . . .' Mifuyu said thoughtfully, 'do you believe the Hitotsubashi family was plotting to assassinate you?'

'Hmm . . .'

'It's obvious that Heisuke was in contact with the men at their reserve mansion.'

'Almost certainly, yes.'

'That must mean—'

'Slow down, Mifuyu.' Okitsugu took a sip of the fresh batch of tea that Kohei had poured for them, then continued, 'The Hitotsubashi family is of the same bloodline as His Highness the Shogun. Imagine what would happen if it became public that they had attempted to eliminate a roju who aids His Highness and administers the affairs of the country. I prefer not to stir up trouble in any event – if I can manage it, that is . . . As Iida Heisuke served the Hitotsubashi house before he was moved to mine, it's not inconceivable that someone in that family might have wanted me dead already back then.

'You know – my late brother Okinobu was once the house elder of Hitotsubashi, so I have been acting in their best interests ever since I became a roju. At least, that was my intention. From their point of view, however, perhaps I might have appeared as though I were trying to manipulate the house through our Lord Shogun's authority. That is my failing.'

A melancholy smile flickered across his face.

'I'm planning to make my brother's son, Okimune, a house elder of Hitotsubashi soon . . .' he went on. 'All I wanted was to help my nephew along in his career – no ulterior motives. And . . . besides, Akiyama Sensei . . .'

'Yes?'

'For one engaged in politics, power and influence hold a strange, nigh-irresistible attraction, you see.' That was Okitsugu's honest thoughts, pure and simple.

'I can imagine,' Kohei said.

'However, that doesn't mean I want to rule over the whole country, of course. Put another way, it's the same urge one has when one starts saving money – the more you put away, the more you want to hoard, and there's no end to it... In order to conduct the affairs of the public in just the way we wish, we must expand our influence as far as it can reach – there is no other way.'

'If I may observe... I have heard tell of the present head of the Hitotsubashi family, Lord Tokugawa Harusada, that he is a rather strong-willed man,' Kohei said candidly.

'Yes, he is indeed...'

Okitsugu fell silent.

Hitotsubashi Harusada was the grandson of the eighth shogun, Tokugawa Yoshimune. In 1764, he rose to the martial rank of Jusanmi Sakon'e Gon-no-Chujo and became the head of Hitotsubashi. His wife was of royal descent: the daughter of Kyogoku-no-miya Kinhito-shin'no.

Since Harusada had become the master of Hitotsubashi, he came to resent the shogunate's custom of meddling in the affairs of the house at every turn, which led to a number of clashes between him and the high officials of the shogunate.

Ever since Okitsugu had been appointed as roju, though, Okitsugu had worked so seamlessly with the current shogun and conducted all matters with such smooth, skilful manoeuvring that Harusada never even had a chance to rebel. In recent years, he had in fact become closer to Okitsugu and appeared to be maintaining friendly relations.

Underneath this facade, however, something might have built up in the pit of Harusada's stomach, roiling all the more violently because it found no outlet.

This was what Kohei was hinting at by his remark.

As expected, Okitsugu didn't respond.

He merely looked up at the sky in silence. His wrinkled face was expressionless, but Kohei's sharp eyes could detect something there.

It seems even the roju is at his wits' end when it comes to the Lord of Hitotsubashi . . . Kohei thought.

Some time later, Okitsugu departed from Kohei's home. Before leaving, he proffered fifty gold ryo to Kohei as thanks for his recent work. Mifuyu presented the parcel of coins on a small wooden offering stand.

'Please do me the honour of accepting this,' Okitsugu said with a small bow.

It was offered in such a natural manner, and Kohei received it without any reserve or embarrassment.

'My goodness, this is a wonderful gift . . . Thank you. I will take it with gratitude.'

When Oharu came home around sunset, Kohei was feeding the furnace for the bath with firewood.

'Oh, sensei, I could've done that . . .' she said in surprise.

'Never mind, it's all right. By the way, Oharu.'

'Aye?'

'There's a stand with fifty gold ryo on it in the tokonoma – did you see?'

'Dear me. Really, sensei?'

'A little gift from a certain someone.'

'Good for you, sensei.'

'I'll take care of everything in the kitchen tonight. While I do that, could you go on the boat and take ten ryo from the pile – no, make that fifteen – to my boy?'

'Sure thing.'

'Tell him it's some pocket money from me.'

'I know.'

'How about we take a bath together when you're back?'

'I'd love that . . .'

'I'll scrub your back for you – haven't done that in a while.'

'Just my back? Don't stop there.'

'All right, all right. I'll wash every bit of you.'

'That's more like it.'

Twilight had veiled the little flowers on the moss rose bursting into bloom in the shrubbery by the engawa, and the colours of the garden melted away in the gathering gloom.

Translator's Acknowledgements

While I am unable to cite all the historical and fictional resources that I referenced while working on this book, I would like to acknowledge these texts in particular: the works of Shiba Ryōtarō, translated by Juliet Winters Carpenter, Paul McCarthy and Margaret Mitsutani (edited by Phyllis Birnbaum); and *Strokes of Brush and Blade: Tales of the Samurai* (Kurodahan Press, 2019), an anthology edited by Edward Lipsett. I also thank my parents – especially my father, who is a fifth-dan in kendo, for picking apart some sword-fighting sequences.